THE BLUE STAIN

Studies in German Literature, Linguistics, and Culture

HUGO BETTAUER

THE BLUE STAIN

A NOVEL OF A RACIAL OUTCAST

EDITED AND WITH AN INTRODUCTION BY PETER HÖYNG

TRANSLATED BY
PETER HÖYNG AND CHAUNCEY J. MELLOR

AFTERWORD BY KENNETH R. JANKEN

CAMDEN HOUSE
Rochester, New York

First published 2017 by Camden House
Reprinted in paperback 2018

Original German-language edition: *Das blaue Mal: Der Roman
eines Ausgestoßenen* (Vienna: Gloriette-Verlag, 1922)

Camden House is an imprint of Boydell & Brewer Inc.
668 Mt. Hope Avenue, Rochester, NY 14620, USA
www.camden-house.com
and of Boydell & Brewer Limited
PO Box 9, Woodbridge, Suffolk IP12 3DF, UK
www.boydellandbrewer.com

Paperback ISBN-13: 978-1-57113-999-3 / Paperback ISBN-10: 1-57113-999-0
Hardcover ISBN-13: 978-1-57113-982-5 / Hardcover ISBN-10: 1-57113-982-6

Library of Congress Cataloging-in-Publication Data

Names: Bettauer, Hugo, 1872–1925, author. | Höyng, Peter, translator, editor. |
    Mellor, Chauncey J., 1942– translator. | Janken, Kenneth Robert, 1956– writer
    of supplementary content.
Title: The blue stain : a novel of a racial outcast / Hugo Bettauer ; edited and with
    an introduction by Peter Höyng ; translated by Peter Höyng and Chauncey J.
    Mellor ; afterword by Kenneth R. Janken.
Other titles: Blaue Mal. English
Description: Rochester, New York : Camden House, 2017. | Series: Studies in
    German literature, linguistics, and culture | Includes bibliographical references.
Identifiers: LCCN 2016050884| ISBN 9781571139825 (hardcover : alk. paper) |
    ISBN 1571139826 (hardcover : alk. paper)
Subjects: LCSH: Racially mixed people—Fiction. | Civil rights movements—
    United States—Fiction. | Race relations—Fiction.
Classification: LCC PT2603.E857 B413 2017 | DDC 833/.912—dc23 LC record
    available at https://lccn.loc.gov/2016050884

CONTENTS

ACKNOWLEDGMENTS

As much as the name, or, as in our case, names, on the cover indicate the authors of the book, this volume would not have emerged without the advice and contributions of many colleagues. Hence, acknowledging their valuable input is only a small token after a long journey that all started one summer morning over a decade ago in the Austrian National Library in Vienna, when I discovered and began reading Hugo Bettauer's *Das blaue Mal.*

I might have never found the novel without the initial push by La Vinia Delois Jennings, Distinguished Professor in the Humanities and Professor of Twentieth-Century American Literature and Culture at the University of Tennessee-Knoxville. After all it was she who, as an editor of a volume on whiteness in literature and performance entitled *At Home and Abroad* (2009), invited me to contribute an essay on Hugo Bettauer's best-known novel, *Die Stadt ohne Juden* (City without Jews, 1922). Both Chauncey J. Mellor and I are deeply indebted to her crucial input, encouragement, and guidance as the project moved along.

The undertaking all started with the help of Jonathan Jackson, who worked as an Emory undergraduate student on an initial draft of a translation of excerpts from Bettauer's novel. Toward the end of the project, I was lucky to count on another gifted young student from Emory College, Chloe B. Kipka, who provided helpful feedback.

I would certainly feel less confident about our translation if colleagues from other disciplines and institutions had not provided crucial responses; among them the late Maximilian Aue, a dear colleague from my own German Studies Department at Emory's College of Arts & Sciences and himself a highly accomplished translator. We also appreciated the comments on an early draft by Christoph Irmscher, George F. Getz Jr. Professor in the Wells Scholars Program at the University of Indiana-Bloomington. Likewise helpful were the remarks by Reinhild Steingröver, Professor of German at the Eastman School of Music, on the translation's first draft. At my own institution, I could count on the support from my entire department, and the direction of my colleague and friend Elizabeth Goodstein in the then Institute of Liberal Arts (ILA) at Emory. And an additional colleague from the ILA was also instrumental in moving the project forward: I am most grateful for the interest in and kind recommendations for our project we received from the late Professor Rudolph P. Byrd, Professor of English and founding director of Emory's James Johnson Weldon Institute. And special thanks go to the vital input from Carol Anderson, Samuel Candler Dobbs Professor of African American Studies at Emory.

Beyond these wonderful personal encounters with my colleagues, I am also grateful for the generous institutional support at Emory University by both the Laney Graduate School and the College of Arts & Sciences.

I am also most appreciative of the collaboration with Kenneth R. Janken, Professor of History and Director of UNC-Chapel Hill's Center for the Study of the American South. In his substantive afterword, he raises an important critical voice and thereby very much enriches the book as a whole.

Yet, what you hold in your hands would be less thorough if it were not for the critical eye, patience, and experience of Camden House's editorial director Jim Walker.

As instrumental as all these accomplished guardians have been, the translation of the novel would never have seen the light of the day if it were not for the collaboration with my former colleague at the University of Tennessee-Knoxville and dear friend Chauncey Jeff Mellor. Jeff's knowledge of historical linguistics, his superb command of and knack for German, his tireless enthusiasm and energy for looking up words, phrases, and locales, and his attention to every detail of Bettauer's seemingly simple text turned the work into the most enriching and endearing teamwork of which I have been a part. Saying thank you, however loudly, does not nearly convey my deep gratitude for his expertise, patience, and, above all, true friendship.

Last but certainly not least, I would like to dedicate this book to my dear wife Mentewab and our son Paul Iyasu Tesfaye.

Peter Höyng
Atlanta, winter 2017

TRANSLATORS' NOTE

Peter Höyng and Chauncey J. Mellor

T ranslations exist for different purposes and for different audiences and vary accordingly. Fidelity to the original text must be married to the natural fluency of the translated text. Reading the translation should provide readers with the sense that the text was originally written in the language they know and see before them. At the same time, the foreignness of the content must be so engagingly and genuinely expressed in the translation that the readers also experience the distance between their standpoint and that of the original author. *Das Blaue Mal: Roman eines Ausgestoßenen* (1922) provides an especially rich set of crosscurrents for someone translating it into English.

Written by an assimilated Austrian Jew, Hugo Bettauer, with a richly prophetic and perspicacious view of race relations in the United States and his German-speaking homeland, the book reports first on the experience of an archetypically German father and then of his quadroon son successively in Georgia, New York, Vienna, Switzerland, Hamburg, New York, Alabama, and Georgia once again, in the first decade of the twentieth century. The publication of the book in 1922 provides a clear *terminus ad quem* for the scenes depicted and the situations described. Repeated references in the text make it clear that the events transpire in the twentieth century, but astonishingly absent from the work is any hint of the Great War that so pervaded Bettauer's own peripatetic life and the world he experienced. As a journalist, Bettauer was obviously a quick study who brought his intrepid and penetrating insights and European sensibilities to bear on the complex issue of American race relations in an astonishing panoply of locales and social conditions: Georgia plantation society, Austrian university and student society, lower middle-class Viennese society, Hamburg waterfront life, Manhattan milieus—from the Upper West Side, to Broadway and Union Square, to the unionized offices in Lower Manhattan, to the Tenderloin district, to black society on the lower West Side by the Hudson—then to gangs of lumberjack hirelings segregated by race, language, and the immigrant community clearing the North Alabama forest, and finally back to Atlanta in middle-class educated black society energized by the work of W. E. B. Du Bois.

As translators, we endeavored to take account of each of these social, geographical, and physical circumstances in rendering the Bettauer text. The words had to fit the stance of the narrator, a sophisticated, insightful, European academic outside observer, and capture the atmosphere and style of each of the speakers in those bygone days and milieus so absent from our present time.

A very obvious example where such adjustment was required comes in the historical use of terms referring to persons of African descent: boy, colored, mulatto, Negro, nigger, octoroon, quadroon, and so on. Given the circumstances, however objectionable these terms may be, each of them has a place in this narrative, and often in quite close conjunction. When, in the refined Manhattan Hotel St. Regis, a crusty old Southern hotel guest refers to Carlo as "der Kerl," the rendering "boy" captures the kind of speech someone present would have heard. In response, the hotel manager tells Carlo that "Farbige," that is, "colored people," cannot lodge in his establishment.

The title of the work, *Das blaue Mal*, itself gave rise to a number of serious deliberations. The connotations of the term *Mal* include *Geburtsmal*, "birthmark," and *Kainsmal*, "mark/brand/stigma of Cain." As a result, the terms "birthmark" and "mark" were seriously considered before we arrived at the rendering "stain." Two factors weighed heavily in this choice: first, the term "stain" incorporates both the substantive visual aspect of a birthmark and the negative sense of the mark of Cain. Second, the original book cover emphasized with Expressionistic garishness the coloration and hue of the skin under the fingernails of the protagonist, which ultimately tipped the scales in favor of "stain."

Finding the "right," that is, most fitting, translation frequently led us to consult reference works covering the period involved, often to ascertain that a turn of phrase genuinely belonged to the era and context. Among the works frequently consulted were: *Webster's New International Dictionary of the English Language* (2nd ed., 1934), *Webster's Third New International*

Dictionary of the English Language (1961), *Historical Dictionary of American Slang* (A–G, H–O), *The Century Cyclopedia and Dictionary* (1895), *Muret-Sanders Enzyklopädisches Wörterbuch der englischen und deutschen Sprache* (1897), *The New Cassell's German Dictionary* (1958), *Deutsches Wörterbuch* (1852–1961) by Jacob and Wilhelm Grimm, *Meyers Konversationslexikon* (1896), and *Encyclopaedia Britannica* (11th ed.). In addition, both the *Encyclopaedia Britannica* and *Meyers Konversationslexikon* were very useful for tracing the physical locales Bettauer so accurately describes in New York and Vienna.

Of course, consultation with a series of reference sources could never completely resolve issues of social and cultural naturalness, especially across the European-American cultural divide, as the two following instances exemplify. At one point, the narrator tells us that Carlo was to dine with the proper, but socially much more constrained Ortner family, including young Elly, "ein schlanker, hübscher Backfisch mit kurzgeschorenem Haare" (105). Even in Bettauer's time, "Backfisch" carried a rather precious tinge of "boarding school miss," ironically elevating her above her quite modest station. Rendering this with "teenager" would have artificially carried modern-day associations for the pubescent generation. How then to capture the connotation and denotation, and yet avoid modern parlance and simultaneously not sound outdated? In the end, the choice rested on our sensitivity for language that bridged the older text, its foreign context, with the needs for readers of English in the early twenty-first century; hence "schoolgirl" seemed most suitable for this young maiden, despite its being somewhat more bland than the jolly, amusing and slightly belittling term "Backfisch."

Interjections often presented surprisingly knotty issues because they crystallize crosscurrents of emotions in one short burst of speech. At one point, for example, Zeller exclaims "Wehe, wenn mich die schöne Frau Harriett in dieser Situation auch nur ahnen würde" (32–33), when he comes to fear that the patently flirtatious but racist Harriet might sense his growing attraction to her slave servant Karola. Possible dictionary translations for "Wehe" were "alack" and "woe is me," both of which sounded hopelessly stilted and obsolete, reminiscent of shallow melodrama, and out of character for Zeller. "Good grief" was also rejected, because it evokes Charlie Brown's use of this stock phrase in *Peanuts* and the bemusement it conjures up. Reaching beyond dictionaries, we searched period literary texts for equivalences. "Good Gracious" showed up, but seemed a bit too pretentious, British, and possibly effeminate. Similar contexts produced "Good God," which in the end we deemed suitable for a man of Zeller's education, stature, and sensibilities, talking to himself. In our assessment, it captured both Zeller's shock and dismay at his racially charged predicament and carried just enough of the self-pity and apprehension that impelled him to exclaim that one word, "Wehe."

Having addressed the issue of accuracy and naturalness, we must in conclusion briefly address the matter of alienation and the "foreignness" of the content. Some readers may find the punctuation erratic, even bizarre. We have elected to preserve much of it in the belief that it conveys Bettauer's style. Likewise, the very range of venues—spanning two continents and a remarkable range of social circumstances—provides some guarantee that the readers will gain a sense of estrangement when they glimpse into a world and a time that are new and distant to them. Bettauer's daring excursions into sensitive and taboo-laden areas also likely make readers pause, stand back, and reflect. In a sense, an accurate and natural rendering of speech from a world to which one otherwise has had little or no access genuinely inspires the feeling of distance and novelty a good translation must strive for. It reveals the foreignness of the material clothed in words and phrases that seem natural, unforced, and appropriate to the setting. It is that double effect that we as translators have tried to convey in translating a text that itself passes our American society through a European lens and has us see it as at once both familiar and strange.

INTRODUCTION

Peter Höyng

When on the very last page of Hugo Bettauer's 1922 novel *The Blue Stain: A Novel of a Racial Outcast* (originally in German *Das blaue Mal: Der Roman eines Ausgestoßenen*), the novel's protagonist, Carlo, decides to fight for the civil rights of African Americans in Atlanta by joining The National Association for the Advancement of Colored People (NAACP), it is impossible for the reader not to be moved by his late but daring decision. Right up until Carlo makes this choice, the reader is ready to accompany this young man on his return to Europe, where he believed he could leave behind the appalling racism that he had encountered, first in New York City, later in the forests of North Alabama, and finally in Atlanta, Georgia. He longs to shed the role of the outcast, as the subtitle of the novel brands him. Instead, Carlo desires to thrive in Vienna, Austria as he once did, albeit no longer in a reckless and immature manner. He appears poised for a homecoming to a society that had treated him as one of its own, as a somewhat exotic white man.

In this final turn of events, the novel strikes a bracing and stunning chord: Carlo, who was conceived by his white European father and his mulatto mother in Atlanta during the post-Reconstruction period and was raised by his father in Vienna after his mother's death, had for so long insisted on his whiteness and resisted his blackness, but now finally and fully accepts his dual, mixed-race identity. The "blue stain" under his fingernails, a condition alleged to provide evidence of black heritage, remains a visible sign of his parents' miscegenation. Even as Carlo's vicissitudes amaze us, his life story simultaneously reveals its shaping not only of his, but also of our identities: we are born first as human beings, and it is the dominant society that then sees or does not see the color, gender, or other biological characteristics of a person, that determine whether this person is treated by social convention as "normal" or is stigmatized as "other." Should one succumb to the societal norms and values of the majority, or should one resist with all one's might those overbearing pressures and forces? Mustering this resistance leads to the hardest of all choices. In the end, Carlo consciously heeds the summons of his destiny to help *his* people be treated as equal regardless of their race, gender, or culture.

As if this glimpse into the novel's ending does not already provide surprises and lead to the fundamental question of a moral choice, the story line embodies even more intricacies of how race played out in different societies and across nations in such deplorable ways in the late nineteenth and early twentieth centuries. To make matters even more intriguing, *The Blue Stain* also demands reconsideration of the issue of what literature in modern societies should and can mean, how cultural transfer does or does not take place, and how the righteous ideal of humanism depends on cultural translation and negotiation. It is these aspects that I want to focus on in this introduction.

The stories surrounding the novel and its author are almost as fascinating as Carlo's tale itself. It was in 1922 in Vienna that Hugo Bettauer published his fictional account of Carlo. That Bettauer is still known at all, if mainly to historians of German literature, is thanks to his novel *Die Stadt ohne Juden* (The City without Jews), published in the same year as *The Blue Stain*.[1] *The City without Jews* retains its shock value even today because it tackled anti-Semitism in interwar Austria by prophetically imagining what would happen if all Jews were by law forced to leave the country and the state were to seize their properties. Bettauer imagines this outrageous state of affairs in order to demonstrate *ex negativo* what an invaluable and integral part of Austrian society the Jews—who had been granted civil rights in 1867—had become. At the end of this fictitious story, and in a highly fanciful turn of events, all the Jews return to Vienna. Not so in real life, of course. Once Hitler had annexed Austria in March of 1938, the National Socialists purged the country of its 200,000 Jews by forcing them either into exile or brutally murdering them in concentration camps. These horrible crimes render Bettauer's early account eerily prescient, especially considering its subtitle, *A Novel of the Day after Tomorrow* (*Ein Roman*

---

[1] In the first two years after its publication, *Die Stadt ohne Juden* sold 250,000 copies. Cf. Murray Hall, *Der Fall Bettauer*, 24.

von Übermorgen)—except that history proved his fairy-tale ending to be unfortunately just that. But whereas *Die Stadt ohne Juden* was translated into English as *The City without Jews* in 1926, and remains available today in German, *The Blue Stain* has been almost forgotten.[2]

Remarkably, the disappearance of *The Blue Stain* from literary awareness goes so far that it earns no mention in Werner Sollors's extensive study of interracial literature, *Neither Black nor White yet Both: Thematic Explorations of Interracial Literature*.[3] Nor, for that matter, have scholars of German literature even been cognizant of the fact that *The Blue Stain* represents the first novel in German to address racism in the United States in the twentieth century, and "the first representation of a black German American character," as Nancy P. Nenno has added.[4] This is all the more notable since a number of German-speaking authors had openly critiqued slavery in their novels as early as the late eighteenth century and on into the pre-Civil War nineteenth century.[5] However, in the early twentieth century, German-speaking writers either ignored the Jim Crow laws altogether or mentioned them in passing without making racial politics their focus. Arthur Holitscher's travel account from 1912, for example, reports in his chapter entitled "Der Neger" (The Negro), on the despicable segregation and even includes a picture of a lynching in "Oklahoma" [*sic*] and leaves it at that. No less a writer than Franz Kafka was inspired by Holitscher's travel narrative as he began writing his novel *The Missing Person* (*Der Verschollene*), when he imagines his protagonist Karl Rossmann emigrating

---

[2] Nancy P. Nenno's recent essay "Elective Paternities: White Germans and Black Americans in Hugo Bettauer's *Das Blaue Mal* (1922)" is one of only a handful on *The Blue Stain*. Both Lisa Silverman's *Becoming Austrians: Jews and Culture between the World Wars* and June J. Hwang's *Lost in Time: Locating the Stranger in German Modernity* give extensive attention to Hugo Bettauer, but both mainly focus on *The City without Jews*.

[3] This is all the more noteworthy since Sollors identifies in French, American, German, and English literary texts from the 1850s to 1950s the distinct bluish tint at the base of the fingernails referred to in Bettauer's title as a leitmotif that "yield[s] clues to a character's nonwhite racial ancestry. . . ." Werner Sollors, "The Bluish Tinge in the Halfmoon; or Fingernails as a Racial Sign" in *Neither Black nor White yet Both*, 142–61; here 146.

[4] Cf. Nenno, "Elective Paternities," 261. Primus Heinz Kucher recently discovered Arthur Rundt's novel *Marilyn*, which is set in Chicago, New York City, and the Caribbean and features the mulatto woman Marilyn, a modern, self-confident woman who dates a white man, as its protagonist. The novel was published in Vienna's premier daily, *Neue Freie Presse*, in the early fall of 1928. Kucher will soon publish the novel in the Vienna publishing house *edition atelier*.

[5] Cf. Wynfried Kriegleder, "Die amerikanische Sklaverei im deutschsprachigen Roman zwischen 1760 und 1860."

to the States.[6] Instead of merely imagining what life in the United States felt and looked like, in *The Blue Stain* Hugo Bettauer doubtless relied extensively on his own life experiences during the several years he spent in New York, which in terms of turbulent twists and turns seem to have rivaled those of his fictional character Carlo.

Hugo Bettauer

Maximilian Hugo Bettauer was born in 1872, the first son of a Jewish family in Baden, a half-hour's train ride southwest of Vienna. The year and place of his birth is particularly telling insofar as Bettauer grew up during the period of Jewish emancipation, which allowed his father to succeed as a stockbroker and move with his family to Baden, a posh spa town. In a move indicative of his adventurous life to come, Bettauer ran away to Alexandria, Egypt at age sixteen. Likewise unconventional is the fact that at age eighteen, he officially neglected his Jewish origins by converting to Christianity. Even so, his joining the Lutheran Church instead of the Catholic Church, which is dominant in Austria, might well be seen as a further act of defiance and estrangement. After all, Bettauer resisted the prevailing influences exerted on Jews either to assimilate to Catholic norms or run the risk of being treated as the inferior "other." Regardless of the willingness of many Jews to submit to the pressures of the dominant culture and to change their faith, habits, language, and appearance, they continued to encounter stigmatization. Witness for example the situation of such prominent Jewish figures as the composer Gustav Mahler, who had to convert to the Catholic faith before assuming the prestigious role of director of the Court Opera, or the founder of modern psychoanalysis, Sigmund Freud, who was denied a professorship at the University of Vienna by the Ministry of Education because he was a Jew.

Bettauer's conversion highlights a sharp awareness of this complex social environment, and already indicates a rebellious attitude toward its hypocrisy and racial hierarchy. And his running away as a sixteen-year-old to Egypt illustrates his fearless and dauntless attitude towards life, and his habit of escaping from and breaking with social norms, which became a leitmotif. All of these characteristics came into full play when he moved to Zurich in 1896, and then, having inherited a sizeable sum from his father, decided to leave Europe for the United States with his first wife, the actress

---

[6] Franz Kafka's friend and literary executor Max Brod named the fragment *Amerika*, and published it after Kafka's death.

Olga Steiner. While crossing the Atlantic, Bettauer learned that he had lost his entire fortune due to the bankruptcy of a Chicago bank in which he had invested. Because he could not find permanent employment, and despite his naturalization as a US citizen, he returned with his wife to Europe in 1899, this time to Berlin. There Bettauer spearheaded aggressive investigative journalism against police corruption—including a case where a policeman had mistreated a black person—that eventually led to his expulsion from Prussia in 1901 and subsequently to his divorce. In Hamburg, at the age of thirty, he fell in love with the sixteen-year-old Helene Müller, with whom he made another one of his escapes, once again to New York. In fact, he married her while on board in the mid-Atlantic en route to New York. Bettauer's second stay in New York lasted six years (1904–10), during which he worked for various German-language newspapers such as the Hearst-owned *New Yorker Deutsche Zeitung* and the *New Yorker Morgen-Journal*,[7] not only as a journalist but also as a writer of five serialized novels, most of which were detective stories that, while set in New York, exhibited no genuine interest in the city or even in American society. Instead, the city mainly serves as the backdrop for the novels, which are full of clichés concerning the monstrous nature of capitalism, always accompanied by a heavy dose of social criticism from a European perspective. While a certain parallel to Upton Sinclair's muckraking novel *The Jungle* (1906) is undeniable, Bettauer's sensational novels also include some autobiographical elements such as the sudden loss of a fortune. Regrettably, though, we have no personal records of Bettauer's years in New York, and as a result lack a better understanding of his work as a journalist and writer.[8]

What we do know is that he once again bolted for Europe in 1910, this time back to Vienna, where, after some legal complications due to his US citizenship, he continued his career as a journalist for various newspapers, among them the leading daily *Neue Freie Presse* until 1918. After World War I, Bettauer once again reported for the New York Hearst newspapers, though this time from the Old World. And although he had already published his detective novels in German-language newspapers in New York, his true success and breakthrough as an author in German coincided with the unstable years of the first Austrian Republic after 1920. In a brief span of time, in what may be seen as the Roaring Twenties in Austria, he became very successful in writing and publishing a number of

---

[7] Both of these newspapers belonged to the Hearst media group and because of an office fire in 1915, no pre-1911 copies of them have survived. Peter Conolly-Smith, *Translating America*, 78.

[8] Cf. Hall, *Der Fall Bettauer*, 11–14.

popular novels that tackled pressing social and political issues in Vienna, generally resulting from the trauma of Austria's losing its hegemonic position within the Habsburg Empire. Bettauer's tremendous success embodied and characterized the interwar era in that he fully embraced the new opportunities provided by a democratic society, in which breaking with rigid conventions and practicing liberal lifestyles seemed the new order of the day. He embodied a modern *Zeitgeist* as a pioneering journalist, author, and entrepreneur. After all, he invested in new publishing avenues such as the two short-lived but momentous journals: *Er und Sie: Wochenschrift für Lebenskultur und Erotik* (He and She: A Weekly for Lifestyle and Eroticism, February 14–March 13, 1924) and, following legal battles over censorship, *Bettauers Wochenschrift: Probleme des Lebens* (Bettauer's Weekly: Problems of Life), which he introduced in May 1924 and which continued to be published by one of his sons through June 1928 after Bettauer's dreadful death by assassination in March 1925. In both journals, Bettauer was ahead of his time in popularizing some of Freud's notions on sexuality by openly discussing this taboo topic and promoting sex education for adults. What is more, he endorsed the rights of homosexuals, and even argued for legalized abortion. Finally, his journals displayed an uncommonly open attitude towards sexuality by running personal ads that intimated clearly erotic/sexual outcomes, a circumstance that ultimately goaded into action the legal authorities, who were as opposed to these provocative and popular journals as they had been to the first Austrian staging of Arthur Schnitzler's risqué play *Reigen*—known in English by its French title *La Ronde*—in Vienna in 1921.

As unaccustomed as Bettauer's audience may have been to his journals' open discussion of sexuality, a large number of readers, especially the younger generation, nevertheless welcomed it all the more.[9] Consequently the shock for them must have been even greater when Otto Rothstock, a twenty-year-old former Nazi Party member, enraged by Bettauer's liberal points of view, fatally shot Bettauer in his office on March 10, 1925.[10] Bettauer's tragic demise unfortunately carries symbolic meaning beyond

[9] *Er und Sie* had a circulation of 60,000, and up to 200,000 readers. Cf. Hall, *Der Fall Bettauer*, 41.

[10] On March 26, Bettauer died of his wounds. Murray Hall's *Der Fall Bettauer* concentrates on the circumstances of Bettauer's assassination by Rothstock, the subsequent trial, and Bettauer as a victim of anti-Semitism. Cf. Hall, *Der Fall Bettauer* 80–133. Rothstock did not face any punishment but was set free because of empathy by the judges who sanctioned his argument that the murder was legitimate because of the taboo breaking and indecent nature of Bettauer's journal. Today, a plaque near the site of the murder on the *Lange Gasse* commemorates the site of the 1925 shooting.

his individual fate, as it reveals the sociopolitical frailties of postwar Austria. In a sense, his assassination crystallizes two crucial and interrelated aspects of anti-Semitism that permeated Vienna's dominant culture from the 1880s on. First, despite the 1867 law emancipating Austrian Jews, which was extended and improved with the establishment of Austria's First Republic following World War I, Jews continued to be racially ostracized. Second, despite Bettauer's conversion and attempts to become invisible as a Jew, in which we may see a noteworthy parallel to Carlo, he continued to be perceived as one. Furthermore, Bettauer's journalistic endeavors largely supported the ideological link that anti-Semitism had promulgated and incited: the fear of sexuality was married to the hatred of Jews; ergo, being Jewish became a mark not only of the racial, but also the sexual threat to traditional ways of life. Lisa Silverman persuasively links these interrelated causes in *Becoming Austrians: Jews and Culture between the World Wars* when she summarizes Bettauer's assassination:

> Bettauer's status as a Jew, first emphasized at his trial for public indecency, only increased after his death. Coding Bettauer as Jewish in associating him with pornography, prostitution, and sexual perversity helped the Viennese envision Rothstock as a hero. . . . Bettauer's Jewishness was more significant to the audience needing a 'rational' reason for accepting his brutal murder than it had likely been for Rothstock, who needed few excuses to justify killing him.[11]

The traumatic downfall of the Austro-Hungarian Empire in 1918 created, especially for many Austrian males, a strong sense of anxiety and instability, fed by anti-Semitic notions branding the Jews as scapegoats for the insecurities rampant in the dominant culture. In effect, the dominant culture of ethnic Germans in Austria managed to "blacken" the Jews in order to buttress their own identity as pure, white, and male.[12]

By now, it should be evident that Hugo Bettauer, relatively unknown in literary circles today, became one of the vital figures in Austria's capital after the downfall of the empire in 1918. He did not pursue modernist literary style, today associated with writers such as Marcel Proust, James Joyce, Franz Kafka, Robert Musil, or Thomas Mann, but instead reflected modernity in two other substantive and noteworthy ways: He popularized Freud by disseminating many central psychoanalytic points of view in

---

[11] Silverman, *Becoming Austrians*, 55–56.

[12] Cf. Peter Höyng, "A Dream of a White Vienna after World War I: Hugo Bettauer's *The City without Jews* and *The Blue Stain*."

groundbreaking and popular journals, and he was an author unashamed to write for the working-class *and* the bourgeoisie—a mass audience craving plot-driven, accessible literature reflecting their daily, often unconscious, concerns, fears, and desires. As June J. Hwang rightly observes, Bettauer "educates the public to facilitate an atmosphere of acceptance and challenges notions of morality that unnecessarily restrict an individual and the life he or she wishes to lead."[13] To put it differently, Bettauer managed both to tap into the collective desires and to channel them towards an enlightened outlook. As both a journalist and an author, he understood how to combine capitalistic forms of publishing and entertainment with socially relevant and progressive ideas, and hence, one can see him as an heir of enlightened thinkers and writers of the eighteenth century. Or one can, as Hwang does, interpret Bettauer in a larger context of urban modernity, as a "privileged stranger," and view his writings as "an insistence on the possibility of agency within the modern city and on the ability of an individual to decide how to live his or her life. . . ."[14] In fact, Bettauer's son Helmut marketed his father after his murder as a "martyr of enlightenment" who fought "for freedom and equality, against arbitrariness, oppression and prejudices."[15] Of his twenty-one novels, fully nine were adapted for the silver screen,[16] most notably his novel about the extremes of economic depression after World War I, *The Joyless Street* (*Die freudlose Gasse*, 1925), a classic of the silent movie era, directed by G. W. Pabst and starring the young Greta Garbo. What makes Bettauer so intriguing today is his keen instinct for addressing controversial issues in his works, such as sexuality, the fight for social justice, sexism, or, in *The Blue Stain*, racism.

The Blue Stain

Innovative as Bettauer was when choosing and portraying topics that many regarded as inconvenient, he nevertheless narrated his texts in a traditional manner, as is the case of *The Blue Stain*, where the story follows the established conventions of the *Bildungsroman*, in which a male protagonist

---

[13] Hwang, *Lost in Time*, 184.

[14] Hwang, *Lost in Time*, 183.

[15] The quote is from Helmut Bettauer, who attempted to continue his father's journalistic endeavors, from an advertisement for the weekly *Bettauers Wochenschrift* on the last page of Hugo Bettauer's posthumously published novel *Der Kampf ums Glück*, 319.

[16] Cf. Hall, *Der Fall Bettauer*, 187–92.

finds, through the course of hardships, his place in society, or in this case, his "true" identity as a black person.

In the first and shortest part of the novel, "Georgia," Bettauer introduces Rudolf Zeller, a Swiss German by birth and well-known professor of botany at the University of Göttingen, Germany, "who had accepted a call to the venerable German university in Prague just before his trip to America." Zeller travels to provincial Irvington, Georgia, during the era of Jim Crow in order to meet a fellow botanist, Colonel Whilcox, a plantation owner and a resolute racist. While being welcomed into the home of the ostensibly genteel Southerners, Zeller soon feels alienated, primarily because of the rabid racism of his host family, most notably Lady Harriet Whilcox, a transplanted Bostonian, who foments race baiting and a lynching to take revenge on Zeller, who ignores her sexual overtures, but instead is attracted to the housemaid's daughter, the beautiful sixteen-year-old Karola Sampson. While Zeller feels pity for the disgraceful treatment of African Americans in general, he initially constrains his sexual desire for Karola, whom he treats paternally. After witnessing and narrowly escaping a lynching, Zeller and Karola manage to flee to New York City.[17] During their first sexual encounter, which occurs in Atlanta while they are en route to the North, they conceive Carletto, the protagonist of the rest of the novel. Soon after, they find their way to New York City, where Zeller becomes aware that Karola cannot be an equal partner, not only because of their age difference and cultural gap, but also because of the laws restricting interracial cohabitation. Karola becomes pregnant, and when months later Carletto Zeller is born and his mother dies in childbirth, Zeller immediately decides to return to Europe with his baby after he has been offered a professorship at the University of Vienna.

Bettauer sets the second part of the novel, "Carletto," many years after the first part, in the altered cultural space of Vienna. The reader encounters Carlo shortly after his father's death. He is now a handsome law student with "olive complexion," "black eyes, sensual mouth, and beautiful teeth"—foreign features that make him look like a "Spaniard or Latin American." Carlo frequents cafés and has affairs with married women of the upper bourgeoisie. One of these profligate affairs leads to a duel that, following

---

[17] "Between 1882 and 1930 the American South experienced an epidemic of fatal mob violence that produced more than 3,000 victims, the vast majority of whom were African Americans. More than 450 documented lynchings occurred in Georgia alone. *Lynching* refers to the illegal killing of a person by a group of others. It does not refer to the method of killing." E. M. Beck and Stewart E. Tolnay, "Lynching," *New Georgia Encyclopedia*, accessed August 15, 2016, www.georgiaencyclopedia.org.

his victory, not only significantly enhances his social prestige among his friends but also causes his debts to balloon. His circle of friends believes that he can afford to lead the carefree life of a dandy as they do, while his guardian reluctantly and only partially provides the financial means to do so. The rest Carlo borrows from a loan shark. After his various glamorous and expensive love affairs and the death of his guardian, and after he has abandoned his pursuit of a law degree, Carlo becomes engaged to Lisl, who embodies the proper and truly affectionate virgin, but who is of a lower class. Carlo's precarious financial situation makes it imperative for him to leave Vienna for New York with the hope of succeeding in the New World, where Lisl already has moved to join distant relatives.

The third and longest part, "The Colored Gentleman," starts in New York City, which functions both as the mythical space where anyone may succeed by hard work, and as Carlo's place of birth. Carlo is, however, unprepared in more than one way to go back to his birthplace. For it is in New York that he is, for the first time in his life, instantly marked as a "colored" person and that the elaborate tabulations of degrees of blackness (mulatto, quadroon, octoroon), which pervade not only the American South but also the North, are immediately applied to him. In a short period of time, a con artist steals all his money and he loses Lisl, who is forced by social circumstance to deny the man she loves because of his race. In short, he loses everything familiar and valuable to him. Gone are his easy and high-class lifestyle, his successes with women, his ability to adapt to the prevailing social and cultural codes, and his financial means.

Absolutely penniless and friendless, Carlo ends up in a black neighborhood close to the harbor and experiences acceptance for the first time since arriving in New York months earlier. Yet, even now he refuses to accept that he is considered black, insists on his whiteness, and wishes nothing so much as to be back in the accustomed white world of Vienna. In order to obtain money to return to Vienna, Carlo indentures himself as a lumberjack and joins a crew bound for northern Alabama by train. It is only there that Carlo, after having stayed and identified with white co-workers at first, turns to his black fellows, who live in segregated barracks. Although he enjoys their "negro" music after a day of hard work and is curious to learn more about his fellow black workers and "how they thought and felt, what they wanted from life and what they hoped for," he clings proudly to his European whiteness, a whiteness that his black co-workers affirm in him as well. Carlo begins to teach them basic skills of hygiene, geography, and history and in return they call him "professor," first mockingly, and then with increasing respect and gratitude.

With his whiteness and desire to return to Vienna still intact, Carlo scrupulously saves enough money for the trip "home," and then fatefully encounters a woman on the train from Birmingham to Atlanta. Jane Morris is an attractive, sophisticated, French-speaking, educated African American woman who teaches orphaned girls, is active in the NAACP, and works for its premier African American publication, *The Crisis*. She compares her race work to that of the emancipation of Jews and argues that Negroes should develop pride in their own race.

Jane eventually becomes the catalyst for Carlo to accept his "black" identity. Bettauer paints the picture of Carlo's inner resistance to his blackness against the backdrop of the city where he was conceived, Atlanta. Only after Carlo witnesses a brutal fight between blacks and whites, in which he is seriously wounded, and only after Jane has saved his life, does his racial conviction assert itself: He decides not to return to Vienna after all. Instead, he commits himself to assisting a black activist group in fighting racism in the South. Thus, his personal crisis of racial identity resolves itself as a political and public fight against racism.

Translating Intercultural Transfers

By definition translation is a positioning process, intentionally transforming content from a point of departure to a new destination. In order to successfully take this something and transport it from one site to the other, the translator has to be aware of and familiar with both places. And while the translator as a courier conveys this something in as unaltered a way as possible, she or he must constantly anticipate how it will be perceived differently in its new environment. The translator therefore sees a dual perspective, and works with a double consciousness. The translator's task is thus challenging in that one transports something that must stay the same in the full knowledge that it will necessarily be perceived differently at its new site. The translator constantly traverses in her or his mind the space between one site and the other while transporting this item, being painfully aware of the unattainability of preserving it unaltered. This continuous transfer loop, however, affects the positioning and task not only of the translator but also of the reader, to the extent that she or he leaves the familiar culture and enters unfamiliar grounds and needs to calibrate or translate between the accustomed and unaccustomed.

Translating *The Blue Stain*, however, adds yet another layer to these intercultural transfers. Whereas in 1922, Bettauer communicated in *Das blaue Mal* a great portion of US racial politics and culture for his readers in German, translating *The Blue Stain* into English in 2017 is in effect shipping a view of American culture back from the Europe of 1922 to the United States of today. It allows American readers to look into their own history and society as perceived by a European, and hence to learn about themselves through an "other," quite apart from whether that other's perception is correct or incorrect. In fact, the resulting misperceptions can generate a productive dynamic of ongoing reflections, either between these cultures or from within one of the two. Hence, whereas I as an interlocutor was initially motivated to present to an American audience a work of modern German literature that tells a story of a racist US society, I needed to pause and ask myself who in the States needs to learn from a white European author who chronicles discrimination against African Americans in Georgia and New York City during the Jim Crow era? To answer this question one needs to welcome this neglected novel by this neglected author because it provides such a rich opportunity to engage in intercultural transfer. To put it even more pointedly, the translation of *The Blue Stain* offers a chance for intercultural dialogue not despite but because of its various misunderstandings and even contradictions resulting from Bettauer's good intention of spurring the fight against inequality, prejudice, and racism. After all, its transnational and transcultural misperceptions provide an opportunity at the beginning of the twenty-first century for probing the all-too-simple idea of a universalized culture and universal humanism that the age of globalization and the internet seems able to effect. In short, besides telling a compelling story with a well-intended noble ending, the translation of Bettauer's work unintentionally tells us a number of other stories resulting from its multiple levels of intercultural transfers across the Atlantic, the decades and the racial perceptions.

For one, Bettauer unconsciously provides a prime example of whiteness and blackness being first and foremost cultural constructions; that is, they are connected to skin pigment only in a relative sense. As long as Carlo has control over his life in Vienna, he is white—a social status that is primarily determined by education, behavior, mentality, and economic status. Once he enters the United States he is seen as black and deprived of his privileged position. While Carlo's physical appearance remains identical, the social value ascribed to his body changes according to whether the given society sees him as white or black: His identity is imposed onto him and changes in each cultural milieu. Although Carlo is a mixture of German and African ancestries, Anglo Americans in the United States treat him as black because of racist views such as Whilcox's assertion that "one drop of Negro blood and the whole generation is negroized. . . . To mix means to kill the white person in oneself and to create an accursed race!" It is as if being a quadroon represents a third race, one that, in the eyes of white supremacists such as the Whilcoxes, threatens whites more than does the black race, which, after all, can be controlled by the oppressive laws known as Jim Crow. And, opposite to Whilcox's views, the "quadroon" finds himself in an impossible position in US society: while Carlo assimilates to the dominant culture, the dominant culture does not allow for full integration because of the signs his body broadcasts; they make him an outcast. Simultaneously, the minority culture sees him as the "other" precisely because of his cultural assimilation. For his poor black fellows in the woods of Alabama Carlo is the "professor," black like them and yet exotic due to his education and upbringing in a different part of the world. Both Anglo and African ethnic groups in the United States treat him as the "other," while in Vienna he is only seen as "white," and thus he can blend in as part of the dominant culture. These varying social positionings also help explain why Carlo refuses for so long to accept his black identity: Doing so would make him the other *to himself.* Social circumstances push him to reinvent his conception of himself. In that sense it is a traditional *Bildungsroman,* albeit a unique one, since race is the determining factor for his new identity.

Bettauer's portrayal to his fellow Europeans, nearly a hundred years ago, of an American society then largely unknown to them, can help open our eyes today to the ways in which society generates racism precisely because Bettauer operates as a translator who conjures up a point of view from the outside peering in. Bettauer had traversed both cultures, but here operated as an interpreter when he depicted for his German-speaking audience the period of Jim Crow laws that continued racial inequality after the Civil War at the state and local level by segregating and discriminating against the African American minority.

Bettauer's narrative demonstrates his knowledge of early civil rights activism in America that he wishes to impart to his audience in German-speaking cultures. Particularly, Bettauer's direct references in his last chapter to William Edward Burghardt Du Bois (1868–1963), known by his initials W. E. B., show his familiarity with Du Bois's exceptional biography: He became Harvard's first African American graduate in 1890, founder of modern sociology in the United States,[18] and first editor of *The Crisis* (1910), the monthly journal of the NAACP, which Du Bois helped to found in 1909. It is most likely that Bettauer had read some of Du Bois's works, including

---

[18] Cf. Aldon Morris, *The Scholar Denied.*

his groundbreaking volume *The Souls of Black Folk* (1903) and drew from it ideas and even some statistics that Bettauer has Jane share with Carlo en route to Atlanta. When Jane fervently asserts that "we have struggled with all the weapons of our intellect for our advancement, our unity, and our true liberation," she echoes Du Bois's approach of urging African Americans to "fight for political power, insist on civil rights, and also provide higher education."[19] That Jane sides with Du Bois is all the more obvious when she dismisses Booker T. Washington's preference for first achieving social and economic independence for African Americans rather than challenging Jim Crow segregation.

As much as Bettauer was aware of Du Bois's defense of and call for higher education for African Americans, he must have been aware of Atlanta University, one of America's earliest black institutions of higher learning, where Du Bois taught at the time of the novel's action and where he had established the Department of Social Work. And when Carlo joins the rioting crowd to save Jane in the novel's stunning and melodramatic climax, the scene exhibits too many parallels with Atlanta's race riots in September 1906 to call them coincidental.[20] Whether Bettauer only read about Atlanta's race riots in the newspapers or whether he had actually traveled to Atlanta and the Southeast remains unknown. But by including in his narrative these direct and indirect connections to the existing black movement of his times, Bettauer enlightened his German-speaking readers, however with the implication of white European supremacy, as I will elucidate further.

---

[19] W. E. B. Du Bois, *The Souls of Black Folk*, 41.

[20] "On the evening of September 22 [1906], whites, aroused by false and exaggerated reports of arguments between blacks and whites, massed on Decatur Street. Word spread, and whites attacked streetcars and destroyed black shops and businesses on Auburn Street, then invaded black neighborhoods, with halfhearted resistance by or the support of city police and local militia. Black homes were pillaged, and five blacks were murdered. Blacks put up some resistance but were overwhelmed and outnumbered in pitched battles with armed whites. On the following night, state militia troops arrived, but many joined the white mob, which headed toward Brownsville, the city's middle-class black college suburb, and attacked its black residents. Police arrested and disarmed blacks who attempted to defend themselves. The next morning, police and militia entered Brownsville homes, supposedly to hunt for guns and arrest rioters; they beat and arrested affluent blacks. White rioting continued every night until September 26, when order was finally restored. Twenty-five blacks had been killed (as well as one white), and hundreds had been injured or had their property destroyed. More than a thousand blacks left Atlanta during and after the riots." Greg Robinson, "Atlanta Riot of 1906," *Encyclopedia of African-American Culture and History*, Gale Virtual Reference Library, accessed August 5, 2016, Web.

Bettauer's novel can be seen as indicative of a growing interest by Europeans in the United States after World War I, and the need for translating its culture to them as was done by a number of travel reports in the twenties such as Arthur Holitscher's *America Today and Tomorrow* (*Amerika heute und morgen*, 1912), Arthur Rundt's *America is Different* (*Amerika ist anders*, 1926), Ann Tizia Leitich's *America, You Have It Better* (*Amerika, du hast es besser*, 1926), and Egon Erwin Kisch's *Paradise America* (*Paradies Amerika*, 1930). Many were fascinated by America's sheer forward-looking energy, its self-confidence, the magnitude of the country—symbolized by its skyscrapers—its modern way of life, and its "exotic" culture, exemplified, for example, by African American jazz.[21] Arthur Rundt, in his 1926 travel report *America is Different*, was, for example, deeply impressed by the Harlem Renaissance and the progress in higher education that African Americans had experienced.[22] His enthusiasm was, however, mixed with a strong realization of the challenges facing the African American community in the form of the social inequality and persistent racism that he found. And Rundt was not alone in this ambiguity towards the United States. These ambivalent feelings could easily slant towards a perceived threat to European culture, and were sometimes fanned by exponents of nationalist ideologies into outright anti-Americanism. This was the case, for example, when Ernst Krenek's opera *Johnny spielt auf* premiered in Vienna in 1926, calling forth a backlash by the nascent Nazi Party, which denounced the entire music drama as a jazz opera because the main character is a black jazz musician.[23]

As emphasized before, translating is a two-way process: While embracing the new site, one cannot completely shed the views of one's original point of departure. In that sense, Bettauer not only translated for his principally Austrian readers how the United States appeared to him, but by having published *The City without Jews* the same year as *The Blue Stain*, he also made his Austrian citizens aware of how fragile the status of equal rights for Jews was after centuries of discrimination. Yet, in regard to *The Blue Stain*, it is as if Bettauer proudly wants to proclaim how liberal, tolerant, and progressive Europe has become vis-à-vis the United States. Startling as it is, he projects racism as existing only outside

---

[21] Cf. Siegfried Mattl's essay "Hugo Bettauer's *The Blue Stain*: American Blackness in the Viennese Mode."

[22] Arthur Rundt, *Amerika ist anders*, 71–78.

[23] Cf. Dan Diner, *America in the Eyes of the Germans: An Essay on Anti-Americanism*. For an early example of such anti-Americanism, see Adolf Halfeld's report *Amerika und Amerikanismus* from 1927.

Europe. The opposing views on Austrian society—that it was anti-Semitic on the one hand, and free of racism on the other hand—beg for some further probing.

Early on, the novel positions Zeller as an educated and morally superior European vis-à-vis US society. After his first tour of Whilcox's farm, and the discussion that ensues with Whilcox after they have encountered the housemaid's daughter, Karola, who will later become Zeller's wife, the narrator continues: "The Colonel's remarks about the brown girl incensed the Swiss German beyond all measure, this cultivated person living outside the realm of all prejudice. And as far as Boston was concerned, well, Zeller had visited there once, and he had become convinced that the members of the orchestra, from the conductor on down to the lowliest flutist, were Germans or Slavs; . . . and that the high society, which considered itself the best educated in the world, possessed just that amount of average sophistication that is worse than having no education at all." Thus from the novel's beginning, the European reader assumes a superior position vis-à-vis the racially repressive US society. While American society is above all sharply criticized for its race-based hate crimes in the South and the blatant racist discrimination in the North, Bettauer implies that Vienna is a place free of racial intolerance and inequity, a condition he had shown to be false in *The City without Jews*. Zeller is incensed to observe how disrespectfully his host Whilcox treats African Americans and to learn that even Whilcox's more enlightened friends do not see them as human beings since they "have no past, no history, no tradition, they are . . . like the baby that has just started crawling." Thus, Zeller embodies the enlightened, educated, sophisticated, and ostensibly non-racist European—and thus Bettauer is able to convey to his white European readers a picture of US society as being everything but enlightened, tolerant, and modern. In short, Bettauer establishes a Eurocentric hierarchy, or as Nenno observes, the novel "undermines the fascination with the New World at the same time as it reasserts the superiority of the Old World."[24]

While witnessing a lynching in the American South, Zeller himself poses the question whether the United States in the late nineteenth century is, in fact, just like during the Middle Ages, when witch hunts and pogroms against Jews were ever-present dangers. Thus Bettauer insinuates, perhaps desperately, that the discrimination against Jews is something belonging to the Old World past, and therefore no longer an integral part of modern Vienna and Europe. Of course, Bettauer must

---

[24] Nenno, "Elective Paternities," 274.

have been aware how contrived this implicit supposition was, since he not only has Carlo make a comparison between forms of racism against Jews and blacks but, moreover, has Carlo's mother, Karola, die in New York so as to avoid portraying the introduction of a mulatto woman into polite Viennese society. After all, Zeller asks himself, "Should he take Karola along? Have her admired in Vienna like some exotic little animal [Wundertierchen] while placing himself in an awkward social position?" Therefore, Bettauer must erase the mulatto and thus darker-looking Karola from the narrative prior to Zeller's return to Europe in order to spare her the role of the quintessential exotic "other." Karola's forced obliteration at the end of part 1 proves that Bettauer knew all too well his prejudice-free Vienna hardly corresponded to reality. This is also evident when Jane reminds Carlo that his fantasy of a racism-free Europe is just that, a fantasy: "Oh, I well know that people there don't do any wrongs to the Negro and the Negro race [Negerstämmling] there. Because they hold him in high regard? Not one bit! Because he is a rare curiosity! Take ten thousand Negroes to Vienna or Berlin, then hate will suddenly flare up against them. . . ." It is with this kind of assertion, which occurs even more prominently in *The City without Jews*, that Bettauer shows his awareness of latent and even overt racism and discrimination in Austria and beyond. And it this racial cognizance that also helps to explain why Bettauer deemphasizes Carlo's mulatto features by describing his complexion as olive, which makes him look like a Spaniard or South American, a level of exoticism that is amenable to the European context. From then on, there is no further mention of Carlo's physiognomic features suggesting his African ancestry. Bettauer suppresses the bodily signs of "otherness" for the sake of his antiracial argument. When living his spendthrift lifestyle in Vienna among a wealthy group of friends, Carlo does not fully fit in due to his lower social class, but he does not "look" or "behave" like a "black," and hence is part of the white majority in regard to race.

Curiously, though, one recurrent theme is his aroma, reminiscent of cinnamon and exotic spices, which European and American women alike comment on, and which even Carlo professes to notice. It seems that the social behavior cannot obscure bodily differences, be it its scent or the blue stain, the two physical features on which Kenneth R. Janken eloquently elaborates in his afterword to this edition.

One is compelled to wonder why the author of *Das blaue Mal*, who in the same year published *Die Stadt ohne Juden*, a novel in which he openly addresses latent and manifest forms of anti-Semitism in Vienna, presented racism as relatively absent in Vienna, Austria, and Europe and yet used racism as *the* marker that distinguishes between the Old World and the New World. What might be the reasons, one wonders, for creating a story that repositions "the Old World as the source of enlightenment, rationality, and progress"[25] while being aware that that description is at best only partially the case?[26]

Searching for reasons for this faux fault line between two opposing societies, one arrives at an unintentional form of racism that is enveloped in a sort of universal humanism. For one can argue that Bettauer did after all uphold the dominant white culture. Carlo's final acceptance of a black identity is a disguised form of white validation since it is only acceptable when African Americans acquire, like Carlo, the education that whites provide according to their norms. This educational canon according to the standards by and for whites becomes particularly apparent in the case of Jane, who "learned at home with the other white children" while also helping her mother, who functioned as a servant. Drawing on Richard Dyer's notion of whiteness in visual culture, one can argue that we witness a form of educational colonization—that is, white people facilitate the transfer of canonized knowledge, and create their "standards of humanity," even if not necessarily "maliciously."[27] We can witness this structural educational disparity when, for example, the self-educated Jane can indeed carry on her conversation with Carlo in French, "though not with a 'faultless accent.'" Conversing in a (white) European language marks, on the one hand, sophistication and also implies superiority towards those who are unable to do so, but Jane's not fully mastering French, on the other hand, leaves the social and, in this case, racial hierarchy untouched. That Jane can increase her social capital by having read the modernist Viennese author Arthur Schnitzler furthermore indicates that it is the white Europeans who set the standards by which one is able to raise one's social standing through *Bildung*, or education.

Zeller's views on racial politics also reveal a paternal, colonial attitude, regardless of how well intended it is. Via an analogy between flowers and the human races, Zeller, the botanist, sees every plant as legitimate and holds that one cannot discriminate between them; thus "for him, Negroes were just human beings with a different skin color, but not at all inferior." Yet Zeller maintains the notion that the other race is "on a lower plane of

---

[25] Nenno, "Elective Paternities," 262.

[26] Cf. Peter Höyng, "A Dream of a White Vienna after World War I: Hugo Bettauer's *The City without Jews* and *The Blue Stain*."

[27] Cf. Richard Dyer, *White*, 9.

civilization from which the white gardener could raise them with mercy and love." What makes this well-intended attitude problematic is that the "white gardener" places himself in the position of a benevolent caretaker, and therefore remains in a superior position. Like his father, Carlo also argues that the emancipation of blacks can and will take place by the "systematic education . . . until he has reached the level the German, Anglo-Saxon, Romance, and Slavic peoples have attained." Accordingly, Carlo teaches and treats his black fellows like children since he assumes that they have the "desire to ascend [emporzuwachsen] to the level of white people, to become their equals in the best sense."[28] And whereas any education thrives on the premise of the student eventually reaching full maturity by following the teacher's skill and knowledge, Bettauer's view, expressed by Carlo, nevertheless implies a structural imbalance in that the "black fellows" have to first reach the canon of knowledge as developed by whites in order to be called equal. Implicitly, African Americans are barred from contributing to the canon of knowledge at least as long as they need to earn their educational equality."[29]

Only after he has established whiteness as a universalized and superior concept in the name of equality and tolerance—two pinnacles of an enlightened humanism—does Bettauer have Carlo accept his black identity. In other words, blackness is acceptable only if one acts according to the standards of Europe's humanism, powerfully encoded, for example, in Beethoven's Ninth Symphony when the choir celebrates its fresh brotherhood with the words of Schiller's "Ode to Joy" after having defeated the injustice of despotism and tyranny.

In the end, what the readers of Hugo Bettauer's *The Blue Stain* hold in their hands is a translation of the very first novel in which a German-speaking author of European birth addresses racial politics in the United States in the early twentieth century informed by his own firsthand experiences living in New York. It is also one of a kind because it chronicles European-Americans' discrimination against African Americans in Georgia and New York from a European perspective. To reflect today's awareness, it seemed most sensitive to add the attribute of "racial" to the original subtitle, a "Novel of an Outcast." There is, however, an irony regarding the book. While Bettauer tells a story that sanctions a white European liberalism with respect to race, the novel's plot nevertheless exhibits its

---

[28] Cf. Nenno, "Elective Paternities," 267.

[29] According to Kendi's groundbreaking study on racism in the United States, Bettauer's anti-racist stance can be viewed as assimilationist. Cf. Ibram X. Kendi, *Stamped from the Beginning*, 2.

own brand of racism by promoting, ostensibly, universal humanism while still asserting that Americans of African descent need extensive Western cultivation and enculturation to aspire to the sophistication valued by persons of European lineage. The novel, therefore, serves as a unique historical account of flawed transnational and transcultural perceptions of racial identities in the early twentieth century, both in the United States and in Europe, that continue to create interracial polarities and reverberations throughout our present globalized world. One can only hope that the rediscovery of the novel also helps readers of all backgrounds to come to terms with racial inequality not as "a trendy issue" but unfortunately as "an entrenched issue" that begs to be fully pondered.[30]

Bibliography

Beck, E. M., and Stewart E. Tolnay. "Lynching." *New Georgia Encyclopedia*. Accessed August 15, 2016. www.georgiaencyclopedia.org.

Bettauer, Hugo. *Das blaue Mal: Der Roman eines Ausgestoßenen*. Vienna: Gloriette, 1922.

———. *The City without Jews: A Novel of Our Time*. Translated by Salomea Neumark Brainin. New York: Bloch, 1926.

———. *Der Kampf ums Glück: New Yorker Roman*. Vienna: Verlag Bettauers Wochenschrift, n.d. [1926].

———. *Die Stadt ohne Juden*. Vienna: Gloriette, 1922.

Blow, Charles W. "The State of Race in America." *New York Times*, June 30, 2016: n.p.

Conolly-Smith, Peter. *Translating America: An Immigrant Press Visualizes American Popular Culture, 1895–1918*. Washington, DC: Smithsonian, 2004.

Diner, Dan. *America in the Eyes of the Germans: An Essay on Anti-Americanism*. Translated by Allison Brown. Princeton, NJ: Markus Wiener Publications, 1996.

Du Bois, W. E. B. *The Souls of Black Folk*. 1903. New York: Barnes & Noble Classics, 2005.

Dyer, Richard. *White*. New York: Routledge, 1997.

Halfeld, Adolf. *Amerika und der Amerikanismus: Kritische Betrachtungen eines Deutschen und Europäers*. Jena: Diederichs, 1927.

Hall, Murray G. *Der Fall Bettauer*. Vienna: Löcker, 1978.

Holitscher, Arthur. *Amerika heute und morgen: Reiseerlebnisse*. Berlin: S. Fischer, 1912.

---

[30] Charles M. Blow, "The State of Race in America."

Höyng, Peter. "A Dream of a White Vienna after World War I: Hugo Bettauer's *The City without Jews* and *The Blue Stain*." In *At Home and Abroad: Historicizing Twentieth-Century Whiteness in Literature and Performance*. Edited by La Vinia Delois Jennings, 29–60. Knoxville: University of Tennessee Press, 2009.

Hwang, June J. *Lost in Time: Locating the Stranger in German Modernity*. Evanston, IL: Northwestern University Press, 2014.

Kafka, Franz. *Amerika: The Missing Person*. A new translation, based on the restored text. Translated by Mark Harman. New York: Schocken Books, 2008.

Kendi, Ibram X. *Stamped from the Beginning: The Definitive History of Racist Ideas in America*. New York: Nation Books, 2016.

Kisch, Egon Erwin. *Egon Erwin Kisch beehrt sich darzubieten: Paradies Amerika*. Berlin: Reiss, 1930.

Kriegleder, Wynfried. "Die amerikanische Sklaverei im deutschsprachigen Roman zwischen 1760 und 1860." In *Nordamerikastudien*, edited by Thomas Fröschl, Margarete Grandner, and Birgitta Bader-Zaar, 78–89. Wiener Beiträge zur Geschichte der Neuzeit vol. 24. Vienna: Verlag für Geschichte und Politik, 2000.

Leitich, Ann Tizia. *Amerika, du hast es besser*. Vienna: Steyrermühl, 1926.

Mattl, Siegfried. "Hugo Bettauer's *The Blue Stain*: American Blackness in the Viennese Mode." In *Imagining Blackness in Germany and Austria*, edited by Charlotte Szilagyi, Sabrina K. Rahman, and Michael Saman, 43–56. Newcastle upon Tyne: Cambridge Scholars Publishing, 2012.

Morris, Aldon. *The Scholar Denied: W. E. B. Du Bois and the Birth of Modern Sociology*. Oakland: University of California Press, 2015.

Nenno, Nancy P. "Elective Paternities: White Germans and Black Americans in Hugo Bettauer's *Das Blaue Mal* (1922)." *German Studies Review* 39, no. 2 (2016): 259–77.

Robinson, Greg. "Atlanta Riot of 1906." *Encyclopedia of African-American Culture and and History*. Gale Virtual Reference Library. Accessed August 5, 2016. Web.

Rundt, Arthur. *Amerika ist anders*. Berlin: Volksverband der Bücherfreunde, 1926.

Silverman, Lisa. *Becoming Austrians: Jews and Culture between the World Wars*. Oxford: Oxford University Press, 2012.

Sollors, Werner. *Neither Black nor White yet Both: Thematic Explorations of Interracial Literature*. New York: Oxford University Press, 1997.

THE BLUE STAIN

PART ONE

GEORGIA

"It's a fine country you're coming to, Sir; just too many of these damned nigras! If only we had one Dutchman of your blond kind for ten of these black devils, it would be paradise. It's a blessed country, Sir, this Georgia, the jewel of the South, and so the jewel of the world!"

The blond, blue-eyed gentleman—despite his impeccable elegance, even at a hundred paces, one could spot him as a European "greenhorn"—listened in bemusement to his fellow traveler. He enjoyed the boundless self-satisfaction of Americans, who, no matter whether they came from New York, Illinois, California, or in this case Georgia, praised their native state as paradise on earth. At the same time, the tirades against blacks—which became increasingly harsh and brutal for every degree of latitude he traveled further south—irritated him. Brushing his hair off his forehead with his stubby fingers, he said with a shrug: "Just what do you all want from these poor Negroes? I've gotten to know them as barbers, shoeshine boys, servants, conductors, and deckhands, and I find them quite handy, considerably more polite than the hired help of our own skin color, and they are always in a good mood and jocular. I actually quite like them."

With great virtuosity, the American spit right past the German into the spittoon.

"First of all, sir, my compliments on your excellent English. More refined English than us here stateside. By God, these Germans can do anything, and whatever they can do, they do right well.—However, with all due respect, you just do not understand the situation with the Negroes; you're talking rubbish there. One Negro is good as a barber, a shoeshine boy, or waiter, very good even, but in bunches they are bad, very bad. When they live in bunches, they are worse than beasts! And they are beasts, and it is unfortunate that those damned Yankees—may they go to hell, even though they are hardworking fellas—have gotten them to thinking that they are not brutes but human beings, just as good or even better than the evil white man who doesn't even grant they are human. Well, that might work in the North where they can be waiters or barbers or house servants, but here in the South it is a different story. Here we don't think: them *and* us, it's them *or* us!—My dear sir, once you have lived in this blessed Georgia for a few months, you will admit that James Brockfield from Atlanta isn't so dumb after all, even though he hasn't studied medicine like you, and grant that the Negro is a black beast!"

The German grew tired of this discussion; he had had these kinds of conversations all too often on his crisscross journeys through the States and on the steamer that brought him from New York to Savannah: the same narrow-mindedness of the people that continually irked him. But since the American had introduced himself by name, even though indirectly, the German for his part felt obliged to introduce himself.

"My name is Rudolf Zeller, a doctor, but not a medical doctor. I'm a botanist."

"Botanist? Hm, what kind of business is that, if I may ask?" Dr. Zeller explained with a smile and added that he was just now traveling to Irvington at the invitation of a gentleman who had succeeded in creating very strange and unique hybrids in flowers and fruits.

"Well then, you are what we call a gardener. That doesn't bring in much hereabouts, at best twenty-five dollars a week; and with that you cannot travel to Europe, so it must pay better in Germany."

Dr. Zeller had kept silent on the fact that, despite being only thirty-eight years of age, he was a European celebrity and a university professor in Göttingen. He gave up trying to explain the relevance of botany to the American, preferring instead to light up an American Key West Cigar and, looking out the tall etched-glass windows, took in the countryside the milk train from Savannah had been traversing all morning—ever so slowly. To the left and right he saw endless cotton plantations interrupted only occasionally by pitiful mud shacks with swarms of black children standing out front, shouting at the train.—Just like Germany, Zeller thought, only the houses there are tidier and more imposing, and the children blond.

Now a Negro in uniform approached the scholar and said in his strange, comically broad Negro dialect: "Next stop Irvington, Sir! I will unload all your suitcases, the small ones here and the large ones from the baggage car." And when Zeller pressed a silver dollar into his hand, black on the outside but dirty grey on his palm, the porter grinned with delight, no longer addressing him as "Sir" but "Massa," and brushed him off with loving care from head to toe. And once again, Zeller could not comprehend how one could persecute with such hate and disdain these harmless good-natured folks.

The train stopped in Irvington, and Dr. Zeller was greeted heartily by a tall, gaunt gentleman with a hooked nose, and a face that was clean-shaven and deeply tanned. This was Colonel Henry Whilcox. In the South, every respectable gentleman is a colonel and owner of a huge cotton plantation, and a floriculturist by passion. Zeller had once met him at a floriculture conference in London, and they had continued to correspond. Whilcox had frequently extended an invitation to the German scholar to visit him. The death of an uncle, who had left him a tidy sum of money, enabled Zeller to fulfill his long cherished desire for a study trip to the United States. He took a one-year leave of absence, traveled to New York, and from there out West, then back to Philadelphia, where he boarded a coastal steamer bound for Savannah. In just under ten hours, the train brought him to Irvington, an aspiring town in the state of Georgia. It was near Irvington, on Colonel Whilcox's plantation and estate, where he found thriving the most unusual orchids, carnation hybrids, coal black roses, tulips as big as his head—and in twenty different hues—as well as violet bananas that tasted like oranges.

Colonel Whilcox greeted the scholar warmly and in a highly theatrical manner: all the same, the tall, gaunt gentleman called to mind a buffoon. While Professor Zeller's luggage was being stowed atop an elegant carriage drawn by two magnificent trotters, the newly arrived guest was able to take a look around.

Irvington's primitive train depot posed a peculiar sight, looking like a wooden shed on the main square in the town center. Then there were two adjoining department stores, with gigantic display windows, garish posters, clothed female mannequins, with bonbons strewn about them. All this was surrounded by four terribly primitive and tasteless churches, only one of which, the Baptist Church, was made of stone, while the others were wood. With their low steeples and gaudy sign boards pitching their Sunday services like shirt sales, it was just possible to discern they were in fact churches, actually Presbyterian, Lutheran, and Catholic churches. Between the churches and the department stores were narrow dwellings, with their ground floors mostly turned into liquor stores and beer saloons. But in at least three, there were pharmacies out of which high society Irvington ladies were streaming, having grown curious, with their dishes of ice cream still in their hands, ready to gawk at the new arrivals. The blond German seemed to make a real impression. They had doubtlessly caught wind of the impending arrival. Curious, penetrating and coquettish glances grazed him, while Professor Zeller somewhat apprehensively noted that virtually this entire array of womanhood was stylishly dressed, slender, high-toned, and pretty.

Meanwhile two Negroes had finished loading the luggage. The black coachman took hold of the reins, the colonel took a seat next to his guest, and the chestnut bays started off. First they rode on the nice asphalt street where Irvington's better society had their houses, but then things changed. The wagon shook on rubber wheels through dirty, neglected streets, and out of the windows and doors of three- and four-story houses, left and right, nothing but the heads of Negroes protruded. In passing, Zeller saw coal-black pure-blooded Negroes, brown mulattos, yellow-brown quadroons, and wonderfully small chocolate-brown Negro children who were tussling half naked on the street; sometimes he also saw young, slim Negro girls whose distinctive beauty caught his eye.

Colonel Whilcox, who had followed Zeller's gaze, nodded: "Yes, of this sort we have plenty! Every year we get more coloreds, who breed like rabbits, while our women bear no children or at best one."

"Does this increase in the black population somehow make itself noticed in an unpleasant way?"

"Actually no, quite the opposite, at least there has been no shortage of hands to help at harvest time in the past few years. And we make plenty sure that this riffraff doesn't get ideas. Our young folk won't tolerate any foolishness in this regard.

"Just a few days ago, there was some rabble-rousing black itinerant riffraff Methodist preacher here who tried talking his racial compatriots into some sort of nonsense about equal rights. Well, before the day ended, he was tarred, feathered, and flogged out of town!"

A cloud of disapproval passed visibly over Zeller's open, bright face. He, who in the world of plants had come to appreciate the legitimacy of every living strand—the development from one level to the next, the growth out of a primal cell—could not comprehend such racist prejudices. He was imbued with the idea that everything in the world had deep significance, legitimacy, and an almost limitless potential for development. For him, Negroes were just human beings with a different skin color, but not at all inferior. At most, they were on a lower plane of civilization from which the white gardener could raise them with mercy and love.

Colonel Whilcox looked at his watch and cracked the coachman on the shoulder with his riding crop: "Hurry up, Sam, get a move on, no falling asleep." And turning to Zeller, he remarked: "We are a little late, and Mrs. Whilcox doesn't like to be kept waiting for dinner."

Zeller couldn't help smiling. So this gaunt, wiry man with his imperious nose was also a henpecked husband like almost all American men. And the fact that in this country, educated husbands only referred to their wives in the third person as Mrs. So-and-So seemed significant to Zeller and by no means empty formality. In Europe one *possessed* a wife; here one was married to a lady.—A fresh evening breeze was blowing, and the carriage hurried on between endless cotton bushes. The colonel pointed to an obelisk stone marker at the roadside: "My neighbor Perkins' plantation runs to here; from here on to the house everything belongs to me."

Small log shacks hove into view, and Negro children and big puffy Negro mammies poured out. Automatically Zeller thought back to those tales from the time of slavery and doubted whether very much had fundamentally changed. The well-kept country road curved, and the horses fell into a slow trot. This made it possible to see up-close a full-bosomed black woman and a young girl, both standing in front of one of the cabins. An exclamation of surprise escaped his lips: this girl, half child, half woman was of such rare beauty that it would have caught the attention of any connoisseur. She was obviously not pure black but of mixed blood, the skin color a muted brown, and her bare feet and her legs naked up to the knees were of most exquisite form. Framed by long thick eyelashes, wide eyes shone from a slender face with a small mouth whose lips were full, but not bulbous. The woman and her daughter bowed deeply and respectfully while a tall gangly black guy just emerging from his garden waved his straw hat in obeisance. Colonel Whilcox nodded faintly. Zeller, for his part, expressed friendly thanks. The carriage flew by at full trot, and the German scholar clearly sensed the brown child's gaze following him. He wanted to pose a question to his host, but Whilcox anticipated it and said, pointing backward:

"A decent, well-behaved woman who used to work in our home. Her daughter is a remarkably good-looking creature; of course her father is some white man. The boy that Bessie, her mother, later married has caused her quite a peck of trouble. A shiftless slacker, always chasing women, drinks like a fish, and beats his wife, who recently confessed to me in tears that she has to keep her daughter away from him—little Karola, the one you just saw.—Well, no matter really, whether it will be him or some other rascal. . . ."

Zeller felt a dull anger rising, but he successfully subdued it. Different way of thinking, he reflected. I first have to get some insight into these customs before I can differentiate here right from wrong, moral from immoral.

By now the carriage had pulled up to the front of the "big house," as these villas of the plantation owners were still called, in contrast to the homes of the Negroes. The beautiful white, two-story, rambling edifice beamed in their direction. A mighty front terrace, the so-called "porch"— supported by slender columns—extended around the raised ground floor of the stone building. From the veranda, the main entrance led into the cool, spacious hall that was surrounded by the living quarters, the dining room, the library, and various smaller parlors for entertaining guests. A carpeted staircase stained dark brown led to the second floor, where the bedrooms, guest rooms, and bathrooms were situated, while the garden steps descended to the kitchen and servants' quarters. All these country mansions in the United States exhibited almost the same layout and architectural design and differed from one another only in size and construction materials used. The great mansion of Colonel Whilcox was truly a princely estate of snow-white sandstone, comfortable and sleek from the outside, and majestic and solid from the inside.

Mrs. Harriett Whilcox, the spouse of the cotton plantation owner, received the gentlemen on the veranda. A gorgeous presence she was, a typical "American Beauty" of high society, tall, slender, her body well cared for with every finesse of the toilette, her evening gown elegant, yet simple. But for German tastes, she wore too many pearls and diamonds in her rich chestnut hair, over her plunging neckline, in her tiny ears, and on her long, slender fingers. She looks like a picture, Zeller thought, but a picture without mercy. And he sensed that behind her snow-white forehead, almost too high, a willfulness and a domineering spirit lay in repose that could make an American man his wife's compliant servant.

"Mr. Whilcox has told me much about you, and I am pleased to make your acquaintance. But Henry truly is not gifted when recounting details, because he described you very poorly. I expected to have as a guest a venerable German professor with a long beard and glasses who always leaves his umbrella behind, and instead—well, I don't want to give you any compliments."

"Madam, your husband told me almost nothing about you, but I had sensed that here in the Southern states I would meet a typical representative of the Nordic beauty of the northern states, and my senses have truly not betrayed me."

"Oh, how charmingly you pay court to a person, Professor," she laughed.

After this idle banter, Zeller betook himself to his assigned room, quickly took a cold bath that dissipated all his fatigue, and in the American manner, more strictly observed in the South than in the North, put on full dress, and was guided by a black servant to the dining room.

Later that night, the German botanist leaned against the window and breathed in the mild soft spring air, his head still heavy from the dinner wine. The many impressions of the past few weeks passed before him, and his thoughts came to rest on Mrs. Harriett Whilcox, who, in saying good-night, let her hand linger in his for several seconds as she all the while fixed him with a strange penetrating gaze from her grey iridescent eyes. Passion boiled up in him. He shook it off. "For shame—my host's wife! One must banish such ugly thoughts, the very thought makes you a scoundrel."

Rudolf Zeller, who as yet had no concept of the secrets or the depths of American flirtatiousness, slept restlessly and dreamed strange dreams: The beautiful lady Harriett and the young Negro girl from before stood in front of him. The former took off her pearl necklace and offered it to him. He, in turn, reached for a meadow flower that the black child had offered to him. Then the white woman smashed her fist into the Negro girl's face and screamed: "Get out, you are not human, you must not look at a white man!" And she hissed at him: "How dare you look at a black woman when I am here.—Oh, you Germans are fiends, like the Negroes, it is only we Americans who embody the human race."

Zeller awoke. Outside the sun glowed white-hot in a cloudless sky. Laughing at his stupid dream, he dressed quickly so as to learn about Colonel Whilcox's famous plant and fruit cultivation that had lured him to the American South.

About half a mile from the plantation house, on a rise facing south, Colonel Whilcox had his unusual nursery. It was the very time when the flowers were in full blossom and offered the botanist an abundance to admire. After years of effort, with limitless patience and care, the Colonel had, in this nearly tropical climate, by applying artificial fertilizers, man-aged to crossbreed plants of the most varied species, magically conjuring up the most remarkable plant types, even managing to make them capable of reproduction. As a consequence one found flowers that were neither carnations nor roses, but both; turf-rooted plants that were grafted onto trees and bushes; mignonettes growing on trees almost as tall as a man; carnations as large as a child's head in seven different colors, red forget-me-nots, yellow violets. He succeeded in producing creeping vines that were unimaginably complicated and mysterious and in uniting the most various kinds of fruit on a single tree.

The two gentlemen stayed in the garden for hours; the professional interest of the scholar and the joyful pride of the happy planter over his recognition were so great that they paid no attention to the grueling sun which had almost reached its zenith by the time little Karola Sampson, the mulatto girl from the day before, came and presented the gentlemen with two giant Panama hats.

"The lady sends me with these because otherwise the sun might could burn the head of the gentleman," she said laughing, while giving off an air of freshness and precious grace.

While the Colonel took his hat without a word and replaced his Scottish cap with it, Zeller gave thanks with a smile and ran his hand over Karola's bluish black hair that was uncovered and simply tied back with a red headband. And so he learned that her hair was not woolly, but tightly curled and silken. Strangely shocked, Karola looked at him with the large and knowing eyes of a child holding still, like a chicken being petted. With a quick glance at the Colonel, who was already busying himself with clippers on a bush without looking around, she then said: "German mister should not stroke Karola. If the lady see this, she get very angry and never shake hand with German gentleman, but beat Karola's face with stick." And then she said with a soft voice full of concern: "Mister not can stay in sun, your face already very red, Colonel used to sun in Georgia, but German gentleman come from country where no sun be, must be careful."

Now the Colonel stood upright and turned to his guest, and Karola hopped away in great leaps. Her skirt flew up so that one could see her light brown legs in all their slenderness.

Zeller walked in silence together with the Colonel towards the mansion, and suddenly he said: "What a complete beauty this girl is, you know! What will become of her around here?"

The Colonel had to laugh: "Well, I think, first of all, she'll be your lover! But you'd better hurry, Professor, or some dirty nigger will get that little beast before you do. But take care that my wife doesn't notice. She gets very sensitive on these matters and detests anything that comes even in distant contact with a Negro. She would actually prefer to have white servants if it weren't so impossible around here. She is from Boston, and there the ladies are even more particular than other places. Fabulous city, that Boston, best university, best orchestra, the best educated people in the world."

Zeller made no reply. He did not want to, because to do so would have violated the bounds of politeness. The Colonel's remarks about the brown girl incensed the Swiss German beyond all measure, this cultivated person living outside the realm of all prejudice. And as far as Boston was concerned, well, Zeller had visited there once, and he had become convinced that the members of the orchestra, from the conductor on down to the lowliest flutist, were Germans or Slavs; that the students played impressive baseball but had no clue of real scholarship, and that the high society, which considered itself the best educated in the world, possessed just that amount of average sophistication that is worse than having no education at all.

At the luncheon, Lady Harriett wore a pale blue, very low-cut voile dress, with deep-red roses at the décolleté. And the way she sat teetering in her rocking chair after the black coffee, her legs crossed, so that her dainty feet came to full effect in her amber patent leather shoes, she was a perfect beauty. Moreover, in the way she raised her arms from time to time to adjust her hair, so that her lithe figure stretched and gave some hint of the loveliness of her breasts, she embodied ideal beauty. She wouldn't have needed at all to flirt to get the German's blood raging against his better judgment.

One could hear the arrival of a carriage, and immediately following a servant announced Mr. and Mrs. Jackson. A young married couple entered the parlor, and soon thereafter an older gentleman, Dr. Dobb, the top physician in Irvington, arrived on horseback; and from then on one carriage after another arrived, most of them steered by a lady. Actually, all of Irvington was downright curious to make the acquaintance of this blond German who had traveled halfway around the world to admire a few plants. On the veranda, where the rocking chairs were carried, a lively chaos ensued, sounding like chirping in a birdcage.

Zeller again made the same observation as he had done in the East and out West in the States: the gentlemen looked more or less all like brothers; each of them possessed a jovial good-naturedness, although almost none of them had any kind of original idea, intellect, or meaningful education. The women, by contrast, embodied more individual natures; they were superior to their husbands in regard to education and reasoning, were fully aware of it, and formed among themselves a kind of freemasons' guild in their struggle against men, who were to be subjugated. And another thing Dr. Zeller noticed with an agreeable smile: whereas the Englishman is closed off, reserved, and discreet to a point of being inaccessible, the average American, especially those who are not viewed as Yankees, exhibits an astonishing degree of indiscretion. Without being asked, he blurts out the most intimate things in his life and interrogates a person he doesn't know like a detective. And so, Zeller actually had to tell why he had come to America, tell most of what was worth knowing, and more or less recount a full autobiography. But there wasn't a whole lot to tell. He came from an old, noble family in Basel, but had studied in Germany and considered himself German through and through, even more so since his parents had passed away long ago and he had lost touch with the land of his upbringing. He had been a professor of botany at the University of Göttingen for a few years but had accepted a call to the venerable German university in Prague just before his trip to America. The next fall semester, he would be in the capital of Bohemia.

His narrative, however, did not come off all that smoothly. Most of his audience had no clue where Göttingen was or what its significance was, and Prague was for them just another German city, and when he explained that it was the capital of Bohemia, the confusion really peaked. Because Bohemia called to their minds a *bohemian*, and consequently a gypsy, who played the fiddle in coffee houses in the big cities, therefore Prague could only be the capital of Hungary. At any rate—all of this confusion was suitably clarified with a dose of good humor, and the conversation flowed on in an amusing way. The professor for his part artfully used every opportunity to ask questions to get some idea about the general conditions in the Southern States.

The whole time the black servant served soundlessly and nimbly; with extraordinary adroitness he filled glasses with iced drinks, balanced the full tray with the dexterity of an acrobat; appeared when one of the gentlemen wanted to light his cigar, and disappeared instantly when there was no immediate need for him. Zeller involuntarily observed the skillful and graceful moves of the Negro with aesthetic appreciation and thought the moment was right to shift the conversation onto the delicate issue of race. "Ladies and gentlemen," he said when the conversation was about to ebb and the servant had moved out of range of hearing, "Despite my best efforts, I cannot comprehend this general aversion to colored people. What I have seen so far of them, I like. In the vaudeville shows, they are splendid dancers and comedians; as servants they seem to be more willing, adept, and friendlier than their white counterparts; they are reckoned to be among the most tender and self-sacrificing caregivers of children, they are good cooks, barbers, and coachmen.—So, I have to ask myself, where does the extreme disrespect and hate originate that is shown them everywhere, up North, out West, and most especially here, down South?"

These words set off a lively debate. Professor Zeller was rapidly bombarded with a crossfire of protestations. Men surrounded him, pushing in on him, and even the ladies abandoned their reserve and participated in the discussion.

Negroes are well-trained servants, barbers, and shoeshine boys, but they are not human,—from birth on, a Negro is lazy, thieving, and stupid and remains so until death—God intentionally created the Negro different from the white man—the Negro is culturally on the same level as a monkey.—These and similar remarks swirled towards Zeller until some calm emerged and a middle-aged gentleman seized the floor. He had studied at Yale and appeared from his looks to be every inch a European aristocrat. Lewis Sutherland, that was the gentleman's name, who had brought his blond and very elegant wife from England, said:

"With all due respect, dear Professor, you have put your finger on our most sensitive spot and you must not be taken aback by this temperamental American outburst. The issue you have brought up is as horrible as it is complicated and tragic. We, the citizens of the South, and undoubtedly our Northern neighbors as well, are paying for the sins of our fathers and grandfathers. It was a horrible criminal deed, unworthy of human dignity to drag Negroes here in masses like cattle from Africa. But once they were here, it seemed natural from the Southerner's perspective to treat these humans, standing on the lowest level of civilization and utterly foreign to us, as slaves, that is, as purchased property. And it was equally natural that one day the North, which had no experience with the Negro question, would rise up against slavery. And the fact that we lost that fratricidal war, which actually started because of the slavery issue, that was not from some accident or because of poor leadership or even because of treachery, but because of the iron rules of logic, because we fought for an issue that could not be defended. So then, the Negroes were emancipated, and not satisfied with that, some hysterical women and men even declared them to be equal to us in every respect. However, they do not possess equal rights with us, not at all and under any circumstances. I do not mean that they are less than we are; I wouldn't think of placing them on the same level as apes, but I assert that they act toward us as little children do toward adults. They have no past, no history, no tradition; they have only just become human like the child just beginning to crawl. And who would consider giving such a child equal rights? Who would allow it to involve itself in the affairs of adults? If one were to do this, then these children would develop into disgusting and mean tormentors instead of into reasoning human beings.

And this is rather similar to the way it works with Negroes. They are thieving, lying, greedy, and, if one does not keep them on a short leash—impudent. All of these are simply characteristics of children, as any mother can confirm. What can we learn from this? That the Negroes first have to traverse the path toward becoming full-fledged human beings, that they have to be reared and educated for centuries. If one does this, and I am very sure of it, the Negroes will one day be a rather close second to the white race in regard to intelligence and morals.—But how are we to reach this goal? It is a virtually unsolvable problem. Like a small child, the Negro just won't understand that he must first be educated. Well, when bringing up children, you can put them in a corner or even use corporal punishment, but with Negroes you can't do that. Have them educate themselves? That won't work, and because of deeply ingrained feelings of race the white man will not tolerate the childish misbehavior of the Negroes. Especially not here in the South where to some extent we are outnumbered by the black race. If we were actually to grant them in practice the equal rights they have on paper, then not long after that here on the veranda of this beautiful mansion in Irvington it would not be white people conducting conversations of this sort, but Negroes who would be discussing what to do with those inconvenient white people.—

So, what is the way out of this dilemma? There are three possibilities. First, one could ship the black people back to Africa! That is unworkable, both technically and judicially, since our Constitution gives them equal rights, and one cannot force them to return. Second, one could change the Constitution and declare the Negroes once again slaves. That won't work because the old and young, the female and male milksops all over the world would howl and cry out loud to express their pity. Therefore, there is only one solution, and that is the one that we Southerners and actually the Northerners also take: to make the Negroes second-class citizens in order to keep them socially and absolutely distinct, deny them access to the vote, and give them jobs that limit them to their physical capabilities. However—I will admit that this is no real solution, but simply a sort of expedient, and that the coming generations will most certainly have a tough nut to crack on the unresolved Negro question."

Once again, a lively clamor of voices arose. An old gentleman who looked like the very embodiment of Uncle Sam shouted: "We are criminals if we leave our children with this kind of heritage." Another person talked of a plague to exterminate the Negroes that would have to be artificially propagated. And the cynically inclined Doctor Dobb said with a smirk: "I know of a wonderful means, painless when applied to newborn Negro boys, but I cannot go into details with the ladies present." Since all the ladies knew what he meant, they pretended to be appropriately shocked but couldn't refrain from hearty laughter.

Zeller dared to object by saying: "And wouldn't it be possible to arrive at a simpler solution and, overcoming all racial prejudice, tolerate the Negroes gradually becoming part of white society?"

A deep silence fell on the veranda of the large mansion. Zeller noticed by the partly indignant, partly ice-cold expressions on their faces that he had expressed something outrageous to their way of looking at things. An old gentleman, with a vein of rage protruding on his forehead, interrupted the embarrassed silence by saying in a coarse voice: "You are a foreigner, young man, we'll grant you that liberty. If a Yankee had suggested something like that, especially in the presence of ladies, it would have aroused grave displeasure."

Colonel Whilcox, who could not allow his guest to be chastised so harshly, intervened:

"You speak as a scholar, as a botanist, who has just witnessed the wonders of unusual plant hybridizations. But if we were to apply such an experiment to us, this would mean giving up ourselves; it would mean the Africanization, the Negroization firstly of all America and then of the entire world. For as you know, Doctor Zeller, one drop of black blood creates a Negro. We in the South know this all too well to quibble about it. The brown mulatto woman whose father was a white man unites again with a white man. Their child is a quadroon, no darker than a sun-tanned white person, handsome and slender. If it is a girl and unites again with a white person, then the child is an octoroon whom you only recognize by a bluish tint on its fingernails that it has Negro blood. And if it again is a girl who once again unites with a white man, then it happens that the child turns out to be an ugly, grey-black Negro! One drop of Negro blood and the whole generation is negroized. You can't do anything about that, can't want to change that. The blood of Ham is stronger than all the others. It will always show through! To mix means to kill the white person in oneself and to create an accursed race!"

It had nearly turned dark when the handsome Negro appeared quietly, gently tapping a gong to announce that dinner was awaiting the guests. And the modest discord the discussion had engendered soon yielded to a warm and pleasant mood. Professor Zeller was sitting next to the beautiful lady of the house, and it seemed to him that from time to time her knee touched his, or her foot found his. Afterwards, when everyone was promenading in the garden through the hot Southern spring air, the lady Harriett, for a moment, cuddled against the blond German and whispered to him: "I would never forgive you if you were to approach the black brood! And you can't conceal it from me; I catch the scent that these animals leave clinging to everything!"

July approached and with it, scorching heat waves, unbearably hot nights, rendered even more unbearable by swarms of mosquitoes that emerged at sunset, making it impossible to be out in the open. The veranda and all windows had wire screens, and black servants relentlessly waved smoking incense to disperse any and all invasions of these blood-sucking invaders. Time was passed lounging in rocking chairs and drinking iced drinks on the veranda. But July also brought new life to Irvington. Summer break at the universities in the East and West had started right after Independence Day, and now all the sons and nephews came home from college to the South to be thoroughly lazy in the bosom of their families. It was too hot for any kind of sports during the day. Therefore, during the day, the young people lolled in their rocking chairs, went to bars, engaged in their little flirtations, and in the evening they went out for a stroll that usually ended with hunting down Negroes. Out of pure and unmasked racial instinct these college boys hated Negroes—though they nevertheless relentlessly pursued the adolescent Negro girls. The daughters of the blacks were fair game; game which, however, does not customarily flee the hunter but willingly seeks refuge in confinement. The pitiful living conditions under which Negroes barely eke out a living in the South, even more than in the North, assure that their sexual morals are on a very low level. And usually a Negro girl feels very flattered to be approached by a white man, especially if he is of the gentleman class. She feels this even though she knows that the man who embraces her is doing nothing, absolutely nothing, but satisfying his sexual appetite.

The young white men liked strolling through the streets of the small town, shoving Negroes who were not quick enough to escape, and beating them miserably on the pretense that they had heard disrespectful remarks being uttered. They even played judge and jury, following up on thefts committed by blacks, and could scarcely wait for a chance to tar and feather somebody.

One day a few chickens disappeared from Colonel Whilcox's henhouse that were highly valued as breeders. At once the vacationing college boys of Irvington took up tracking them with a dog. The foxhound soon found the right scent and guided the group of about twenty boys to a Negro cabin in which an entire black family was just about to enjoy a delicious chicken soup. Quickly a kangaroo court was convened that sentenced the Negro head of the family to tar and feathers. The poor devil had to undress, was rolled all over in a mass of tar, coated with chicken feathers and wool tufts, and then flogged through the streets. By chance Professor Zeller witnessed the scene and was profoundly enraged; yet being a foreigner he could not decide to intervene. With great disquiet, he noted that elderly Negroes and Negro children joined the white boys in trailing and humiliating the man. But soon afterwards Zeller saw a group of young Negroes and in their faces he saw nothing but hate, their faces gone grey-blue in helpless rage. And he overheard one of the boys say to the others: "The day will come where we will tar those white dogs in their own blood."

That evening there was a grand party on Colonel Whilcox's veranda. Almost all the college boys attended as guests and boasted of the little heroic act they had perpetrated against the chicken thief. Now Zeller could no longer hold back; with sharp words he expressed his utter displeasure at their brand of justice. The older people kept embarrassingly silent; the younger ones protested; one of them even muttered something about "sentimental German nonsense," and there was no shortage of hurtful, malicious remarks. Zeller finally ended the embarrassing exchange when he said: "He who sows hate, will harvest hate. And all of you are sowing an overwhelming measure of hate. Believe me, this is no way to deal with races and people! You can't expel and can't exterminate your Negroes; therefore, you have to find a *modus vivendi*. And tarring and feathering as a punishment is only then acceptable if it is incorporated into the legal system and applied equally to white chicken thieves."

The mood was spoiled. Casual conversation could not get going again, and Zeller felt quite superfluous on this evening. Even though the beautiful lady of the house tried to engage him in conversation, and while doing so, repeatedly placed her hand on his arm, Zeller sought out his bedroom to retire early. Inside, it was very hot and muggy, while outside a cool breeze from the east off the ocean cooled the air. Zeller put on his Panama hat and, to avoid being seen, exited the house by a small garden gate. The evening air made him feel comfortable, and he strode briskly along a meadow path, which ran more or less parallel to the road, leading towards town between endless cotton fields and under beautiful American oaks. The moon above shone silvery and penetratingly; the cicadas chirped unnaturally stridently; and Zeller was overcome by a longing for his homeland. He felt that his behavior today had earned him the reputation of being an impossibly patronizing German and had provoked the displeasure of his host. And consequently it no longer seemed wise for him to stay. For, even though Colonel Whilcox had been too courtly and gallant to give his guest even the slightest hint of ill temper, would it not be a failure of tact on his part to impose further on him and tarry while discord loomed? And then there was the beautiful Harriett Whilcox, who made it seem advisable to retreat expeditiously from the Colonel's wondrous gardens. Zeller sensed that the allure of the American lady was inflaming his passion so much that the moment would soon arrive when he might most crudely abuse the hospitality accorded him. Zeller was not vain, but he was also not naïve, and clearly observed that Mrs. Whilcox was preparing to transgress the generous boundaries of American flirtatiousness. And with him precisely because he was not an American constrained by a thousand prejudices, but a man who thought more freely on these matters and who would not scorn her even if she were to commit adultery with him. All this would lead either to humiliating lies and detestable treachery or to catastrophic results if the hot-blooded Colonel were to gather even the least suspicion. All right, I've got to get away from here, he thought, and the sooner the better!

The meadow path opened onto the country road close by the Negro Sampson's house. Suddenly, as if conjured out of the soil by magic, the young Negro girl Karola was standing before him, the young girl who had so fascinated him at his arrival with her style of beauty. He uttered a few words of greeting and asked her whether she was not afraid to be alone on the road at night. Karola shook her head causing her loose hair to fall over her forehead and said with a soft melodious voice:

"It is too hot inside, and there are too many of us in one room. If it had been someone else coming by, Karola would have quickly fled back into her house. But the great German professor is a good man, and she is not afraid of him."

With a laugh, Zeller ran his hand over her thick hair, which felt like raw silk:

"How do you know I am a good person?"

The girl laughed with a high pitch and cooed:

"Karola feels that! The German man is different than the Yankees. He does not hate or despise the poor black."

"No, Karola, I really don't. And why should I? Surely there are among you colored people as many good and bad people as are among the whites, yellows, and reds. But you, Karola, you probably don't like white people?"

"Oh, I would like to love them, the whites. Blond is the most beautiful thing God created! But they hate us and so I hate them."

There was no objecting to this kind of logic. Zeller laughed and said:

"Come, Karola, let's go for a short walk, and when we are far enough from your home, you can sing one of the lovely sad songs of your people!"

Zeller had taken the girl by her hand, and nearly took fright when she pressed his hand to her lips and kissed it saying softly:

"Oh yeah, Karola like to be with you and take you to a spot where no one can hear or see anything."

The moon shone silvery, quiet, and solitary around them.

The scholar almost felt ill at ease as he strolled through the incandescent night, hand in hand with this beautiful, slender child of nature. His blood surged. If I were to drag her over between the cotton bushes and take her as if plucking some red fruit off a tree, he thought, no one would think the least bit of it, she herself perhaps least of all . . . Who knows how many had already done so, what ugly black guys, or those college boys who must have been struck by her brown beauty, or maybe even that immoral dog of a step-father had done it who, as Colonel Whilcox had said, had been stalking her. A raging envy grew in him and with a hoarse voice he said as he leaned over to her:

"Have you experienced love-making, Karola? Have you ever given yourself to a man?"

The mulatto girl looked at him with wide eyes:

"No, Sir. If one of our kind gets too familiar, I scratch and spit at him, and I hide from the white students. I smell when they are coming, and run away before they catch me. I don't want to make love with anyone, no one, nobody! Not the dark ones because they are stupid and ugly, and not the white ones because I will then have a baby that has no place with us nor with the white ones and would be as unhappy as Karola."

"Are you truly unhappy, Karola? And why is that?"

"I would like to be a white lady, sir!"

In these words Zeller sensed the whole tragedy of a half-breed who feels rejected by the white race. Without thinking, he laid his arm across the shoulder of the child who was blossoming into womanhood and pleasingly felt the sweet nakedness of her young body clothed in nothing more than a blouse and skirt. Karola did not pull away, but instead snuggled up to him like a cat. Their walk took them through the dense underbrush to a small grove of hazelnut bushes, decrepit oaks, and tall thorn bushes. Karola now led the German by the hand deeper and deeper into the tangle until she loudly and gaily exclaimed:

"So, this is my bench!"

There indeed was an uprooted tree, beaten by storms and felled by age that lay there in fact making a bench on which one could comfortably sit. At first Karola sat in silence next to Zeller, then she jumped up, and nestling in a bush so that he barely could see her contour in the moonlight stood right in front of him and began in a gentle melodious voice to sing old Negro melodies, concluding with the beautiful "Old Folks at Home."

Zeller closed his eyes and listened in reverie, as he laughed to himself:

"What a strange, pretentious, and illogical world we live in! If I took the beautiful, brown child with me to Berlin or Vienna, educated her a bit, and dressed her exquisitely, then she would be the great sensation of the day! Princes and millionaires would vie for her attention; all the men would be at her feet, and she could lead the life of a queen. But here she is a miserable mulatto girl with whom some white man can at best satisfy his fleeting desires, but nothing more! Good God, if the beautiful lady Harriett were even to suspect a situation like this! That would put an immediate halt to her friendship and flirtation!"

Karola sat next to him again, and so close that he could feel her body on his arm. He threw his arm around her neck, pulled her over gently, bent her head back, and kissed her full and luscious lips. She returned the kiss and tenderly stroked the blond hair of this man and whispered into his ear:

"Karola instantly liked the good German man when she saw him for the first time . . . and if he wants, he can take her all the way.—But no one is allowed to know about it, otherwise Missus Whilcox will be very angry and kill me."

That awakened the primeval German in him, the protector and helper, and his lust morphed into fatherly tenderness. He stroked her as one strokes a dear little child and kissed her on the eyes that she closed with joy. And he did not accept the gift that she had offered.

From that time on, Zeller sneaked out of the mansion at night very often only to whistle the tune of "Old Folks at Home" near Sampson's cabin. And then it took mere seconds before Karola jumped up from the straw mattress on which she slept in the cabin and silently slipped outside to Zeller, to walk hand in hand to the wild grove where both of them, now tightly enshrouded in a fine-meshed mosquito net, sat on the fallen tree. Zeller often had her tell stories about her old plump mother who had spent her teen years still in slavery. In this way, he gained a profound insight into the dull life of these American Negroes who lacked tradition and whom the whites had first trapped like animals in their primordial state and then carried off. The conviction grew ever more firm in him that it was a prejudice to see and treat Negroes as a despicable lower race, a people, simple in its infancy, and lacking history, despite the millennia of their past. They were like putty for anything, for good or ill, like children in whom all characteristics are mingled awaiting fertilization and development at the hands of the seasoned white preceptor. But the latter had no desire to fulfill his mission and instead desired to keep this uprooted people in eternal infancy. And Zeller was involuntarily reminded of jugglers and itinerant buffoons who stunt the growth of circus children with alcohol.

One evening after dinner, the residents of the great mansion were sitting with their guests on the veranda. Again, there shone a full moon, and the whole group was outfitted for an excursion, by horseback or carriage, to visit the neighboring estate about eight miles away where an iced punch would be served at midnight. With a seemingly guileless smile, the lady Harriett turned to Zeller as he was helping her into her saddle:

"Actually, our nightly excursion must disturb you, Professor, since it prevents you from taking your nightly stroll."

Zeller struggled against his embarrassment and replied nonchalantly:

"Oh, so that hasn't gone unnoticed after all? Well, it actually does me quite a lot of good to stroll around by myself at night in order to gather my thoughts. It is just too hot to fall asleep before the early morning hours."

The American lady gave a shrill and caustic laugh as she swung into her saddle:

"I'm afraid that in your solitude something terrible might happen. Maybe the Negroes will come prowling after you."

"What makes you think that?"

"Well, I told you that I can catch the scent of a nigger from a great distance, and you bring their smell with you. It still clings to you, even after you have taken a bath in the morning."

Shrugging his shoulders, Zeller explained: "That actually might be more a figment of your imagination," as he turned this very uncomfortable conversation in a different direction.

They started off with the horses at a brisk trot, while the carriage horses leaned into the traces. After little more than an hour they arrived at the home of Colonel Stoddard, the Justice of the Peace, whose home was festively illuminated with lampions. A generous cold buffet ensued, and then a delightful ice-cold punch was served, made out of select, first quality peaches and champagne and, since the majority of their society were young folk, things soon turned very lively and jolly. Then suddenly, the lady Harriett, who was extraordinarily agitated, began monopolizing the conversation by complaining that the colored rabble had in the last few weeks become nasty and demanding in glances, demeanor and deportment.

Her comments gave the cue for a nigger hunt first in words and then in the raging threats the young men expelled. They virtually vied with one another in curses against the blacks. Each one of them vowed his intent to tan some Negro's hide at first opportunity. In vain Colonel Stoddard admonished them not to disturb the peace. The students declared in unanimous agreement that something finally had to be done to show this black riffraff once again who was in charge. One of the youths who was obviously courting the lady Harriett emphatically declared that the disciplining of some Negroes was absolutely necessary, otherwise the ladies would be at the mercy of nasty looks or be exposed to even worse from the Negroes once the young men departed after their summer break. This view drew the acclamation of the others, even that of some of the young girls, while the lady Harriett extended her hand to the protector of white innocence.

Without a word, but in anxious attention, Zeller listened to the conversation, and his thoughts wandered to the dear, brown child of nature that he knew in his heart was without fault and more pure than all of these controlling and flirtatious women and girls. He sensed disaster in the offing and resolved to warn Karola and to limit to the absolute minimum his nightly encounters with her. And once again the thought stirred in him to whisk Karola off with him to Europe in the fall.

From that moment on, unrest was brooding in Irvington and its environs. Daily the young Americans caught some Negroes under some pretense or other and flogged them; and day by day the attitude of the young Negroes who worked on the cotton plantations became more defiant and more threatening. And it always was the lady Harriett who spurred the men on in the evenings to new nigger hunts with her applause and by renewed stories that this or that Negro had impudently grinned at her. At the same time she treated her guest more coldly and had long since ceased flirting with him, so that Zeller felt that it was only her proper upbringing that stopped her from being outright rude to him. As much as he appreciated the quiet and likable Colonel Whilcox, he cared that much less for his beautiful and coquettish wife. Nevertheless, he began to feel very ill at ease and resolved to cut short his stay in the state of Georgia earlier than intended and to return to New York by September and from there go on to Europe.

Then an event ensued that scattered all his intentions and plans to the winds.

One late afternoon near the end of August the lady Harriett in riding habit and showing every sign of agitation appeared in the hallway of the Georgia Clubhouse where the whole *jeunesse dorée* of Irvington customarily enjoyed rounds of poker and bridge and summoned out some gentlemen of her acquaintance, including her husband and Dr. Zeller, who were passing time in the library. Breathless, she reported that she had just suffered a horrible affront. Right in front of the house of the nigger Sampson her horse's saddle girth had broken, and Sampson, who was lounging shiftlessly in front of his cabin, quickly repaired the damage. When she attempted to remount her horse, the black beast, under the pretense of adjusting her stirrup, took the liberty of touching her shamelessly. And when out of indignation she struck at him with her riding crop, the mulatto girl, who supposedly was not only his step-daughter but also his whore, observed the event and shouted while clapping her hands: "Go ahead, Pa, grab her, give her a good squeeze." Close to collapse, the lady Harriett quickly galloped to the clubhouse, and now she was entreating the men of Irvington about what must be done to properly discipline Sampson and his daughter.

While Zeller stood there bewildered and dumbfounded—knowing with absolute certainty that the story was a lie, at least as far as Karola was concerned—a horrible tumult ensued. The men shouted heatedly in confusion, pistols were drawn, even Colonel Whilcox clenched his fists and yelled: "This rabble must be exterminated!" Lady Harriett's young suitor stepped up, after the commotion abated, and asked Mrs. Whilcox to rest at ease and go home since her honor was now in good hands. A tribunal would immediately be constituted to decide what steps needed to be taken.

Zeller was so aghast at all this that he lost his quiet composure. Instead of riding immediately to Sampson's house, he attempted conciliation. Since the young men had immediately locked themselves up in a room, he turned to the lady Harriett who simply listened to him with frigid harshness and finally declared with a shrug: "Your attempts to serve as a Negro lawyer, won't be of any help since our boys won't tolerate any meddling in these matters."

Zeller turned in vain to Colonel Whilcox, to Doctor Dobbs, who had joined them, to the pharmacist, and to the other elder gentlemen. They, too, flatly declined to intervene. This was a very blatant case of a Negro assault against a lady and, therefore, justice must be carried out at once, as is usually done in these matters in the South. That was the tenor of their responses.

During these time-consuming discussions, Zeller had not noticed that the young men of Irvington, twenty in all, had stormed away on horses and wagons to avenge the lady Harriett's honor on the Negro and his daughter. When he learned of their departure, he could find neither wagon nor nag to borrow to race after them. And in his frantic anguish for Karola, there was no alternative but for him to cover the long distance on foot in the glowing summer heat. It took more than an hour for him to make it to the cabin, covered in sweat, breathless, and completely exhausted. Long before that, however, he scented acrid smoke and suspected that something horrible had happened. Now he was finally standing in front of the cabin—actually no, in front of the place where the cabin had stood just an hour before! Only a few smoldering beams lay on the ground in the middle of a small trampled yard.

Zeller looked around, and his blood started to freeze in his veins: there, right in front of him, the body of a lynched Negro dangled from the branch of an old apple tree. But his face was not black, but a strange greenish grey. And out of his broad gaping mouth his tongue hung so that it seemed that the hanged man were about to grimace. Cold sweat ran over Zeller's forehead and he stared at the dead body as if lost in thought. Was this possible? Would civilized young men, students who would one day occupy official and honorable positions, really murder a person who at worst had committed an act that could adequately have been punished by a sound beating? Was he living at the end of the nineteenth century or in the Middle Ages? Instantly, Zeller remembered the Jewish persecutions of past centuries, along with witch-hunts and inquisitions.

The sound of horse's hooves snapped him out of his horror. Cross-country over the cotton fields, the self-appointed judges came riding. When they saw the German, they shouted their jolly hellos as if nothing had happened, dismounted and one of them said laughing:

"So, Professor, you don't have anything like this in your old, easy-going Germany! You should be thankful that we have shown you how we in these parts exercise proper justice without courts."

Zeller controlled himself with great effort. He knew that if he showed his disdain to these people, he would make a fool of himself and excite their hatred of him, which would do nothing to save Karola, dear, little

Karola—assuming she were even still alive. And so he entreated the young gentlemen to recount to him how everything had taken place.

The lady Harriett's new lovesick swain obliged him.

"Well, we all galloped at top speed to this place and sure enough found all of the riffraff gathered round. Without dillydallying, we first grabbed Sampson and tied him up with some rope. Then we tried to catch that little beast, his daughter, but unfortunately she was quicker than us; she ducked away quick as lightning, ran between our legs and was away like a wildcat. A couple of us followed, but it was impossible to catch her as she disappeared into the bushes. Well, the main culprit was Sampson himself, and luckily we had gotten him. Meanwhile he howled proclaiming his innocence and his fat wife kept crawling around on her knees so much that we finally had to boot her out of the cabin before pronouncing sentence over the guy. Some of our boys used their revolvers to keep the Negroes at bay who in the meantime had started to gather, while the rest of us dragged Sampson out to the apple tree by the road and quick as you please he was hanging in the noose. When that boy stopped making noise, we torched the whole place so that nothing would be left of this scandalous hovel. And now we have started looking around again for that little whore, but no luck. The old lady ran to town to hide with her black kin. But we are not concerned about her since Mrs. Whilcox had nothing to say against her. But that girl we'll find. Jimmy will bring out his bloodhound tonight and she can hide wherever she wants but we'll track her down."

"And what will happen to her?" Zeller asked, seemingly calm while he felt his heart pounding.

The young boys looked at one another with a grin, then the guy who was called Jimmy responded:

"Well she is a devilishly cute hussy, and young! And since we are young too, we will draw lots to have our fun with her before lashing her soundly and putting her in the stocks in the town square."

Zeller nodded and left. He would not have been able to control himself for another moment, and in an instant would have drawn the pistol that he too, according to the custom of the place, always carried and would have shot down the first lyncher he happened to see. Having already walked a few steps away, he turned around:

"Well, gentlemen, I might just participate in the search for that girl, at least from a distance. When will it start?"

"We'll be riding back to town now, then notify the sheriff, wash down a good dinner with a good swallow of claret, and set out from here with the dog around nine o'clock. 'Tiger' picks up the scent best at night."

Zeller left and traversed the short distance back to the "big house."

He again began to think calmly, clearly, soberly and methodically as if solving a scientific problem. Karola had to be saved, at any cost, even that of his own life. He felt a warm and loving feeling grow in him. His thoughts of Karola were filled with tenderness and longing. "That dear girl," he said to himself, "I would rather have her die by my own hand than abandon her to these brutal beasts."

After he had arrived, he looked at his watch. Five o'clock—all right, time enough. Quickly he washed off with cold water, had the black servant come, who made a disturbed, hate-filled impression, and ordered him to pack his suitcase as quickly as possible. The herbaria he had gathered in Georgia he packed himself. Then he went down to the veranda where Colonel Whilcox nervously and rather embarrassedly greeted him.

"Colonel Whilcox, for almost four months I have been your guest and never in my life will I forget the friendship and genteel hospitality which you have accorded me. But I can no longer stay. What I have witnessed today is simply too much for my German sensibilities. A bitter exchange of words will soon and inevitably come between me and the young men who have eradicated one of God's creatures, and that I must avoid. If you would be so kind as to have my luggage delivered to the depot so that I can take the night train to Macon and from there on to Atlanta. There I shall stay for a day and take the express train to New York and board the next steamer to return to my old-fashioned homeland."

Taken aback, but with perfect dignity, Colonel Whilcox shook hands with the German scholar and assured him that he profoundly regretted his early departure, while understanding completely and honoring the professor's reasons. Now there was only one thing left to be done: bid farewell to the lady Harriett, but this did not take place. The beautiful lady had excused herself and retired early saying the day's commotion had made her feel unwell. So, all alone, Zeller left an hour later for Irvington when the glowing red sun had set, declining in a friendly but firm manner Colonel Whilcox's offer to accompany him.

Not far from the place where only hours before Sampson's piteous cabin had stood, he asked the coachman to stop, got off, and gave the order to have his luggage stored at the train station, and afterwards for the driver to return to the Whilcox home. He had a headache, he said, and would like to go the rest of the way to town on foot. It seemed, however, the black coachman knew that something unusual was about to happen; he looked deeply at the German with trusting eyes and said while shaking his head:

"May God protect and bless you, your Honor, since you are not like the gentlemen around here who hate the Negroes like dirty beasts!"

In feverish anticipation, Professor Zeller walked to the oak grove in which he had spent so many strangely romantic hours with little Karola at night. In vain, he peered into the semi-darkness; the natural bench on which Karola was accustomed to snuggle against him was empty. Deathly silence surrounded him, and the air seemed to be venting off steam. But when Zeller anxiously shouted "Karola" aloud, there was a rustling, and out of the thickest underbrush the contours of the girl emerged, who at the next moment fell around his neck sobbing.

While he was kissing, caressing, and consoling her, Karola told him that her mother had escaped to relatives in town but that she had hidden for hours in the underbrush, determined to sever her arteries with her teeth in the event her pursuers discovered her. But an inner voice had told her that the tall blond German would come and save her. The little mulatto girl assured him and swore by her eternal salvation that she had no notion whatsoever of an encounter between her step-father and Mrs. Whilcox, and that she had only learned from Zeller's narrative why the men had killed Sampson in such a gruesome way.

Now not a minute could be lost. Zeller had planned out everything very precisely in advance. Under no circumstances should the girl take the road to town because she could immediately be captured by one of the lynching party there. Without any delay, she was to hurry across the plantations to the first stop that the local train from Irvington to Macon would make at nine o'clock and then travel with this train to Macon in the attached car for colored people. Zeller would be aboard the train, traveling to Macon, where she would find him waiting for her on the platform. Zeller gave the girl money, who agreed to everything, kissed her tenderly, and then hurried along the country road to Irvington while Karola snuck through the underbrush and cotton bushes on the two-hour journey to the train stop outside of town.

Everything went off without a hitch. In the small town of Macon, Zeller and Karola found each other, and both boarded the express to Atlanta. He, of course, traveled in the Pullman-section while she used the car for colored people. It was almost midnight when they were standing on the street in front of the Atlanta train station.

But now what? The express train to New York left at eight o'clock the next morning, and Zeller would under no circumstances leave the shivering young girl alone in a dirty, dubious Negro hostel. He could not take her into his hotel since she was of color and therefore had no claim to accommodation in a hotel in which white people resided. But Zeller knew what to do.

"Karola, both of us are not ready for sleep. So let us go eat something and then look for the central park that I have noted in my guide and wait for dawn. I won't let you leave me, you poor, little girl." She did not reply. Silently she pressed his hand against her feverish lips while a silent soft sobbing shook her young body.

In a dubious saloon, the appearance of Zeller with the mulatto girl evoked a grin from the solitary waiter. But steak, eggs, fresh lemonade, and fruit were soon served, and the two of them, who had not eaten in the last twelve hours, were able to still their hunger and strengthen themselves. Hand in hand they walked through the great, silent park. They left the paths and looked for a secluded place on the grass, between hedges and bushes, to stretch out.

The night was hot and silent. Karola nestled against the white man who in her confused state appeared to her like a Savior. The blood began to throb in his veins, and his hot hands caressed the hot, virginal body of the girl from a different world who welcomed her deflowering by the man she idolized with a soft, cooing shout of jubilation.

As he had done months before, Professor Zeller again lodged at the Waldorf-Astoria in New York, the world's largest and most luxurious hotel at that time, while he found for Karola room and board with the family of a black Methodist preacher whose wife not only had no objections to the daily visits of the German professor but actually felt honored by them. Living together in a hotel or in a bed and breakfast was impossible even in New York for even though Negroes usually could use the same streetcars, as they generally can in the North, they are nevertheless excluded from the residences and the luxurious life of white people, as they are in the South. The dividing wall is lower but no less rigid: black and white, that is not a problem here, but it is a fact that no one dares challenge.

Zeller was thinking about their next encounter. He loved the child with all his being. He was aware that she could not be a partner in the higher sense of the term but his feelings did not wane and he could not be without her any longer. In Karola's arms, he shed all of life's burden, at her young breast, he found the most complete redemption, utter sensual bliss. And he would not have been a European, especially not a German, if he did not morally feel himself to be inseparable from Karola in this time. But what was he to do? In two weeks at the latest, he had to return to Europe in order to assume his newly endowed chair in Vienna. Should he take Karola along? Have her admired in Vienna like some exotic little animal while placing himself in an awkward social position? Or did he have to tear himself away from her and leave her behind in the care of her racial peers?

Could he do that without mortally wounding Karola, who was devoted to him with a tenderness of which a European woman was barely capable? All these questions found a surprising solution. The newspapers had reported Zeller's arrival in New York City. Reporters questioned him about his observations and studies in the South, and a large scientific society named him an honorary member. One day, barely two weeks after his arrival, the Trustees of Columbia University in New York offered him the prestigious position of an endowed chair.

The offer was a fateful sign. Zeller ran up to the brownstone townhouse on 48th Street in which Karola lived and swung her jubilantly like a doll in the air.

"Karola we shall stay together! One year, two years, many years!"

And then Karola, sobbing and laughing from happiness, uttered her first German words to him:

"Ich danke Dir und dem lieben Gott."

Christmas in New York was a snowstorm. Early in the morning the weather had been as mild and warm as Germany in May. By midday, however, icy frost descended that by afternoon had turned into a blizzard. In less than half an hour the gigantic city was transformed into a snowy Northern landscape. First the streetcars, then the elevated rail system came to a halt. Enormous masses of snow fell from the heavens, and the hurricane-like north wind blew in pedestrians' faces, piling up drifts on the streets to such mountains that the house doors could not be opened and those seeking admittance literally sank shoulder deep in the snow.

Laboriously, Professor Zeller made his short way from the spacious university buildings to the modest house he had rented at the end of Columbus Avenue. He was genuinely indignant at the weather, which he declared to be unscientific, out of place, and against the laws of nature. New York was at the same latitude as Naples, an avowedly Southern city. Besides, this region by rights should have an oceanic climate—so why and wherefore did it have a tropical glow in the summer and Siberian snow in the winter? Moreover, there were other circumstances that put

him in a foul mood. In this weather, Karola would be unable to make
her way to his house. Not only was it Christmas Eve, which he wished
to celebrate according to German tradition in his own home and with
a Christmas tree, but it also was Karola's sixteenth birthday. Zeller had
spent the entire day at the university library putting the finishing touches
on the botanical work that his publisher in Jena was expecting. Now
five o'clock had come. And instead of lighting the Christmas tree which
Karola was to have decorated, only dark rooms and the good-natured but
rather simple-minded old Negro woman he had taken on as housekeeper
would be awaiting him.

The storm howled more and more fiercely, threatening to blow the
wanderer off his feet. It blinded him and hurled clumps of snow in his
face. It was so gloomy that the scholar only found his way home with difficulty. It took the epitome of acrobatic achievement for him to climb up
the five steps leading to the entrance. But at that moment Karola's gentle
arms enfolded him as he stepped in the warm parlor where a green tree
stood glowing with a hundred candles. The girl had struggled against
snow and storm on a three-mile trek, decorated the tree, lit the candles,
festively set the table in the adjoining dining room. And now she stood
before him, clad in an unpretentious black velvet dress whose neckline
partially exposed her lovely bosom. A gentle blush rose in her brown
cheeks, and she looked entreatingly at her lord and teacher with her
great, innocent eyes.

In the distribution of Christmas presents, the old black servant got
money and sweets and the necklace of colorful stones she had wished for.
Professor Zeller received from Karola's hands beautiful, tasteful ties in
muted suave colors since she had cast off the Negro's love for motley, garish
colors and developed a range of stolid bourgeois tastes that tolerated nothing of wild color in her clothing.

Zeller rushed into another room and came back with a large white box
that he handed over to his companion. And when she had untied its rib-
bons and lifted the box's cover, she saw a wonderful mink coat with a muff
and a cap. Karola rejoiced and danced around, slipped into the mink, made
inarticulate cooing sounds from the Dark Continent, but then she nestled
against her benefactor, kissed the hands that he only reluctantly extended
and said with a droll pronunciation and cute sense of importance:

"Rudolf, ich danke dich von ganzes Herzen, und werden dich lipp sein
bis in allen Ewigkeiten!" ["Rudolf, I am thank you from the bottom of my
entire heart, and I will be loving you four all eternity."]

Zeller was flabbergasted and stood silent in astonishment.

"Karola, my dear!" he then exclaimed in reply, likewise in German: "What has come over you? You speak German like an old Reichstag deputy! Who taught you to speak like that?"

Touched and enraptured, he now learned that the mulatto girl with the help of a tutor had been studying German daily, and for the past three months had been working on her German late into the night. By now she had made so much progress that she could read this and that political story in the *Staatszeitung* and was able make herself tolerably well understood in conversation.

Zeller pulled her over onto his lap, kissed her, and said tenderly:

"Karola, you lovely, sweet child; this won't go unnoticed. And we shall stay together until death do us part, won't we?"

He was serious about this; for at this moment he decided once and for all never again to be separated from the black girl.

Karola, however, started, weeping bitter tears at his statement and through her sobs she revealed:

"Oh, my love, that won't take very long because Karola will surely die when she delivers the little baby she has from you!"

So, it was only now that Zeller learned of this, too! Sixteen-year-old Karola was carrying his child under her passionate and loving heart. Back then in Atlanta, on that passion-filled summer night, she must have conceived this child, and in May, when New York's temperatures would again make it a Southern city, she would deliver that baby into the world.

After Karola had regained her calm under the tender caresses of this strangely moved man, she said:

"Dearest, is it possible that our small child won't be a Negro, or a mulatto, or a quadroon but a completely white human being like you?"

"Possible? No, that won't be possible! The child might be much, much lighter than you but always those who know something about these things will sense its black blood.—But that doesn't matter, Karola! The child won't grow up here but in my German homeland where people don't have these prejudices, where no one will belittle, let alone vilify him because of his descent. And now let us write to your mother in Irvington and tell her to join us and take care of her daughter and assist her when her grandchild is expected."

Months passed. Her mother, Sarah Sampson, had long since taken up residence at the preacher's home with her daughter whose young body matured for the blessed event.

And another blizzard came, and yet another, and suddenly overnight it turned wonderfully warm. And when May was acting like mid-summer in Italy, Karola's most difficult and last hour arrived, for it was then that the German doctor, who had with the assistance of a German midwife helped a little boy enter the world, whispered softly to the father:

"Professor, you must be prepared for the possibility that the poor dear little mother might be snatched away from you in death!"

And yet, there was just barely enough time to send for a German notary from the neighborhood who despite his astonishment and disapprobation nevertheless did the unheard of thing and joined the blond, white university professor and the mulatto woman in wedlock! Then Karola lost consciousness; her brown cheeks turned grey, her eyes grew dim. And the baby Rolf Carlo Zeller, who had just begun crowing like a young rooster, had lost his young brown mother.

For Professor Zeller, there was now no longer any reason to stay in America. The story of his wedding appeared in the newspapers, and at the university the gentlemen were very compassionate but at the same time also so measured and cool that he could not fail to comprehend. Quickly Zeller handed in his resignation, hired a sturdy, young, coal-black wet nurse, accepted the professorship at the University of Vienna, and bade farewell to the country that might not have ancient castles, but did retain some neat age-old prejudices.

PART TWO

CARLETTO

About noon one sunny day in May, Carlo Zeller, called Carletto by his friends, and Clemens von Ströbl strolled down Herrengasse towards Michaelerplatz. They came out of the venerable gray building where the legal exams were held, and where Carlo had just passed his first state exam. He had not exactly distinguished himself with an excess of knowledge, but the professors had at least judged his knowledge adequate.

His friend Ströbl, a few years older, roughly twenty-six years of age, blond and stocky, with a short-clipped mustache, full cheeks, and sly, insolent, grey eyes, had made a point of attending and witnessing the exams. As had been previously arranged, they now went to Hotel Sacher so that Carletto could regenerate and restore himself after the exertions of the last hours.

Over his tails Zeller had on a black topcoat and wore a top hat and white kid gloves. He was a gorgeous young man: mid-size, slender, very lithe, with narrow hips and sloping shoulders; jet-black melancholy eyes shadowed by long eyelashes shone from his elongated, olive-complexioned face, as did a smooth, bright red, hedonistic mouth, over which a short upper lip revealed his beautiful white teeth. His whole appearance seemed attractive and exotic like that of a Spaniard or Latin American, and this interesting young man obviously caught the eye of the women, for they sent him very friendly glances.

Next to him, Clemens von Ströbl, embodying the very picture of a genuine Viennese dandy, thrust his arm into that of his friend:

"Well, it seems to me you could make a friendlier face now this stupid exam is over and done with!"

"You know, Clemens, all this folderol is still getting me down," retorted Carletto. "We must stop by the telegraph office; I want to send a dispatch to Graz."

"Why such a rush?" objected Ströbl. "His Honor, your trustee will simply learn of this joyful event a few hours later."

"But I specifically promised the old man that I would telegraph him immediately."

"Your devotion is really touching!" Ströbl said, laughing at Zeller. "We've got to wean you of this, you're not a kid any more. First we've got to eat and drink properly and then for all I care you can telegraph love poems to Graz for Professor Wendrich." With these words he energetically dragged Carletto away, who had remained standing irresolutely in the Michaelerplatz.

The headwaiter in Hotel Sacher, who knew Clemens von Ströbl, led them into one of the small, red-festooned rooms where only four tables stood, none of which were occupied at the moment. "Excellent," shouted Ströbl, "the peace and quiet will do you good, Carlo!" He then set up the bill of fare, ordered a bottle of Chateau Lafite and already had a bottle of Beuve Cliquot put on ice. "The victory must be suitably celebrated," he said. Zeller, who objected to drinking champagne before noon, had to relent.

The two young men rehashed the exam as they dined. This was just the first exam, five more were to come. Carletto sighed deeply.

As he had frequently done, Ströbl remonstrated with him about the senselessness of such worries:

"You are well off, after all, and you do know that my old man will get you a position at a bank—if you absolutely want to enter that career—if it suits you, even without the doctor's title."

"But what if my guardian insists that I get my doctor's, and what if this was simply the wish of my late father?"—replied Carlo, who inwardly would all too gladly have adopted his friend's view and would have given up his studies sooner rather than later, which were hard for him and gave him no particular joy.

"Oh, Professor Wendrich!" Clemens said dismissively. "It certainly is a matter of conscience to respect the wishes of your father. But could your father, God rest his soul, not anticipate that you just can't get legal studies into your head?"

It was actually somewhat uncomfortable for the frivolous Ströbl to have his devoted pupil and carefree crony whisked away for hours devoted to his studies. Carlo's future concerned him just as little as his own, which to be sure seemed far more secure than that of his friend, since he was the only son of a rich industrialist.

"Can't you guess how I imagine we should spend the rest of the afternoon?" he asked. "After our meal we'll drive over to your place, rest a bit, and around half past four go down to the Prater and into the Krieau. I have arranged to meet two young ladies from the Ronacher Theater over there, the ones I recently told you about."

Carlo, somewhat embarrassed, remained silent at first and then said: "You must excuse me, Clemens, but I already have plans for this afternoon. I expect a visit."

"Who from?"

"You can well imagine who."

Ströbl lit a cigarette and grumpily blew out the smoke. "This story is starting to get boring, my friend. It's already been carrying on since last summer. So, how much longer is this going to go on? Why not just get married right now?"

"But if I like her . . ." said the other earnestly.

"Oh Lord, you can like anyone who is pretty, nice, and chic. At your age you don't want to tie yourself down so tightly. If we at least knew for certain who this demonic woman is who's been keeping you on such a tight leash for so long."

A wrathful spark in Carlo's dark eyes smoldered, and raising his voice he said: "You know you can't get anything out of me on this. Why do you keep pressuring me?"

"It seems to me that I have earned enough of your trust to learn at last the great secret of your life," Ströbl responded irritably.—"Or must I remind you: Who accepted you most cordially when you first came to the club? Who walked you through your first steps in the big city? When I think of how you looked, how shy you were, the high-school graduate from Graz . . . Stubbornness like that can really anger a person."

It saddened Carlo Zeller to see his friend hurting so. Comforting him, he laid his right hand on Ströbl's. "I know, Clemens, I know, but what cannot be, cannot be. I gave my word of honor to be discreet, so don't be mad at me."

"Good, we won't talk about that anymore, maybe the moment will come when you will confide in me of your own accord. Anyway, affairs that last that long don't always end neatly.—Cheers!"

The champagne flutes rang against one another and the ill feelings between the two soon dissipated.

A half hour later they left the restaurant and shook hands cordially. Zeller climbed into an automobile and drove home to Reisner Street.

He possessed a very nice three-room apartment and had made his place comfortable and cozy with the furnishings from his father's living quarters. An old servant, Franz, kept the small household in order. From a nearby restaurant he brought the meals Carletto took in at home. Now Franz complimented the worthy gentleman on passing his exam and helped him change. It had been Ströbl who back then had introduced old, bald Franz into Carletto's household. Of course, it was Ströbl who had taken care of everything. He had found a servant's quarters that opened onto the great park of an aristocratic palace, had selected the wallpaper and placed the furniture. It was also Ströbl who, with a great deal of coaxing, had convinced Carlo last year to give up living in a pension and set up his own home. Ah, Ströbl! He truly taught me how to live, thought Carletto, while he lay comfortably on a sofa smoking in his study awaiting Hella.

When Carlo was in his sixth year of high school, Professor Rudolf Zeller died from a severe stomach malady following a brief illness, leaving his only son quite alone. Rudolf Zeller had appointed as guardian the zoologist Professor Wendrich, his former colleague at the university and his closest friend, who had been living in Graz since retirement. Wendrich, a confirmed bachelor, immediately rushed to Vienna and spent the rest of the school year with the boy in Vienna, and thereupon dissolved the Zeller household and took Carlo back to Graz. There, Carlo had finished his two remaining high school classes. It had been Wendrich's plan for Carlo also to attend the university in Graz. However, the young Zeller had resisted this most resolutely, because he did not feel comfortable in the provincial city, and living with the kind and wise, but quirky and reserved, old man greatly depressed him. Carlo was not a very simple character to deal with either; usually compliant and readily flexible, he could become determined and unyielding once he got a goal in his head. So Professor Wendrich, who well knew the disposition of his ward and no longer commanded much willpower, gave in and let Carletto depart for Vienna.

Young Zeller at first took up quarters in a modest pension. There he lived by himself and spent the first semester quite alone. Athletically gifted and interested in all sports, he registered in the Palace Fencing Club one day. Upon his entry into the club a radical change occurred in his lifestyle. The young people that he got to know took him under their wing and soon turned him from a timid provincial into a dashing dandy. Especially Clemens von Ströbl, who played an enormous role among the members of the sports club, took charge of Carletto. He introduced him into society, pulled him into fun-loving circles, brought him together with all kinds of easy women, and dragged him quite often from nightclub to nightclub.

Professor Wendrich could not help but notice Carlo's metamorphosis, above all because the young man could not find the means to sustain his new way of living on his modest allowance and repeatedly asked for an increase. However, since the young Zeller's financial circumstances were actually quite favorable, and Carletto's demands remained within manageable limits, Wendrich had had no cause to intervene.

✳   ✳   ✳

Wearied from the excitement of the exam and somewhat numbed from his imbibing, Carlo had fallen asleep on the loveseat. He had fallen into such a deep slumber that even a knock at the door had not brought him to his senses, whereas a kiss on his forehead finally did.

"Hella!" he shouted jumping up and passionately embracing the tall, slender strawberry blonde standing in front of him.

"First of all, my dear Bubi, I congratulate you on passing your exam," she said kissing him on his glowingly fresh, boyish lips. "Franz has already told me everything."

She had gray-green, dewy, shimmering eyes, a finely shaped nose, and a small doll-like mouth. Carlo wanted to help her take off her hat. "No, no," she said, warning him off, "I can't stay long."

Only now did he notice a certain distress and consternation in her demeanor. "What's wrong, my dear," he asked with concern as he pulled her down to his side.

"Nothing, Carlo, nothing of any importance, I just have one more errand to run." And with a smile, which was intended to put him at ease, she added: "But I can stay long enough to drink tea with you, meanwhile you must tell me how you spent the last twenty-four hours and how the exam went."

He let himself be taken in by Hella's disarming and seemingly cheerful words. He rang Franz to serve tea and, while they sipped, nibbled, and nestled, he chatted away. Then suddenly he broke off. He had noticed that Hella was only listening to him with one ear; her gloomy gaze dwelt musingly somewhere off in the distance.

"Where have your thoughts strayed to, Hella?" he asked her intrusively. "Something's happened; why don't you want to tell me?"

She shook her head and forced a smile.

"You're seeing apparitions, my little Bubi, maybe I'm just a bit nervous today, that's all."

But now he didn't believe her any longer. He jumped up agitatedly, seized her hands and forced her to look him in the eye. "I want to know the truth, the truth, you hear me!"

Her gaze eluded his. "You're torturing me . . . let go of my hands, you're hurting me!"

But irascible as Carlo was, he squeezed her right hand even more tightly and with fiery eyes shouted: "You must tell me!"

"You're forcing me. I didn't want to tell you because I didn't want to upset you. Thomas received an anonymous letter today—"

He felt his color change. In sudden shock he took a step back: "Your husband? . . ."

"Somebody put him on to our relationship. There was a terrible scene. I denied everything of course, but I very much fear that he will be having us shadowed now. Yes, my dear boy" she said sadly, "we will have to be careful. We will not be able to meet so often anymore." She ran her hands caressingly through his silky, black, slightly wavy hair.

Carlo, who sat down by her side again, let his head droop: "Terrible, now he will torture you and I must stand idly by not able to come to your aid." Then he reached out and stretched, and from his eyes shone boldness and a lust for battle. "Oh, if only I could confront him!"

"Be reasonable, Carletto, you must be reasonable, for the sake of my honor. Above all, I must avoid anything that could make him distrustful. For Thomas will of course be very wary. Not out of love for me," she said, smiling bitterly, "but from vanity. That's why I consider it best for us not to be seeing each other at all for a few weeks." These last words she brought forth hesitatingly, fearing that they might cast Carlo down into utter despair.

Indeed, he nearly cried out: "What, not see you anymore?—That I can't do, Hella, I can't." A profound, genuine aching trembled in his voice. Mrs. Bühler, who had already stood up in preparation to leave, had to sit down again. She pulled Carlo to her, leaned his head against her shoulder, and stroked and consoled him:

"Just for a few weeks, my darling, you just have to be strong enough to endure it, just until he has forgotten that wicked letter."

"But you also risked coming to me today," he objected.

"Thomas has taken the car out this afternoon to the factory in Mödling.—I will call you Carlo, every day, and you shall not wait even one hour longer for me than I deem necessary."

With a heavy heart and glistening tears in his long curved eyelashes, he submitted to the inevitable. They kissed long and tenderly, and then Hella left.

Carlo leaned out the open window, which opened onto the park ablaze with lush blossoms, and mused. Had this visit meant farewell? Was everything over now?

In his mind, he ran through the whole course of his relationship with Hella Bühler. He had gotten to know her at the Madonna di Campiglio where he visited a family of friends of his. At first it had only been a flirtation. She was six or seven years older, the wife of an industrial tycoon, famed in Vienna, and she was a much sought-after beauty. On his own, Carlo would scarcely have dared set his sights on this woman. But it had been Hella herself who gradually gave him to understand that she found him exceptionally attractive, she whose advances had emboldened him and made his blood boil.

A shrill ringing tore him out of his dim, melancholy daydream. He heard voices in the anteroom; a visitor at this hour, who could that be? Franz stepped in and, with a timid look, presented him a card: "Commercial Councilor, Thomas Bühler."

For a moment, Zeller's heart stood still.

"The gentleman appears very upset," a concerned Franz whispered, "perhaps it's better if you do not receive him, milord."

But Carlo had already regained his composure. While he turned his back to the servant so that he could not observe his actions, he removed a revolver from the desk and stuck it in his outer jacket pocket. With a firm voice, he said, "Please show the gentleman in."

A few seconds later Thomas Bühler and Zeller stood opposite each other, eye to eye. Carlo's features were immovably rigid. Only his cheeks were redder than usual. He stood fully erect, leaning at attention against his desk.

Commercial Councilor Bühler was a thick-set, barely average-sized man in his mid-forties, with a protruding hooked nose, thick brown mustache, and bristly hair shorn short and graying at the temples.

Barely suggesting a formal bow, Carlo asked: "How may I be of service, Mr. Commercial Councilor?"

Bühler smiled sneeringly and cunningly. His eyes shimmered dark green under thick brows grown together: "Are you not able to guess, Mr. Zeller?"

The latter shrugged: "Indeed, I am in no position to do so!"

Bühler looked around: "Nice place you have here, very nice. And how splendid it smells here.—Ambre antique—ah, what a bachelor!" He burst out laughing again: "If these walls could talk? Probably witnessed a lady visitor just a short while back?"

Carlo's face began to darken and express increasing impatience: "How may I be of service? What visitors I receive is none of your business, Sir!"

Bühler took a step forward. "So you think so? You think even my wife's visits here are none of my concern?"

Carlo said haltingly: "Your wife, I don't understand!"

"What, are you still attempting to deny that my wife left only a few minutes ago, you cowardly scoundrel?"—Distorted by rage, Bühler threw himself at Zeller with his fist raised in attack.

But Carlo had already grabbed his arm and threw the attacker, who probably was not prepared for such physical strength in an opponent of almost delicate proportions, back a few steps. "Stop your attacks, otherwise I'll shoot you down!—I'm at your disposal!"—He pointed to the door commandingly with his hand and shouted: "Now, out!"

"You'll hear from me!" hissed Commercial Councilor Bühler disappearing.

Carlo dropped into an armchair. His head was in total confusion. The rapid succession of events numbed him. Only gradually did he come to his senses and become fully capable of assessing the embarrassing position in which he suddenly found himself, reflecting on it in all its ramifications. Of course his mind had not directed his first clear thoughts to himself, but to Hella, whose fate aroused great concern in him. He considered for a few moments whether he was bound to offer her his hand. But then reason finally reasserted itself; he was twenty-two, she was close to thirty. He had no social position and had nothing to put forward in life. His wealth was too modest to be able to meet the requirements of such a coddled woman.

Above all, he told himself as he calmed down, he needed to prepare for the duel. He wanted to put the entire matter in Ströbl's hands, whom he still hoped to meet up with in the Krieau, since it was only half past five. He snatched up hat and gloves, bolted out of the house, summoned the first coach he saw, and rushed down to the Prater.

At this hour, quite a few people were taking their coffee at the Krieau Meierei, among them many friends of Carlo, who waved to him and shouted. But he didn't stop for anyone, just kept his eyes on the lookout for Ströbl, whom he finally found in the company of decked-out, heavily made-up young hussies. Ströbl, most joyously surprised, hastened towards him, setting about to drag him over to the table.

"No thanks, Clemens," Carlo declined.—"I beg you, bid the two girls here goodbye for today and give me the rest of your day, I have serious and urgent matters to discuss with you."

Taking a careful look at Carlo's face, Clemens von Ströbl could no longer be in doubt that it had to be an important matter. So he complied with his friend's request, bade goodbye to his companions, and left the coffeehouse with Carlo. While they both walked down the Prater Boulevard, Zeller narrated the whole afternoon's events.

"Thunderation, the beautiful Hella Bühler! You lucky devil," was the first response Ströbl gave to the news. "But you did come to me with this matter after all, and faster than I thought," he said continuing with obvious satisfaction.

Zeller assailed him to preserve discretion.

"As your second, I am bound to do so!" Ströbl said calming him. "As alternate deputy, I suggest Lieutenant Colonel Baron Rakossy. Be assured, you can leave all matters to the two of us."

Ströbl was almost cheerful to have his friend be so intricately ensnared in such a spicy and fashionable affair. "You're coming right along, my boy, you're coming right along!" he assured him time and again.

The duel took place at the Officers' Riding Academy in the early dawn hours. The harshest conditions had been set. Cavalry sabers, slash and stab without bandaging, until no longer fit for combat.

On the drive out to the Riding Academy, Carlo was so nervous that Ströbl and the tall Hussar lieutenant exchanged worried looks. However, upon entering the great, echoing hall, a calm and poise came over him. His hand tightened firmly on the saber's grip, and his dark eyes flashed self-confidence and assurance.

Thomas Bühler, a former student cadet, attacked with verve. Calmly and artfully Carlo parried off the hard and raging blows. It was quite a sight to see: his bare, smooth, sinewy upper-body in a dominant game of strength, bending and flexing, stretching and tightening. The first round produced no results. Mr. Bühler's sweat ran over his cheeks and chest; the corpulent man was already quite exhausted and breathing heavily. Carlo's breath, however, was easy and steady, and there was not a drop of sweat to see on his skin. At the start of the second round, Baron Rakossy murmured to him: "Go for it!" Zeller's lips echoed a slight smile and he nodded. He took Rakossy's advice and quickly shifted to an attack position and with one blow low on the left side of Buehler's chest put him out of commission.

Thomas Bühler was severely injured, but it was not life-threatening. When Ströbl disclosed the doctor's findings to Carlo, who was waiting in one of the corners in the hall, he breathed easy again. For all the hate he felt for the man, his conscience would have severely suffered if he had slain him.

The Zeller-Bühler duel did not go unnoticed in Viennese society. It even caused a substantial sensation and formed the topic of conversation in certain circles. As so often happens, sympathy almost everywhere resided with the younger man, the victor. The young well-to-do gentlemen, the girls in their teens, the cocottes, and the young, misunderstood wives all admired Carlo Zeller and made him the hero of the day. This admiration soon reached Carlo directly. Flowers were sent, letters of congratulation came from women whose acquaintance he scarcely remembered, perfumed notes rained in, and the telephone jangled all day. The always helpful Ströbl organized and sifted through the correspondence and determined on the spot when an answer would be appropriate or not, because, for one thing, Carlo had little interest in all these proofs of suddenly reawakened interest. He felt very unhappy in those days. Hella had disappeared from Vienna, and nothing of her fate was known to him. At one point it was rumored that she had retired to her parents' home in Bohemia: then again, that she had gone on a journey; some said that the divorce had been initiated, others that a reconciliation between the spouses had been set in motion. Zeller received not a single sign of life from her.

But his circle of friends, first and foremost Clemens von Ströbl, could not abide Carlo's withdrawal from society, something Carlo himself would have preferred. For all the young people were now proud to be able to count themselves as one of Zeller's friends. Everyone wanted to be seen with him and boasted of their trusted relationship with him. Of course, Ströbl was the proudest of all, who could boast with full authority of having discovered and molded Carlo into celebrity status.

So it came to pass that Carlo almost against his will became involved in a swirl of carefree life, which finally numbed him and made him forget Hella, and pleased him more and more, for he was young and fun-loving, naïve, and very vain.

It was perfectly obvious that his allotted annuity could no longer sustain the merry life he led. He began to put even more emphasis on clothes and ran up debts with tailors, boot makers, and linen services. He gave small social gatherings, organized by Ströbl, which were lavish and devoured quite some money. Considerable sums went to the champagne inns, the carriages, and the chauffeurs. When the tailors and shoemakers urged payment, he had no other choice but to appeal to his guardian for a raise in allowance. Professor Wendrich wrote a very angry letter but was in the end moved to increase the monthly check a tiny bit. However, he emphasized that Carlo now had the full advantage of his wealth, and that a further raise was no longer possible.

Zeller was barely able to satisfy the most unpleasant lenders. When however even those lenders who had been patient up to now also approached him, his embarrassment resurfaced. However, he could not bring himself to cut back, to live again within modest means. He feared the mockery of his friends, male and female, and he even lost the willpower to forego his accustomed pleasures.

In his distress he confided in Clemens von Ströbl.

Naturally, Ströbl knew what to do. "So borrow money somewhere. How long will it be before you are of legal age and can have full power over your own allowance? A fellow like you need not fear the future, who are you skimping for, anyway? You will be able to make a good match with plenty of wealthy women."

Ströbl's argument made sense to Carlo. And in his naïve artlessness, he asked: "Would you be a friend and help me out with 10,000 kronen?"

But Ströbl immediately made a very long face. "That wouldn't work," he explained in protest. The rather high sums that he withdrew from the factory were barely enough to cover his own needs. "However, I do know a Mr. Herlinger, Friedrich Herlinger. He is a café owner on Schönbrunner Street, a very trustworthy man whose pleasure it will be to give you a hand. Of course he also wants to get his cut. But I can only assure you, he is a rare bird among his peers. He has helped me out, yeah, even Rakossy and Kehlhausen, actually, he has helped all of us at the Club."

So they immediately sought out Mr. Herlinger; Zeller got money and was from that point on in the clutches of a usurer.

The small band was playing a slow waltz in the hall of the Lido Palace Hotel. It was after dinnertime, the guests were sitting in wicker chairs chatting and sipping cold drinks; the ladies were dressed lavishly with loads of jewelry, the gentlemen in tails. Outside a starlit summer night shone blue and the sea murmured gently.

In the middle of the hall just one couple was dancing, all eyes admiringly following them: Beate Salagna in the arms of Carlo Zeller. Salagna, a

racy and slender brunette, supple as a cat, and Carlo Zeller were indisput-
ably the best dancing couple in the hotel. Time and again they were called
on to perform by general demand, and when the two stepped up to dance
the pliant, hovering Boston, the temperamental Mattchiche, or the grotesque Cakewalk, the other couples simply vanished into thin air.

And when everybody around kept following the lovely pair with their
eyes, they kept buzzing this question: "Is she his lover?"

No, Beate Salagna did not yet belong to Carlo, even though he
wooed and assailed her more and more each day. But a Beate Salagna
was not such an easy conquest. She was flirtatious and clever, and if she
at one moment favored Carlo over all of her other suitors, to the extent
that he had to believe he had already achieved the goal of his desires,
she conducted herself in the next moment so coolly and dismissively
that he was utterly perplexed. However, in the opinion of those who followed in suspense the development of the relationship between the two,
and this was more or less the whole rest of the hotel audience, Carlo
Zeller surely had the best chances. He had undoubtedly better chances
than Capitano Alberto Alberti—one of the most tenacious, most fer-
vent suitors of the singer Beate Salagna—an ugly, broad-shouldered
man with a black, combed mustache, a short flat nose, and strong teeth
with the protruding lower jaw of a predator. He was of that sort of brutal manliness to which easy triumph with women is allotted, and he
hated the young, pretty boy from Vienna who made victory so difficult
for him on this occasion.

The waltz had ended. The couple, who were enthusiastically applauded,
returned to their table. There a fairly large group was sitting, sipping champagne: the Captain, Clemens von Ströbl, and Guido Kehlhausen, another
friend of Carlo's from the Club. In addition, there was Liane Lenoir, a Parisian
actress, whom Ströbl had conquered, Felix Freiherr von Rheinsperg, an
elderly white-haired distinguished gentleman, a bon vivant and owner of
race horses from Hamburg, and his nephew Walter Rheinsperg, cavalry
lieutenant colonel from Bamberg, Miss Elinor Pearson, the famous flame
dancer, and Fedor Obolensky, a fat landowner from the Crimea. They discussed the inconsequential events of hotel life, and contrived pleasures and
trip plans for the coming days: "I propose a ball outdoors for tomorrow
evening," shouted Liane Lenoir, a lively, dainty blonde.

"Postpone this ball until the day after tomorrow," Captain Alberti
responded. "There is a tournament committee dinner at Danieli tomorrow
evening that I must attend. Plus, Mr. Zeller dare not be absent, am I right?"
he said, turning his artificial, ingratiating countenance to Carlo.

Carlo had participated in an international fencing tournament and had won a prize: "Very true, I am attending the dinner as well," he said providing this information while turning to continue his conversation with old Baron Rheinsperg.

Felix von Rheinsperg, who had taken an obvious liking to Zeller, whispered to him: "A person might really be frightened if he saw the hate-filled gazes that fellow casts your way when he thinks he is not being watched. But surely it is well known that you know how to use your saber and know no fear."

Carlo shrugged his shoulders with a scornful smile: "Just let him come, if that suits him."

Just then, following Miss Pearson's encouragement, the rest got up to take a short stroll along the beach. A glance from Salagna summoned Carlo to her side. Between him and the Captain, she strode out of the hotel entrance into the mild moonlit night, on past the colossus of a nigger porter grinning almost good-naturedly as he humbly tugged his cap.

Clemens von Ströbl soon joined the three. He engaged the captain in an animated conversation, and when Ströbl and Alberti finally fell back a few steps, this was not just by accident. Ströbl was always striving to help Zeller get undisturbed personal time with the female singer.

Carlo and Beate disappeared behind the nearest cabana. Arm in arm they strode over the deep, soft sand that yielded under their feet like a thick rug. A gentle breeze rippled across the silvery sea. Far out on the horizon some fishing boats stood immobile like black silhouettes towering into the night.

From the hotel, the sound of the Monte Christo waltz wafted over on the breeze.

Carlo pressed Beate's arm tighter and tighter to his, which she tolerated silently smiling. His feelings were intensely aroused, but he did not speak a word. Often, very often, he had laid his love out at her feet and begged her to hear his entreaties.—Each time in the end, she chided him with subtle mockery to be reasonable. There was wild defiance in him now and the fear that her reserve might carry him away and lead him to speak foolishly, for he knew and feared his nature, which, once agitated, was capable of the most intemperate forms of expression.

After a while she said: "I think that we have been silent long enough."

"My heart is too full for me to talk.—Why do you torture me so, Beate?"

"Am I torturing you?" she asked in a coquettishly mocking tone that was already driving Carlo to despair. "Maybe you torture yourself because you get things in your head which are not so easy to attain."

"Not so easy?—Difficult to attain they may be, but I very well do have the will to attain them!"

"Maybe they won't be attainable at all!" Beate said frostily.

He stopped: "Vouloir c'est pouvoir, did you not tell me this, when you told me of your sad youth, of your struggles, of your difficulties in rising in society? Please permit me to have that be my motto as well." And with a sudden, unexpected movement he seized her and, before she could fend him off, embraced her and kissed her.

But his kisses, these hot, imploring kisses of ravishing youth, aroused her passion as well. She returned his kisses, languishing in his arms with closed eyes and heavy, surging breaths.

Oncoming footfalls wrested the two out of their blissful absorption. Beate straightened up. Immediately she resumed her mocking attitude, or at least acted so: "You are very impudent, my dear friend. Don't think of this as something special because you nabbed me in a moment of weakness."

But Carlo heard through the false tone and laughed happily: "Yep, I do think of this as something special," he retorted pleasurably, "for one thing I know is that a woman such as you doesn't let someone kiss her if she is indifferent towards him. She'll slap him in the face instead."

Captain Alberti, along with Ströbl and Liane Lenoir, was standing in front of them.

"Sheer foolishness, Capitano!" Salagna replied. "Or are you forbidding me that?" She hung herself on the Italian's arm, and pulling him a bit over to the side, looked around triumphantly at Zeller just to irritate him again and drive him mad.

But her game wasn't working anymore. He smiled calmly after her with the certainty in his breast that he would soon attain his goal.

The next evening Carlo journeyed to Venice in a vaporetto. The whole gang had escorted him down to the small steamer. Amidst the jokes and jests of those staying back, he set off. Miss Pearson called after him: "Don't come home with too much of a hangover after celebrating your victory!" and the fat Obolensky growled a Russian farewell song in his deep voice.

The grand dinner in the great hall of the Danieli Hotel went off splendidly. The Count of Turin, the honorary president of the tournament committee, chaired the affair, and the cream of Venetian civil and military authorities, all of whom sat on the committee, were all present at the festive occasion. The prizewinners and the Maitres d'assaut, among them also Capitano Alberti, were present as well. Alberti was especially friendly to Carlo on this evening. When Carlo was about to take the last vaporetto to decamp at eleven thirty, it was the captain who ultimately held him back and urged him to stay.

"Take a gondola, the night is young," he advised.

"And you?" Zeller asked.

"I'm spending the night in the city. Major Idoni, my old comrade from military school, you see him over there, the lanky gentleman with the goatee. He is posted to the city headquarters here and just an hour ago was so kind as to place a bed in his living quarters at my disposal." Major Idoni and Alberti were going the same way.

After a while Carletto finally left as well.

At the steps of the piazzetta, which were completely deserted at this hour, a few gondolas lay at anchor. Almost all of the gondoliers were asleep. Of the two or three who were still awake, only one especially small, nimble man pushed up to Carletto. "Where does the gentleman wish to go?" he inquired busily, and when Carlo named the Palace Hotel and Lido as his destination, the man took him by the arm and pulled him swiftly into his black barque.

The two officers saluted and turned off towards Piazza San Marco.

As the gentle gliding and monotone ripple pleasantly lulled him, the overtired Carlo soon dozed off. When he awakened, probably from an increased rocking of the boat, he was in that instant utterly unable to say how long he had been napping, or where he was. Bewildered and gradually coming to his senses, he looked around. Far, far back stood the city tower. Back and to the right, away from the direction of travel, he could just barely make out the Lido. He found himself on the open sea, which was no longer calm out where he was. Clouds flew across the heavens and temporarily blanketed the moon's disk, so that an unearthly, dark night surrounded him.

"Where are you taking me?" Carlo said turning around to the gondolier, not exactly frightened, but somewhat agitated all the same. "The Lido lies there to the right." He spoke Italian fluently, as well as French and English. He had an exceptional talent for languages, and the study of foreign languages was the only thing that had ever interested him, perhaps just because he had a natural talent for it.

"Quite right, Sir, quite right" the rower replied assiduously. "But one must make a detour at night."

"A detour?" He had already gone out too often at night in a gondola not to find this answer suspicious. "Turn right immediately," he ordered in a sharp tone, glaring at the gondolier.

Now he burst out laughing in scorn: "I'll go as I please."

"No, do as I command!" cried Carlo jumping up while preparing to bound over the backrest of his seat; for it was clear to him he had to stay out of range of the long oar.

"Stay down, you dog!" the gondolier screamed to him, already tearing the oar out of its lock. "Stay down or I'll knock you down and chuck you into the sea."

After these words Zeller could no longer be in doubt of what this ride was supposed to mean for him—a death ride.

But he had already agilely jumped afore and stood next to the gondolier on the bench before he could prepare to strike. Even though Carlo had no weapon, he was determined to engage his opponent. He went for his throat: "If you don't keep rowing this instant, I'll strangle you!" Sliding the oars back in the locks and bending far back, the gondolier had evaded Carlo's grasp. Cursing he reached into his right trouser pocket and began flashing a stiletto in his raised hand.

However, Carlo had expected such a move. Already grasping the gondolier's wrist, and because he was considerably stronger, succeeded in taking possession of the stiletto after a short tussle. Now he was armed. He jumped back a step in the gondola and swinging the dagger, he called: "Now over to the Lido or I'll stick you with this!"

Threatened by the weapon and intimidated by the passenger's power and courage, the gondolier was obliged to seize hold of the oar once again. Carlo stood close to him, not letting him out of his sight for one moment.

Only when the gondola drew very close to the dunes did Carlo return to his seat again with all appropriate caution. He had the following plan: as soon as the boat came to shore he would spring out, call for help, and wait for people to come who could take custody of the gondolier.

Not far from the Palace Hotel the gondola slid onto the sand. The gondolier still had the audacity to say: "That will be five lire, Sir." But Zeller had already jumped out of the vessel and, grasping the prow from below—and in his opinion protected by the prow—screamed at the top of his lungs: "Help, help!"

But to all appearances he had not kept himself well enough protected after all. The gondolier lifted the heavy oar upwards and with all his might, summoned by his fear of death, smashed it down on Carlo. He hit him on the head. Unable to utter another sound, Carlo sank down. The gondola quickly took off, disappearing out to sea in a few seconds.

At the hotel, all lay in deep slumber. Only a single person was still awake to hear the calls for help from the beach. It was the huge black porter who discovered the situation when he was about to lock the front portal. He listened intently for the noise outside: no more shouting, nothing; but it was as if he were hearing the sand crunching under a departing boat. Fearless and without delay, he reached in his chamber for a hanging lamp and with a sturdy stick rushed out in the direction from which the screams had sounded. The lamp's strong gleam illuminated the ground before him. And there, he almost cried out for fear. He saw a figure lying on the ground before him, his feet nearly covered by the sea since high tide was approaching. He kneeled over the fainted man and recognized Carlo Zeller. Blood trickled over his forehead.

"Poor, poor young man." Tommy breathed as he felt for the unconscious man's pulse with unskilled fingers. When he shone his lamp over Carlo's hand his eyes fell on the blue half-moons on the quadroon's nails. Deeply moved, he pulled the slender hand to his lips and following an involuntary impulse he kissed it, the hand of his brother.

Now his zeal to help and summon rescue redoubled. He lifted the young man in his strong arms, his lamp between his teeth, and bore him up to the hotel vestibule where he laid him out on a leather bench. He immediately awakened a groom, ordering him to fetch a doctor residing in the hotel as well as Mr. von Ströbl, for he knew that he was the close friend and travel companion of the injured man. The doctor, a gentleman from Berlin, appeared very quickly, and von Ströbl, who again had drunk rather too much that evening and had been difficult to awaken from his deep slumber, arrived somewhat later.

Together they carried Zeller to his room, where Tommy unclothed him and laid him in bed with a degree of care one would not have expected from such an unwieldy giant.

After that, the doctor washed the blood off his wound to examine it. He found a laceration extending from the left front area of his skull to the forehead just over the eye. Nowhere was the bone injured, and the doctor was able to assure von Ströbl that with regard to the bloody wound it appeared more harmless than it had at first seemed.

Clemens von Ströbl spent the night on the sofa in the room. Carlo, who had already begun to run a temperature, recounted the adventure in fits and snatches. Ströbl was already beginning to wonder who the instigator of this attack might be and wanted, in Carlo's interest, to avoid a scandal.

Zeller awakened in the morning, still running a fever.

"I would recommend hiring a nurse, even though so far we are dealing only with a common fever from a wound," said the doctor, who had already appeared once more at Carlo's bedside by 8 o'clock. Ströbl sought out Kehlhausen, to whom he reported the occurrences of the previous night. Then together they went out looking for Salagna. When Beate learned of the misadventure, she turned pale and began to tremble. After recovering, she was seized by extreme outrage toward Capitano Alberti, who, as they all agreed, stood behind this foul deed.

"If that guy tries to come near me today, I will publicly slap him right in the face and turn him over to the police." Ströbl and Kehlhausen had great trouble calming her.

"We must look for a nurse now," Clemens von Ströbl said, as he and Kehlhausen turned to leave.

"Why a nurse?" Beate Salagna held the two back. "I will care for him," she firmly declared. And noticing the look the two exchanged, she added with a contemptuous laugh: "Think whatever you want, it matters nothing to me."

They led her over to the injured man. When he caught sight of Beate, his eyes lit up and he spoke his first words: "I'm so happy, I'm so happy . . ." while attempting to kiss her hand.

This she resisted, however: "Stop that, I am going to nurse you back to health." Turning to Ströbl and Kehlhausen, she said: "I believe that it doesn't help to have so many people in the room. Perhaps Carletto wants to sleep again. But send the doctor right up so that he can give me instructions for nursing him."

She straightened up Carlo's pillow with a gentle hand, let down the Venetian blinds again, and, withdrawing to the balcony with a novel she found on the table, monitored the slumber into which Carlo soon lapsed with a contented, blissful smile on his lips.

The two Rheinspergs, outraged as they were, but on the other hand too correct to accuse someone of such a serious crime without evidence, traveled to Venice in order to pursue their own investigation. What they uncovered left virtually no room for doubt that the gondolier who had taken Zeller for a ride had been a creature for hire. Carlo Zeller had no adversary in the vicinity other than Capitano Alberti. By questioning the gondoliers at the piazzetta, the Rheinspergs learned that the gondolier who had virtually forced himself on Carlo was utterly unknown to the men there and had never before docked at the piazzetta. He docked at the steps, they said, around half past eleven. Passengers who had approached him he denied a ride using all manner of excuses. From far off, out of a group of three gentlemen who had come over after midnight from Danieli to the anchorage, a few whistles, the first bars of a well-known song, were heard. Upon hearing this whistling, the gondolier immediately jumped up and offered his services to the gentleman in civilian clothes.

The barons brought back this news in the noon hour. They kept it secret from Zeller so as not to upset him.

Alberto Alberti was so bold as to appear on the hotel's coffee terrace at teatime. The circle of friends, to the extent they had been let in on the situation, received him with striking reserve. When the captain heard of Carlo's accident, he gesticulated full of sympathy and most indignantly. He promised to initiate an investigation himself at the police station and wished to obtain information from Miss Salagna about the state of Mr. Zeller's health. Since no one made a move to accompany him—and when the other members of the group, Obolensky, Liane Lenoir, and Miss Pearson, noticed the behavior as well, they too showed frosty reserve—he went up alone. He summoned Salagna via the room maid. A flood of questions seemed just about to wash over her. But after his first expressions of sympathy, she cut him off, measuring him from head to toe.

"I admire your nerve!—in the future, kindly spare me your salutation." She turned her back on him and returned to the room.

Capitano Alberti discolored: "What do you mean, miss?" he asked hoarsely.

But the door had already clicked shut behind Beate.

Without bidding adieu to the coffeehouse group, the Capitano left the hotel immediately and two days later left Venice as well.

Carlo's fever abated slowly, but he grew chipper again and was on the way to recovery. Beate nursed and cared for him tirelessly and most solicitously, guided not only by her awakening love but also out of remorse. For she accused herself of raising false hopes in Alberti with her coquetry and of foolishly having made him jealous, thereby indirectly being guilty of the profound misfortune which had befallen Carletto.

The incident had dampened the desire of the whole group to extend their stay much longer. In consideration, they merely awaited Zeller's recovery before departing from the Lido in all different directions.

As it happened, Carlo and Beate were the first to depart. In order to escape an awkward leave-taking, they left surreptitiously one day at the break of dawn, leaving behind lighthearted regards to their friends. They went to Riva on Lake Garda. At the quiet shores of this lake with its most wondrous deep blue under sycamores and cypresses and amid ripe, swelling grapes, they enjoyed the first weeks of their young love untroubled and free from spying. Ultimately a letter in September to the singer from her director, calling her back to Vienna to study a new role, put an end to these days of absolute bliss and raging passion.

Carlo overwhelmed Beate with precious gifts in Vienna. He felt deeply in her debt for so much pleasurable delight. It was his heart's desire to give concrete expression to his gratitude.

However, the month's end brought a time of nasty worries for him. First of all, the debt to Mr. Herlinger fell due, and he did not look as though he would grant an extension.

"Yes, my friend,—now it's time to go to Graz and confess," Ströbl said, although not without inwardly gloating over seeing Carlo in such a fix. This, because his friend's successes had gradually awakened his envy after all, and he sensed as well that Zeller was gradually outgrowing his dependence on him, just as any pupil slowly outgrows his teacher. "I suggest you confess right off to 15,000 in debts, because that is the amount I'm estimating you are down for."

"It's even more," Zeller responded dejectedly. He had counted up his debts, and arrived at a sum not much under 20,000 kronen. At the moment he was financing his lifestyle, which was in no way different from what it had been, by borrowing money from his servant, the good soul Franz.

So he traveled to Graz.

Professor Wendrich—markedly aged and declining in the last year, was both surprised and delighted by the visit. And Carlo, ashamed at Wendrich's praise of him as a good boy, had for two days not ventured forth with the truth. It was genuine torture for him to have to report on the progress of his studies, his circle of acquaintances, his way of life, intentions, and plans. But the time came when he had to show his true colors: his summer trip had gobbled up a great deal of money. His accident, the fall from the boat, also had cost him plenty. The foreign doctors were very expensive, and a suitcase of his with valuable wardrobe items needing replacement had gone missing; also some repairs and new purchases were needed for his apartment—in short, he badly needed 20,000 kronen.

The old man leaned back in his armchair, lips turning pale, almost gasping for breath. The 20,000 kronen was a small fortune to his way of thinking. When he had recovered from the initial shock, he could not refrain with severe reproaches and became more agitated than Carlo had ever seen him.

"You seem to be leading quite a nice life! You've become a good-for-nothing, a spendthrift who is headed for a bad end. No, uh-uh, you will get nothing from me!"

The cold sweat of fear broke out on Carlo's forehead. He had pledged his word of honor to everyone. Herlinger would immediately turn to Professor Wendrich, and, even if he sold all his furnishings, he would not be able to make good on his debt.

"Well, what will you do now, if I don't put 20,000 kronen at your disposal, hmm? What will you do? Revolver, huh?"

Carlo did not give an answer. He sensed the lurking fear from Wendrich's question and took advantage of it. He nodded, dropping his head.

"You have borrowed money here and there, and now they're coming after your hide!"

Carlo began to plead and beg. He promised to stop, to do better. After long, long pains he finally succeeded in softening up Wendrich and wheedling a check out of him for 20,000 kronen.

The next morning Carlo set off on his journey home. Professor Wendrich would have it no other way than to accompany him to the train station. He now strode back and forth on the platform, a bent and shrunken little man with a snow-white goatee, a big, black, broad-brim slouch hat over his long silvery hair. He gave Carlo admonishments and instructions on his journey, extracting from him once again the promise of a fundamental change for the better. Suddenly, breaking off in the middle of his speech, he stopped and doffed his hat before two ladies; one of them old, tall, and quite corpulent with gray hair, and the other one a young, pretty, fresh blond with blue eyes.

"What a surprise! Are you once again here in Graz, Madame Colonel? Ready to depart?—And you haven't found it worth the trouble to seek out your old friend Wendrich?"—He threatened with his finger. "Miss Lisl looks splendid, this child keeps getting prettier and prettier."

"You must excuse my neglect, my dear Professor," said Madame Colonel Ortner. "We only stayed here for two days and had no opportunity to leave my father's home."

"Yes, yes, I heard, Mr. Privy Councilor Braun was feeling poorly. But permit me, ladies, to introduce you to my ward, Mr. *studiosus juris* Carlo Zeller."

The ladies offered their hands to Carlo, who until now had stood around seeming rather bored.

"Ah, the son of your friend in your youth, Professor Rudolf Zeller?," the Madame Colonel said benevolently.

"Indeed, that he is."

They promenaded now in a group of four over the platform awaiting the express train's arrival.

"Carlo, who is also going to Vienna, certainly will place himself at the ladies' disposal with pleasure," Professor Wendrich said, who with this remark gave Zeller very little joy, for he had little fondness for so-called family ties, or association with honorable, bourgeois officers' widows and their daughters. He had also grown accustomed to traveling first class, and one could tell by looking at the two ladies that they definitely traveled second class. Yet he had no choice but to say: "Indeed, it will be an honor for me!"

Carlo went on ahead with Miss Ortner. She told him that they customarily lived in Vienna, where her father, who passed away a few years ago, had headed a department in the Ministry of War; she mentioned her brother, who was about to complete his studies at the Military Engineering Academy, and her little sister, 15-year-old Elly, who was attending commercial school. She chatted quite nicely and Carlo also found her appearance not at all unpleasant. She had a genuine cute Viennese face, animated and full of grace, and her small feet and hands, like her supple budding figure, could satisfy even his pampered tastes. But her manner of dress, so unfashionable, so shabby,—this cheap, washed-out linen smock, this miserable straw hat with daisies, obviously everything fabricated at home! While he observed her more intently, he in his unblemished elegance almost felt ashamed to be seen at her side.

Then the train came rolling in. He helped both women into the coupe. With an ironic smile he stowed their luggage: their small traveling basket, which already seemed to have put in many years of service, the umbrellas bound by a leather strap and then their threadbare coats. Of course, they went into the second-class compartment, where they just managed to get the last seats. The travelers surrounding them were of an inferior lot, among them a woman with many children who was just then feeding them eggs and sandwiches. These surroundings continued to annoy Carlo, and it took a fairly long while until he was again in a better mood and able to rekindle a conversation with the two ladies.

It was an entire world that separated him, with his sophisticated ideas and affectations, from the social sphere of the Ortners. However, he was not so strongly entangled in his prejudices to fail to recognize that Madame Colonel was a woman of tact, education, decency and kindness and that Lisl was a splendid and fun-loving creature. He got to know a sphere of society with all its great worries, distresses, and modest joys, which until then had been completely unknown to him. But they held their heads high, hoping for a better future and not letting the day's vexations weigh them down. In a year's time, Artur was to be mustered out of service as a lieutenant, and he could then stand on his own two feet. Elly had a prospect for a position at the state railway.

"Then there's me, I'm a lazy brat and useless mouth to feed, wouldn't you say, Mama?" Lisl said laughing while she bit right into a juicy pear that Carlo had provided for her at the station.

"Well, things are not so bad with you, I am completely content," Madame Colonel said, lovingly caressing her daughter's cheek. "After all, you are very good in financial matters and do very lovely wood paintings, which bring in something as well."

"Yes, things could go much better for Lisl, maybe even very much better."—Madame Ortner had a brother-in-law in New York, her late spouse's brother, who had succeeded in becoming the director of a big stock company. Twenty-five years ago, as a very young engineer, he had gone over to America. He had only one child, a daughter, Lisl's age, and had repeatedly offered to take Lisl into his family.

"But it's so hard to part," Madame Ortner said with a low sigh, "maybe in a few years, when Elly is grown up and I have some support from her."

"And would you like to go over there, Miss, would you have the courage?" Carlo Zeller asked.

"Why not? If it weren't for my mother, I would sooner leave for the New World today than tomorrow."

"Actually, I also ought to go over there once as well, just to see my mother's homeland," Carlo reflected.

"Really, your mother was American?" Lisl inquired curiously.

"I remember now, Professor Wendrich once told me of your father's fate," Madame Ortner said. "A fate that almost sounded like a novel."

"Can't I hear about it as well?" Miss Ortner asked. She followed his words very intensely. Her big, open violet-blue eyes virtually hung on his lips with an expression that revealed more than mere curiosity: sympathy and dawning affection.

"Perhaps I'll go on over, once I have finished my doctor's degree. I don't want to interrupt my studies for a rather long voyage," concluded Zeller, who instinctively found it better to emphasize more the studious and striving student in him than the idler and bon vivant in the company of the two ladies.

When they arrived in Vienna in the late afternoon, they had shared a pleasant trip and had begun to feel at ease with one another. Carlo had begun increasingly to like Lisl Ortner so much that he had nearly reconciled himself to her unsophisticated dressing style. It simply had done him well to speak just once with a young, fresh, unspoiled creature whose eyes radiated harmlessness and purity.

The Ortners very cordially invited Carlo Zeller to visit them sometime, which he also promised to do in this moment of doubtless the very best of intentions.

The experiences in Graz, including his guardian's admonitions and the encounter with Lisl Ortner, still lingered in his mind as he made his way home in the coach.

A contemplative mood embraced him, and he thought it would be nice for once to stay at home this evening, organize the library, set out textbooks and legal writings, and formulate plans for studying.

"Mr. von Ströbl and Miss Salagna are waiting inside," Franz greeted him. "They called at noon inquiring when milord would be coming. They are in a fun-loving mood, I had to cool a bottle of champagne for milord's arrival."

"Three cheers and hurray!" they shouted as he appeared on the threshold. The two guests stood before him, filled flutes in hand. A large bouquet of roses stood resplendent on the table. Salagna seized him by the right arm, Ströbl by the left: "Now, we have you back again!" she laughed.

"Where is the ass laden with gold?" shouted Ströbl.

"Everything's all set!" Carlo replied. He stretched as if chains had fallen off him. He smelled the sweet scent of a beautiful woman and the smoke of English cigarettes, saw bubbling champagne and heard the quiet rustling of silken lingerie: "Yes, you've got me back."

December had come. Carlo drifted gaily along his accustomed path. At Salagna's side, surrounded by his friends, he continued his previous life, ever more breezy and uninhibited.

Even Lisl Ortner, to whom his thoughts turned quite often in the beginning with an undefined yearning, was now forgotten, or nearly forgotten. Only occasionally did her image, now faded, float before his mind's eye when he chanced to see a pretty blond girl resembling her.

Of course he was mired once again in financial woes. This time, however, he no longer needed Ströbl's help: he sought out Mr. Friedrich Herlinger by himself, with a significantly more confident demeanor than before, and since he had proven himself a punctual payer, he succeeded without great difficulty in once again obtaining quite a substantial loan.

Simply put, his relationship with Salagna placed far too great demands on his purse. Not, however, because the singer was demanding gifts from him. Nevertheless the readiness with which she accepted them showed that she did expect them. And even though his feelings for Beate Salagna had already begun to cool—her artistic moodiness and her high-strung manner had already set off a number of fiery scenes between them—he all the same was too vain to retreat from his much envied position at the side of the storied soubrette.

So he looked around for a source of income, and seized upon that source of income that most readily offered itself to the people in his circles: he began to gamble. And in fact, he had beginner's luck. He did not risk much and was content with modest winnings that just permitted him to stay above water.

But it was precisely the gambling that led to his parting ways with Salagna. As it was, he began to neglect her. It was on the evening of a ball in February when their breakup came about. Salagna expected Carlo in her dressing room after her performance. They wanted to attend the ball—the highlight of the season—together. But she waited in vain. The theater had long been deserted, colleagues had left, but Carlo had not yet turned up. Beate telephoned the club and received a message from the servant that Mr. Zeller could not cancel the game at the moment, since he held the bank, and he was requesting that the lady come by for him. In a foul mood, Beate appeared in the club where she was entreated to be patient for a few minutes in the reception room. But again, a rather long wait ensued before Carlo appeared.

His face was completely pale when he arrived, which, given his swarthy complexion, seemed very ugly, almost ashen. Salagna received him with the most stern rebukes for his lack of consideration. Carlo, likewise in great agitation, replied she was the reason he had just lost a great sum because he had been nervous on her account and played inattentively.

"So, who forced you to play at all?" she burst out. "Well then, just keep your hands off the cards."

"Who forces me to play?" he exploded and with raging flashes of anger and beastly rolling eyes he hurled his answer at her: "I'm playing for you!"

Salagna, almost frightened by his wild and altered appearance, shrank back involuntarily: "For me? Then you don't need to touch the cards any more in the future. I will not have myself involved in gambling, if an immature boy loses his smidgen of money, and, so it seems, his mind as well. We're done, adieu."

She whisked out and left Carlo behind baffled and quite ashamed. At first, he wanted to rush after her. But he immediately thought better of it.

Now things had at least come to an end! he thought with feelings of relief. He was now free of various debts, social as well as monetary. Virtually liberated, he breathed easy again, and thoughts of new experiences, new adventures quickly helped him banish the subtle melancholy that was poised to befall him. He hesitated a bit over whether he ought to return to the game room or attend the ball. He decided to enjoy his newfound freedom right away, this very evening.

Noon was already drawing near, a golden spring day shone through the blinds as Carlo awakened.

He had come home late in the early dawn hours. He and a new girlfriend, Germaine de Vermaingaut, had gone on an excursion to Rodaun. They had stayed out under the stars until nearly midnight, the moon gleaming, and the balmy spring night had enchanted them. And here, in this room, she had tarried till four o'clock in the morning. Her silvery laugh still echoed in all the corners. Then he had escorted her home. At this hour, however, she was probably already sitting in the express train to Constantinople.

What a fine piece of femininity this woman was! A sweet enchantress with whom he was now hopelessly in love. He knew it, and in the ensuing hours, free from the direct influence of her personality, he often felt alarm at it.

The Baroness de Vermaingaut was the wife of a French legation councilor who was assigned to the Ministry of Foreign Affairs and under whose purview the inspection of East European and Asia Minor consulates fell. For the major part of the year, he therefore journeyed and sojourned far from Paris and met up with his wife only for a short time in whatever major city lay on the way between the Orient and Paris. So at that time, he had had a rendezvous with her in the first days of March in Vienna. Germaine had stayed for fourteen more days, which she devoted to Carlo. Then in mid-April, Carlo went on an eight-day visit to see her in Paris. And now she again had sojourned almost another two weeks in Vienna.

Yes, he was occasionally terrified as he thought of this love. For the question nagged him in sober moments, where is my fate taking me? He no longer thought of anybody besides Germaine, who was in his blood as no woman had ever been before. When he was with her, his passion completely consumed him. If he was far from her, yearning for her devoured him. But it was time to think of his future, to build up for himself a stable bourgeois existence. He was finally sated from the libertine life he had been leading for nearly four years now. Did he not also see among those in his circle how certain individuals, the better ones, turned on to other pathways? But how could he succeed in this as long as he languished in the bonds of Germaine . . .?

He felt almost hung over when thinking of his situation now.

He got out of bed and rang for Franz to prepare a refreshing bath. The servant delivered the mail to him on a tray, various letters and a telegram.

The dispatch was from Professor Wendrich's housekeeper, saying that the Professor was gravely ill and Carlo should come to Graz without delay.

Zeller was in no doubt as to the telegram's tone, which indicated the old gentleman's final decline.

He left on the next express train. When Carlo arrived at Wendrich's, the old man already lay in agony. He no longer recognized his ward.

Towards morning Adalbert Wendrich again had a few clear moments in which he admonished Carlo to bring no shame over his father's name and to become a real man. With tears in his eyes Carlo vowed to the old man and to himself to finally take these admonitions to heart.

Two days later they bore Professor Wendrich to his grave.

Carlo transferred the settlement of his affairs to a lawyer in Graz. Since he was not far short of his twenty-fourth birthday, he wanted to be declared of legal age so that his fortune could in consequence be distributed to him.

Upon his return to Vienna, Carlo found numerous letters of condolence. A letter from Madame Colonel Ortner and her daughter Lisl was among them, in which Lisl at the conclusion reproachfully asked why he had not kept his promise to visit them.

Somehow, a warm and nice feeling came over him when he thought of this fresh, bright-eyed girl. But then his gaze again fell on the silver-framed photograph of Germaine de Vermaingaut over his bed, and his vivid memories of Lisl quickly paled.

He also found business letters. Mr. Friedrich Herlinger, to whom he owed another rather large sum, sent a reminder, likewise the jeweler Jönig, whom he had gotten to know through Kehlhausen and who had helped Carlo out only a few weeks earlier, though not in an altogether selfless fashion. There were reminders from suppliers and other tradesmen. Carlo took a pencil and made out a list of all of his commitments. It became clear that he had exhausted a good portion of his wealth. After this shattering realization, Carlo now understood that if he wanted to avoid a miserable end, then with all his strength and with utmost dispatch he had to complete his studies and seek a position.

He sought out a well-known crammer in the city, with whom he drafted a study plan for the next months, and from whom he borrowed the notes from the lectures he had missed, which he would use to pass the next exam. At the same time, he registered for a training course at a commercial school.

A time began for him in which he pursued serious activity. It wasn't easy for him to study anymore. His brain had been weaned of this activity; all his thoughts were undisciplined and erratic; he lacked concentration. But as luck would have it, he was left more or less to himself for the next few weeks, so that no diversion, no seduction presented itself. A particularly hot summer had begun, and his friends had left the city earlier than usual this year. Carlo sat by the lowered blinds in his study, cudgeled his brains with legal paragraphs, and sought to grasp the essence of double-entry accounting. Like an ascetic, he dispelled the luring fantasies that his imagination conjured up over and above textbooks and law texts: summer days somewhere out on the ocean or in the Dolomites, summer days in carefree society, out of which always the dainty, tender figure of the Baroness de Vermaingaut most clearly rose up.

Towards the end of November he had successfully completed the commercial course and was able to pass that test with tolerable success. But progress with his legal studies was not so easy. Here it was a matter of material that he absorbed only with difficulty and retained with even greater difficulty. More and more he asked himself whether he was just losing extremely precious time with this agonizing cramming. And when even his crammer discouraged him from continuing his legal studies, he finally gave them up with a heavy heart.

Carlo was very peevish and discontented with himself and the rest of the world in those days. It had been the wish of his late father that his son should achieve an academic degree, and it would also have flattered Carlo to be authorized to bear a doctor's title. With feelings bordering on shame, he even avoided meeting his closest friends.

On a dim winter day he had an encounter that straightened him up again and wrenched him out of his apathy. As it happened, he met Lisl Ortner as he strolled down Mariahilfer Street, absorbed in thought. He almost didn't recognize her in her brown winter outfit, with a cheap fox fur around her neck, which actually looked very good on her.

But it was she who stepped into his path and spoke to him: "Do you keep all your promises like this, Mr. Zeller?—You have not conducted yourself well towards us, not at all." And she pouted a little more and made a face, but was soon appeased.

"Let's go to a café where we can chat comfortably," he invited her.

"To a coffeehouse? If someone sees us together, rumors will fly. And I must be home at eight o'clock at the latest, otherwise Mama gets worried," she hesitated.

"Do we two have something to hide from one another? I'll get you to your house by eight o'clock, and, if you permit, I'll also pay my respects to your dear Mama."

"That is indeed something different!" She followed him to a nearby coffeehouse, where they sat down in a window niche.

The heavens must virtually have sent Lisl Ortner across his path. He poured his overflowing heart out to her; frankly and freely, and from the depth of his feeling, he committed himself to speaking to a sympathetic soul; he entrusted her with his cares as if she were his closest comrade. She listened to him attentively, and only after he had finished did she begin to speak, to console him, to give him courage, and to cast a friendly light over his situation. She did this until trust and hope really took hold in him again. He was actually rather inexperienced in practical matters, but she had the wisdom of a worthy matron. She gave him advice as to how he should organize his household so that he could continue living comfortably, but not so luxuriously.

"What do you need a servant for, Mr. Zeller? Is it not enough if the housemaid picks up and keeps your apartment in order? And close off one room, since you won't be giving big parties anyway. You must carefully parcel out your money, so that it can last until you succeed in finding a sufficiently remunerative position."

And while she spoke, looked at him and gave instructions, he looked at her and delighted in her presence so full of health, charm, and chastity. But when she sensed his admiring gaze, she became somewhat unsettled and blushed.

She glanced at the clock: "Oh, now we must hurry," she said as she stood up.

The Ortners were living rather far out in the Mariahilfer suburb, on Stumpergasse. For a while Carlo walked in silence alongside Lisl. And suddenly he blurted out just what was on his mind: "You know, Fräulein Lisl, this is wonderful: financially pressed jobless wastrel that I am now, I nevertheless sometimes have the feeling that I am destined for something special—please don't laugh at me—some sort of achievement. In these last weeks, where I have found myself, so to speak, I've had moments where the realization came over me that the life that I have been living up until recently is not at all my life, not even a life appropriate for me, and that

I must set off on different, very different pathways. What pathways, of course, that I don't know."

"You must simply wait now until fate gives you some sign," she said.

"And you, dear Fräulein Lisl, could you watch out a bit as well and stand by me so that I don't overlook such a hint?" he asked her impulsively.

She gave him no answer and looked at the ground. But now as he took her hand and pressed it, she replied with gentle pressure.

Despite the late hour, Madame Colonel Ortner, in her uncomplicated and cordial manner, invited him in and obliged him to stay for dinner, which they took, the four of them, with little Elly, a slim, pretty schoolgirl with short-cut hair, at the foot of the table.

"Yes, of course, it'll work," replied Clemens von Ströbl leaning back comfortably in an armchair and lighting a cigarette. "I'll talk to my old man tomorrow, he'll put in a good word for you with Walter, the director of the Manufacturers Bank, with which our company is closely allied. That's smart of you to have finally put pursuing a law degree to an end."

Following Ströbl's words in the Hotel Bristol bar, fourteen days had passed. Carlo had already met up several times with Clemens, who had, however, never again spoken of this matter. Zeller now began to bring it up himself as they stood together in the club's gym preparing to do some weightlifting.

"Tell me, Clemens, how are things at the Manufacturers Bank? You do know that I am in somewhat of a hurry now."

Ströbl was obviously embarrassed. "Yes, dear Carletto, unfortunately there is nothing at all currently available at the Manufacturers Bank. No openings there. Potentially a position in the Clerk's Office may come open, but it's not exactly foreseeable when. I've already known this for a few days, but I wanted to sound out another position for you at the Bank of Austria, where my cousin Robert works in the legal department."

"And, any result there?"

"I haven't yet been able to speak to him, unfortunately; I will look him up over the course of the next few days. Is it really so imperative for you already to have a position?"

Carlo nodded.

"Already running low on money?"

Carlo's sharp ears heard the mistrust lurking behind this question. It had never been so clear to him as in this moment that people would simply drop him if he were no longer in a position to keep up socially. He threw his head back proudly: "No, that is most definitely not the case. But I have already had enough of the life of a loafer. And you are also more active than you used to be."

"Correct. Oh well, if you want to move things along more quickly, you must also make inquiries in other places, you should not set all your hopes on me."

Now Zeller at least knew where things stood with him and Ströbl. And he decided to speak this very day with Kehlhausen, whose good connections were highly regarded. Furthermore, Zeller wanted to speak with the respected Commercial Councilor Anbelang, board member in the Club, a captain of industry who sat on many boards. And Lisl Ortner, whom he was meeting this very evening—as he now did on nearly every evening—in the coffeehouse on Mariahilfer Street, Lisl advised him to try an advertisement in a large daily newspaper as well.

Ah yes, if he hadn't had Lisl in this period! More and more she emerged as his only friend, his best comrade. On the days they could not see each other for whatever reason, he felt very lonely.

Did he love her—did she love him? Love was never mentioned between them, but the tone with which they dealt with one another was assuredly cordial and confidential, though never intimate. There was no flirting in the dealings between them, as he had had earlier with so many young girls from high society, but when he was near her, he felt somehow secure. When he sat next to her, his blood ran faster, and his heart beat stronger, and he was so happy; and often, very often, he felt as if he should clasp her to his breast: "You, you, it is you I have always been looking for, just you alone, and now that I have found you, I'll never let you go."

But why am I speaking of such things? warned an inner voice. He felt that she was sweet on him as well. The possibility of a union was still far away. To inflame each other with confessions would have meant to evoke unnecessary torment for both of them, young and hungry for life as they were. For it would have been a crime to think of any other union than a legitimate one with a girl like Lisl.

For three whole months Carlo had been busily applying for positions, but still no luck. Neither the intervention of his friends, who may well have been quite casual about it, nor his own approaches, advertisements, or proposals had helped. If he had been hopeful that his contacts in Vienna's best circles could help him this time in his advancement, then he saw himself bitterly disappointed. One thought of him as a young man of nice appearance from a good family, with pleasant manners and as a snazzy dancer, but his other qualities were not ranked all that highly. And there was no personage standing behind him to whom one felt obligated to pay respect either as protector, relative, or friend. People put him off, strayed off topic, spoke with him about social or sporting events, and dismissed him with a good, non-committal Viennese phrase: "We will see, my friend Zeller!"

His mood grew more and more desperate. He was now compelled to remain inactive, without income, and to watch his fortune melt away. To be sure, he had imposed certain limitations, but to limit himself radically enough that he could live just on his interest would have required drastic changes in his way of life—giving up his apartment, resignation from the club, withdrawing from his accustomed circle of acquaintances—he would have felt virtually declassé, and his chances of obtaining a position of some consequence, as a clerk or private secretary in a bank or some large industrial firm, in short, a position requiring a respectable, capable, elegant person, would have been even less auspicious.

At that point Carlo thought in his youthful naiveté that he would never have to live through worse days once this crisis was overcome.—

But the Ortner household, too, was plunged into unhappy weeks of sadness and turmoil.

Lisl, who earlier had been so fresh and lively, had for some time fallen quiet and apprehensive in her meetings with Carlo, without explaining to him the reasons for this change in her manner, despite his entreaties. And whenever he showed up at their house, he noticed on Madame Ortner's and Elly's faces expressions of worry and anxiety. When on a Sunday afternoon, it was in early February, Carlo barged into the middle of a family scene, he found Lisl drowned in tears, her hands covering her face, cowering in the corner of a sofa. Madame Ortner stood before her, red with great agitation; Elly shrank into the corner, intimidated.

"What in heaven's name has happened?" were the words that escaped a frightened Carlo.

"Very good that you've come now, Mr. Zeller, very good," said Madame Ortner turning to him: "You are a friend of the family, you should hear everything and advise us." She called on him to take a seat at the round table in the middle, and while Lisl's sobs sounded from time to time from the sofa, she explained:

"You see, Mr. Zeller, we can simply no longer keep on. It is true, Artur is already a lieutenant now in Josefstadt, and Elly has a job at the state railway headquarters. But the poor lad just cannot live on his salary, and Elly's meager wages also don't help much, because, as you know, prices are going up and up every day, groceries, shoes, clothing. And now our rent has been increased. I don't really know a way out any more. And now, another letter came from my brother-in-law in New York a short while ago, we told you about him, and he's written me again, saying that I should ease my burden and send Lisl over. Good heavens, one does not send one's child away that easily, without qualms, you must not believe this, one does not easily send one's darling child across the ocean—but if there is no other way out! It would be a great relief for all of us. Lisl could live carefree, even in luxury, I would rent out a room here, and Elly and I could just barely manage. But now imagine this: Lisl has always said she would very much like to go to her uncle's, but now all of a sudden she will have nothing to do with it; it is *incomprehensible*. She's resisting it tooth and nail! She's giving me no reason at all for her refusal. Perhaps you can get more out of her or put her head straight.—What has gotten into this girl?"

Carlo sat there, effused red with embarrassment and very disconcerted. It seemed to him, as if toward the end of Madame Ortner's agitated explanation of Lisl's incomprehensible refusal, a rather sharp accusation could be heard that was directed at him.

"I will speak with Fräulein Lisl when she has calmed down," he said.

Lisl's tears slowly abated; he sat down at the table and tried to conduct a casual conversation, but progressed only with some difficulty.

"Would you like to do me a favor and come to a movie with me, Fräulein Lisl?" Carlo asked after they had drunk their tea, for he was eager to get out of the house. "It will get your mind off things."

Lisl, who understood him, consented, and, since Madame Ortner had no objection to their movie visit, they soon set off.

They headed in silence across Mariahilfer Straße toward the Ring. They passed by the movie houses with their huge advertising posters. Carlo led Lisl to the central city and an old district behind St. Stephen's Cathedral.

"Where are we going?" she asked.

"You do trust me, don't you? I know an Italian wine bar that should be quite deserted at this hour. Do you want to go?"

Lisl nodded.

They turned into a tight, winding alleyway and after a few steps entered the wine cellar's low vaulted arches. As Carlo had predicted, it was almost completely deserted here. They sat in an unoccupied private booth in which they were quite secluded.

"Why don't you want to go to New York, Lisl?" And when she didn't answer, he added with a quiet voice: "Is it because of me?"

She sunk her head low and breathed: "Yes."

"Lisl!" he nearly cried out and clasped her to him. She bent her head back, closed her eyes, and their lips touched for a long time.

Within the hour they were engaged and pledged to one another for life. And then, nestling closely together, hand in hand, they discussed their future.

Lisl was to go to New York as soon as possible. Carlo would redouble his efforts to obtain a position with utmost speed. Once he was in this position, however, they would make their engagement public, and she would return for the wedding on the next steamer. But if he were not successful in finding a job in Vienna—he would simply follow her to New York! He was young, eager to work, and good at languages; he would not be entering the New World penniless. And why should he not be successful, when so many others had succeeded in gaining respect and fortune over there?

The call from afar—perhaps that is the hand of fate, perhaps my destiny awaits me there!

Lisl Ortner made her preparations for the trip. She stitched and patched and had her hands full in order to be done on time, for her steamship was departing on the tenth of March. Carlo, however, who did not want this little bride of his to go over with such a paltry outfit and be looked at askance, once again was seized by the spendthrift demon, and went grazing through shops making purchases. The most elegant toiletries bag he found and brought to Lisl, presenting it to Madame Ortner innocently as a farewell gift to his dear friend. In secret, however, he slipped Lisl some parcel every day: a dozen silk stockings, a pair of silken evening shoes, a small bottle of French perfume, and a traveling scarf. The engagement ring was also not omitted, but she was only allowed to put it on when she took her seat on the train, for they wanted to declare their engagement to her mother only once they were actually able to be joined in wedlock. They both feared that Mama Ortner might not be particularly edified by their engagement, which at this moment seemed pretty much without prospect. Lisl knew from remarks her mother had made that she nursed the hope that her daughter might make a good match over in America.

The few weeks before Lisl's departure flew by.

It was the ninth of March. Carlo had just arrived home from the small inn in his neighborhood, where he generally took lunch since he had released his servant. He was just about to stretch out on the sofa a little when the doorbell rang. Astonished by a visit at this hour, he went out to open the door. Lisl stood there before him. She was bashful, quite shy, but her blue eyes radiated joy.

"Before I say goodbye, Carlo, I wanted to look at your home so that I can take an image with me of the four walls you live in?"

Aroused and moved, Carlo led her into his study. She buried herself in his chest with a happy smile. Amidst laughter and tears they sat together for two hours. It was no easy task for him to rein in his desires since the young, blossoming creature in his arms surely would not have put up strong resistance to his wishes. But he held himself in check. Her tender looks said thank you to him for his honorable composure and restraint.

The next morning was a rainy March day with almost wintry showers. They all stood by the train, from whose window Lisl Ortner shouted to them her last words of farewell. She was in good spirits, or at least did her utmost not to reveal her emotion and the pain of separation.

Lieutenant Artur Ortner, who had come to Vienna to bid his sister farewell, smiled uncertainly but in a smart, military pose. Carlo Zeller stood somewhat to the side, quite silent. But the last shout, as the train rolled out of the station came from him: "Goodbye, Lisl!"

Carlo continued his efforts to obtain a position, but with ever more meager success. Whenever a job was offered to him, it always was a very inferior one that only seemed humiliating to him and would not have offered him any chances of setting up a household. Those whom he once called his friends and with whom he also still outwardly maintained contact showed no concern at all any more for his private affairs. He did not speak about his private matters with them anymore, since he already knew what little genuine sympathy he encountered among them.

Lisl wrote diligently. She had been lovingly taken in at her uncle's house, was well, and the yearning for Carlo tortured her and clouded her every day. Such letters were of course not well suited to strengthen Carlo's patience. And at the end of June the hour came when he said to himself: "Enough of this fruitless search here, I'm going over to Lisl." In a letter full of trembling passion, he disclosed this decision to her.

He went to sell his furniture, and turned anything he could sell into cash.

But it was this very letter, in which he had announced his early arrival to Lisl, that remained unanswered.

Presumably it had been lost; Carlo repeated the information in a second letter, in which he also complained that he had not heard from her for quite some time.

The revenue from the sale of his belongings, and the remainder of his cash, would for the first while still secure him some measure of independence in America.

He told his friends that he intended to pay a relatively brief visit to relatives in New York; he wanted to avoid bothersome questions and gossip. It very much amused him when he perceived how his reputation had climbed with the news of this journey. They even gave him a jolly farewell evening at Hotel Sacher.

He paid farewell to Madame Ortner as if he were leaving for a summer trip. How the good lady will be surprised when my first message comes from New York!—he thought inwardly full of happiness.

Completely alone, a loner, he departed on an August day from the Vienna North Train Station, sadly aware he was leaving behind no one who would miss him. At the same time, he was also joyous, and happy to be nearing the only person who longed for him.

PART THREE

THE COLORED
GENTLEMAN

End of August. The Hamburg sun has ceased burning, though it still affords warmth and comfort. And the tanned ladies and gentleman sitting at the Alsterpavillon or promenading over to it via the Jungfernstieg take pleasure in this last gift of summer rendering more tolerable the transition from seashore or mountain stronghold to big city life.

Carlo Zeller is lounging casually in a wicker chair observing with interest the lively prospect surrounding him. How completely different from Vienna, where East and West first blend, is this blond German world, he muses: Large, broad-shouldered men, hair bleached almost white from the sun, deeply tanned faces from which friendly blue eyes good-naturedly shine. The women, too, almost without exception, are blond, big, and solid, at thirty already strongly displaying their matronly bearing, for Viennese tastes a little too down to earth, solid and plain. But the girls! Slim and slender with flashing blue eyes that display with every flirtatious glance a hot-temperedness held in check. And do they know how to flirt, these Hamburg girls! "Sonofagun!" escaped Carlo's lips, when he became aware that a considerable number of girlish glances were aimed his way, while here and there, and with increasing frequency, some slim, young thing came slowly strolling by turning her blond head in his direction. How nice to be among blond people and, when all is said and done, that fool in Vienna who published a magazine pitting the blondes against the raven-haired beauties might not be so wrong after all. Carlo's thoughts zigzag first to Vienna and then across the ocean. A warm feeling rose up in him. Lisl, you dear blond girl, soon I will join you where you live and breathe! How devotedly and tenderly she had kissed him good-bye, while the longing of her youthful feelings urged her toward him. If he had wanted, he would have taken her and savored her like a mature, ripe fruit. But no, that would have been forbidden, that would have been a crime! Lisl had to be won honorably, kept safe and happy. Now it was a matter of fighting and struggling over there until he could make something of himself and make Lisl his bride.

Carlo bit his lips and clenched his hands in sudden rage. Was Lisl even still his girl? Why wasn't she writing anymore? In the first few weeks, letter upon letter came, and then, not a blessed word, no response to his last impassioned letter. Had she found another to love over there? No, then she surely would have written him. Was she sick?—Nonsense, she would have had her cousin write him! Carlo banished these frightful thoughts with a wave of his hand. Pah, a letter is easily lost crossing the ocean, she might have written him and received no answer, and he had simply stopped writing repeatedly and constantly when he stopped receiving her news. Now she was waiting and dreaming of their reunion just as he was doing here in Hamburg.

The last angled sunbeam suddenly disappeared. Carlo began to shiver, so he paid and hurled himself into the streaming crowd. He had arrived early today from Vienna. Tomorrow morning the *Alemannia* was setting out from Cuxhaven and he had a cabin on it, so this evening he just had to experience the notorious Hamburg nightlife.

St. Pauli pulsed with its hundreds of taverns and music halls whose garish lights, thumping rhythms, and gigantic billboards lure thousands upon thousands of sailors from all over the world. These sailors are young bloods who after weeks at sea are famished for what promises them pleasure and lust for life, their hard-earned money jingling loosely in their pockets. At Grazienheim flashy high spirits ruled the night. A young, sassy girl with long boyish legs in black silk stockings, her upper body barely covered, was belting out the newest operetta tunes in a shrill and childish voice, all the while underscoring the double entendres in the lyrics with gestures that fit so well that the audience, accustomed to peppery and spicy presentations, howled and roared. Over and over the soubrette, who styled herself Amadea di Risitta, but was surely born on Acker Street in Berlin, was called upon to bow and blow kisses until finally all she had to do was stick her long legs out under the lowered curtain and waggle them in greeting.

Carlo joined all the others in laughter. Here people are cruder and crasser in erotic matters than in Vienna, but at the core there remains the same sheer lust for obscenity that promises everything but renders immediate satisfaction impossible. Carlo was about to continue pondering this topic philosophically, but the flightiness of his temper distracted him. He thought back again to the Viennese women. Lisl, chaste and tender like a fresh young flower, materialized before him. Desire and sultry sensuousness fogged his brain and disrupted his train of thought. He hastily gulped down a glass of wine and was startled when three Negroes overhead raised a gigantic clamor on the podium, hammering the floor with their heavy, yet nimble feet. A pause ensued and the artists mingled with the audience who raised their glasses in greeting. Two portly gentlemen in captain's uniforms escorted the young girl with the wicked legs down front and center; one of the other dancing Negroes strolled over to Carlo, fixed him with his eyes, and set himself down at his table.

Carlo felt somehow unpleasantly affected. The Negro, who was still perspiring from his strenuous dancing, emanated a sharp, sour odor. Carlo pressed his handkerchief soaked in cologne to his nose. A memory flashed through his mind with lightning speed. Once after tennis in Madonna di Campilio, Hella Bühler had sniffed him with her keen little nose and then said: "You know, Carlo, you smell completely different than other men. I would say like nutmeg, cinnamon, and vinegar." He had replied with some frivolous remark or other. Hella gave out with a laugh, and that was that. But now it occurred to him that this black fellow at his table actually did also smell like nutmeg, cinnamon, and vinegar.

Disgusted and insulted, Carlo moved away. And when the Negro spoke to him in a dreadful gibberish and asked whether he always lived in Hamburg, he replied almost impolitely, dryly. What business was it of his, this black fellow's, who came from a completely and utterly different world that was in no way connected with him? None at all—but for one drop of blood. Bewildered, Carlo looked around: Who said that about one drop of blood? It had been his own voice, and heard only by him. "I want to pay" he yelled so loudly that people turned to stare at him. Damn nonsense, the devil fetch this heat and these fumes. Woozy, Carlo ambled back to the Hotel Atlantic. During the night, however, he dreamed of his handsome blond father, of Lisl, of a Negro who seized him and clasped him to himself, and of a spice store that smelled frightfully like nutmeg, cinnamon, and vinegar.

A special train brought Carlo and the other thousand passengers for the *Alemannia* to Cuxhaven the next morning, where the gigantic ship lay at anchor and the last packages and cases had been lowered into its mighty hold. Carlo surveyed his elegant room, first class situated in the middle of the deck towards the sea! Then, he went on deck and mingled with those bidding farewell, the joyful, the sorrowful, the anxious, and the excited. The anchor was weighed and the ship's band played the old tune: "Muß i denn, muß i denn zum Städtele hinaus." Tears, fluttering handkerchiefs, kisses, shouts, a last farewell from a hundred throats, and slowly the white edifice glided out into the North Sea.

Wistfully and with twitching lips Carlo leaned over the railing. Lonely and alone, he detached himself from European soil. The easy friendships, which made life so pleasant for him in Vienna, seemed petty and meaningless to him now. He could scarcely remember any of the names of all the men and women in whose company he had squandered his father's inheritance and wasted his youth. And surely none of them were thinking of him; there was no letter, no post card, or telegram for him in the mountain of farewell cards lying in orderly fashion on the dining hall table. A feeling of profound abandonment, a complete and total sense of self-reliance came over him. To no avail, he sought to conjure up Lisl's image, it faded and dissolved before his very eyes, and a quiet shiver shook his slender body.

Where was his life's journey taking him, what future was he headed for?

The Cuxhaven lighthouse disappeared into the mist. The North Sea swells grew heavier and heavier; they blustered and rolled against the ship, a light drizzle fell and drove the passengers below deck. And while Carlo swayed toward his cabin, he heard a boatswain indifferently reply to a lady's question: "Yep, we're gonna get some real weather!"

That was pretty much the last memory Carlo had of his trip on board the *Alemannia* because a quarter hour later, sea-sickness seized him with all its agonies and terrors and held him captive for eight full days, while the giant ship battled through storm and weather.

✳   ✳   ✳

Pale and even more slender than usual, with his melancholy, dark eyes set deep, Carlo now stood on the deck, dressed in a blue, light worsted cheviot suit, elegant, quite a dandy, staring towards New York harbor, seized with the same feverish expectation as everyone else around him. Green, low-lying Ellis Island lay to the left, that ill-fated island full of torments from which the poor steerage passengers and the cabin passengers, somehow still suspect, first catch a moment to ponder whether the mighty

Statue of Liberty, once a precious symbol, had in the course of the century become an edifice devoid of meaning. Beyond the Statue of Liberty, nearly in reach, thronged enormous buildings, skyscrapers, the strongholds of modern mercantilism, victors over cramped quarters and space shortages. To sharp ears, the pounding surf of an ocean of peoples, the pulse of a city of six million, seemed to resound from the shimmering chaos of stone.

Carlo straightened and stretched.

Before him lay life, his life. Struggle and reward beckoned. There he would have to prove whether he would, like any other superfluous person, sink, or, as one among millions, swim along, or, as one of the blessed, maintain his position at the top. Everything rested upon whether he could transform into coin of the realm everything he had learned and experienced, the languages he had mastered, the education he had enjoyed, and the intelligence that enabled him to see and think more keenly than others.

The gong summoned the passengers to luncheon. Carlo consumed with gusto his first and final meal on board the *Alemannia*, because he had never appeared at table due to sea-sickness. The other passengers ate hastily, rapidly gulping down just a few bites, already torn from the comfortable harmony of life on board ship, already in their thoughts joining relatives, or in their offices, or at the stock exchange.

The next order of business was to pass muster at the immigration authority. American citizens sailed through in no time; non-Americans suffered an indiscreet, ridiculous interrogation.

Born in New York, Carlo was an American citizen who could not lose this privilege even through decades of absence from the States, and so he had little more to do than to present his papers and answer a couple of indifferent questions. But the head of the commission noticed his classical, boarding school English and asked in a friendly manner:

"Weren't you educated over there, Mr. Zeller?"

Carlo nodded. The official looked at him fully in the face now, hesitated, still wanting to ask something, but suppressed the words and whispered something to his co-workers that Zeller didn't understand. Then he was released and, a few minutes later, was able to enter the Promised Land, in Hoboken, where milk and honey flowed as unevenly as it does anywhere else.

Baggage was examined in the horrible, endless customs hall. Hotel employees stood ready to receive their guests. Carlo had reserved his room from Hamburg at the elegant St. Regis Hotel; the uniformed hotel porter took his bag, loaded it onto a handsome taxi and proceeded onto a steam ferry of tremendous proportions from New Jersey over to New York.

Chaotic noise surged and enveloped the new arrival. The mass of pedestrians seemed not to walk, but to be running. Little newspaper urchins flying past bellowed out their editions. Cars filled the street three and four lanes wide. There was ever-present expectation that a Gordian knot would form from the rushing, hooting, cursing people, honking automobiles, and whistling and ringing streetcars. There was always the sense—OK, nothing is going to move, now everything is going to crash together, onto each other and into each other! And again and again the chaos dissolved into forward movement, the stream of people, cars and streetcars glided along into the thoroughfares; and from there onto the side streets, back and forth, over and under, around and through.

They had reached Broadway now at Union Square and Carlo grabbed at his forehead thinking he was losing his senses. At around three in the afternoon, the hustle and bustle grew to enormous proportions. Broadway was black with people and cars, it looked like a revolution, like a battle or an uprising. The streets were paved in automobiles, large and small carriages, mighty six-cylinder vehicles, trucks and tiny open landau carriages. At 18th Street a stream of people merged from right and left to break through the mass of cars, and when an oversize policeman raised his truncheon, everything came to a stop and a passageway opened between the cars, and the horde of people rushed from one side to the other.

There was summer heat, but no sun, which couldn't find a niche to cast its beams down between the buildings stretching up a hundred meters. Carlo was feverish with excitement. He couldn't endure sitting still any longer and playing a stationary extra in this world theater. He reached 20th Street, so he was only about twenty blocks away from his hotel. From his travel guides, he knew that this meant about twenty minutes on foot. He gave the bellboy, who was sitting next to the chauffeur, instructions to wait for him in the hall with his luggage and to remunerate the chauffeur and jumped out quickly and nimbly when the car stopped at the next intersection.

By 23rd Street the scene changed. Here the people were promenading, not scurrying; they were clearly more elegant, the ladies outnumbering the gentlemen. An array of department stores, of the posh world, of theaters, of pastry shops, and of vaudeville houses stretched out. Every second building was a palace of commodities, every fourth a theater, a movie theater, or a music hall.

Carlo looked around attentively, observing the men with intense interest, who were dressed as he was in a nearly identical blue with Caesar-like heads, nasty, squared-off chins, tremendous, emphatic energy, and watery gray eyes, to the untrained eye a muddle so uniform that it was impossible to tell whether this one or that had just elbowed you. A uniform Yankee type fashioned out of a hundred races by the brute force of the machine of life.

From the mighty bronze portal of a department store, femininity in all its nuances and age groups streamed forth. Carlo stopped and stared. He had once observed in Vienna that, of women passers-by, one in ten was pretty, and one in a hundred was beautiful. A quick glance here revealed something different. Almost every one of the young ones was pretty, delicate, slim, and at least every tenth one was beautiful.

In vain, Carlo tried to catch the attention of the women in his Viennese manner. In Vienna every young gal turned round to him, every lady darted a quick glance in his direction. In Hamburg it had been no different. Here the cool, powder gray or translucent brown eyes indifferently passed over him, looked right through him.

Carlo gave a thin smile. Every country has its own way of flirting, one just had to figure out which one worked here.

A couple stepped out of a pastry shop with an Italian name. He was a blond nutcracker like the others, she a fascinating beauty with mahogany red hair. They walked uptown so Carlo followed, walking next to them. He could not divert his gaze from this gracefully slim figure, the alabaster of her cheeks, the burning red of her full, well-turned lips. The beautiful girl noticed his gaze, acknowledged it, and ran her gaze over Carlo in a dry, cold, and deliberative manner. Suddenly she furrowed her brow and turned to her companion, to whom she whispered a few words, whereupon he stopped, glaring furiously at Carlo staring him down and shouting imperiously: "What is it you want?"

Carlo, foreign to this country, and absolutely not prepared for a tussle, disappeared into the milling crowd, and was angered when he felt the light brown of his cheeks suddenly shoot red.

Hotel St. Regis. A colossus, utterly bewildering to European tastes. Stunning and imposing. A twelve-story city with flower boutiques, barbers, bookstores, railroad offices, shoe-shine boys, halls, ballrooms, coffeehouses, restaurants, bars, swimming pools and other amenities for 5,600 people. The mighty hall resounded with hustle and bustle, but transitioned immediately over to discreet, quiet, soundless elegance, with carpets that absorbed the noise.

Now Carlo completely joyous, completely heady from the oxygen of a restless New World traversed the hall completely self-possessed, this pilgrim—a product of two worlds, begotten in tropical heat, born in New York, educated in Vienna—strode by the old and young uniformed Negroes up to the front office.

"My name is Carlo Zeller. My luggage undoubtedly arrived here just a few minutes ago. What is my room number?"

The smartly dressed hotel director in a cutaway bowed politely.

"Of course, Mr. Zeller, Number 934 on the ninth floor. A room with bath. Should it not suit your needs, a change can be made immediately. Here is your key, Mr. Zeller."

A yellow sunbeam skittered through the half-lit office. The manager was already mobbed by other arrivals: questioning, nervous ladies. Carlo turned towards the rank of elevators, where one elevator after another moved up and down quickly and smoothly. He heard however, how a scrawny man with cheeks reddened with age, and with a broad, crude Southern accent barked at the hotel manager.

"What's goin' on? You 're lettin' that boy stay here?"

Noise swallowed the rest of his words. And then the unexpected happened.

Just as he was about to enter the elevator, Carlo felt someone grabbing his arm. The manager stood next to him agitatedly, gawking at him in the face.

Glaring steadfastly at him, struggling for words.

"Excuse me, Sir, there has been an unfortunate mistake—there is no room free for you."

Carlo didn't understand.

"What, the room is not available? Well, give me another room then, I'm not at all insisting on Number 934."

The manager's supple face turned brutal and nasty.

"No, not possible, there are no vacant rooms at all! You must stay somewhere else. We will compensate you for your cab ride."

Carlo stamped his foot down. A few curious folks gathered around.

"What's going on? Are you mad? I reserved my room by wire from Hamburg."

Seeking help, the manager looked around and a few gentlemen grumbled bemused and a lady sighed: "Shocking!"

A hulk of a man, with a low forehead and cheek-bones like a baboon, appeared next to him, laid his hand on his shoulder and murmured to him:

"Now, young man, no commotion! Get your luggage and go to another hotel! Do you not understand? Colored people are not wanted here."

The world started spinning for Carlo. He felt his temper rising, knowing, that he'd become ashen in the face, with bloody spots dancing before his eyes. He lunged, flinging the giant off him slamming him against the elevator gate, then clenched his fist threateningly and roared so loud that it echoed down the hall:

"Scum, idiots, who think that someone who doesn't look like you is a colored man! Fine, I'm leaving, but whoever dares touching me now will get a fist in his eye!"

The manager fled into his office. The spectators melted away, the giant bellowed and looked askance: "The important thing is that you leave!" but did not dare approach Carlo who crouched, ready to pounce.

Breathing deeply, his whole body shaking, Zeller stood before the portal and silently tolerated the loading of his suitcase and valise into the car. The chauffeur leaned toward him questioningly. He did not know what to tell him, until it occurred to him that the Waldorf Astoria was on the same level as St. Regis. As he was about to step into the car, however, a blond, congenial, mature gentleman standing next to him gestured to him.

"Just a word, if you please, young man, just step around the corner if you would. I would like to tell you something that will be of use to you!"

Confused, shocked, and unsettled, Carlo followed.

The congenial gentleman began to speak German now, the good German of a Hanseatic businessman.

"Listen, young man, I observed the scene back there. I'm not a Yankee and I'm not full of prejudices, but come from Bremen and I am just here on business. I would advise you, don't go to the Waldorf. You won't get a room there either."

Rage boiled up in Carlo again.

"For God's sake, why not?"

"Well, you see, young man, in this country everyone notices at first glance that you have black blood in your veins. And you surely do, don't you?"

Tonelessly, as if in a dream, Carlo replied:

"Black blood? I wouldn't say that. My mother was definitely a mix, but my father was a German university professor, and I, myself, grew up in Vienna and have just set foot on American soil for the first time today."

The man from Bremen whistled softly.

"So *that's* it! If your mother was a mulatto and your father a German, you are simply a quadroon, which, according to local understanding, is just as good as being a colored person, a genuine full-blooded nigger. It won't help, young man, spare yourself further humiliation and don't go to the

Waldorf. Even if the hotel manager would want to put you up, he cannot and must not, because otherwise he'll get into a row with his guests. It's stupid, I admit, but that's just the way it is in this country!"

Carlo drooped, his heart and his body quivered, his throat became hoarse.

"I don't understand this—Why did people in Europe take me for a Spaniard or an Italian or the like, and here—"

The congenial gentleman gave a friendly smile.

"Dear friend, the people here just have a lot of practice and can recognize mixed race at a glance into the third or fourth generation, by the hands, the eyes, by everything. And if they don't recognize it in your face, they certainly will recognize it by your blue birthmark, which you will have on your fingernails without fail."

Carlo mechanically stretched out his fingers and saw on every nail the bluish, half-moon at the root of the nails . . .

"Yes, but, where should I stay if no one will put me up?"

"No one? That would be an overstatement! Maybe try in one of the smaller German hotels, perhaps in the Belvedere, they are not so touchy there. Admittedly the best thing would be for you to stay in a"—the old gentleman got embarrassed and nervous! "Well, just go to a special hotel for colored people, there are surely a dozen of them in New York!"

"Never!" Carlo cried up in arms. "I won't have anything to do with Negroes, I am an academically educated German and at least as good as any American."

But he spoke to a void, for the friendly gentleman had disappeared. Carlo went back to the cab and asked to be driven to the Hotel Belvedere. There, in this second-class but clean hotel, which very strongly evoked Europe, Zeller was given a friendly reception—but no room. The hotel owner examined the new arrival, shrugged his shoulders and said with particular kindness:

"Sir, I'm sincerely sorry! Any other time it would have been my pleasure to have you as a guest. But I can't right now because I have four rooms occupied by a family from New Orleans that stays here every year in September. And you of course know,—these people from the South are peculiar people—really, I can't, for my interests as well as in yours, I just can't!"

There was no anger or blind rage welling up in Carlo anymore, just dull despair. He felt stained, as if pelted with buckets of excrement, and looked himself over to find the ulcers and scrapes that people found disgusting. His lips quivered as he murmured to himself:

"My God, what am I to do now, I can't go to a Negro hotel!"

With cordial sympathy, the hotel owner stroked his arm.

"I wouldn't subject you to that either, Sir, truly not, for I see that you are a gentleman. But there is a way out. Go downtown to Second Street on the corner of Canal. There you'll find the Hotel St. Helena whose hotel owner is French. In this decently clean house reside almost exclusively southern Frenchmen, Spaniards, a better class of Italians, nobody will look askance at you there."

Hastily and timidly the Hotel Belvedere owner withdrew just as the family from New Orleans descended the staircase, a white-haired gentleman with a whisky nose and a bushy mustache leading the way while Carlo Zeller departed for the Hotel St. Helena.

At the Hotel St. Helena, whose ugly façade reminded him of a lowest tier hotel by-the-hour, a tattered nigger received him with an amicable grin, for which Carlo would have dearly liked to punch him one, and led him into the office, where a spongy, fat gentleman with an olive complexion and pockmarked face gave him the room key without further ado and charged him three dollars for the day, payable in advance.

The room lay on the third floor and was filled with embarrassing odors, heat, and the stench of cold, stale tobacco smoke. Carlo threw up the window sash and leaned out toward the noisy street. Wherever he looked, he saw nothing but neglected, dirty houses, dust-smudged windows, fire escapes with buckets of garbage on them, smashed dishes, and empty cans lying around. Down below, the people crowded and shoved, streetcars screeched, and car horns honked.

Breathing deeply again, Carlo pulled back into his room. In the next room he heard the low whimpering of a woman, interrupted by brutal French curses from a male throat. In the corridor some employee or other was singing a popular American song with a vapid text and cloying melody. Carlo shuddered and sat down distractedly on the chaise longue draped with a red, unspeakably filthy coverlet. He clapped his hands over the front of his face and burrowed his nails in his forehead for fear of crying out loud.

So this was his reception in the New World; this is how his real "homeland" welcomed him! What he had experienced for the past two hours now all seemed like a horrible dream to him. Of course his father had told him about the American hatred for Negros, and he had read in Viennese newspapers on occasion about a Judge Lynch, but never had this really gotten to him in any special way. He always associated with the word "Negro" a coal black hotel servant, an elevator boy, or at best a minstrel singer in a vaudeville show. He had never felt himself to be a Negro or anyone associated with that race, never suspected that the phrase "colored people" might apply to him.

Carlo stretched out his slim, delicate fingers and inspected his nails. The heritage of his mother, the blue birthmark, shone ghostlike tenfold up at him. It had often attracted attention in Vienna, but never as a stigma. More than one lovely girl had kissed this blue stain, and when his bride, the blond Lisl, for the first time tenderly caressed his hand she exclaimed in amazement:

"How interesting! You surely come from southern blood!"

Lisl! Carlo jumped up, and gentler thoughts came over him. Don't abandon hope! He would seek Lisl out tomorrow, introduce himself to her uncle and other family members, and they would all laugh together over today's grotesque experiences. After all, Lisl's uncle, Mr. Ortner, was Austrian by descent, and even if his wife was American, they would surely be unprejudiced, modern people, not brutish, uneducated hotel clerks clinging to archaic, outmoded rules.

He opened his suitcases, prepared his toilet elaborately, cooled his hot head by putting some ice from the jug into the washbasin, soaked his handkerchief with cologne and left the hotel feeling almost good again. Out on the street, he remembered, however, that he hadn't eaten anything since noon. Hunger and thirst came over him and he quickly checked his notebook for addresses of first-class restaurants that a Viennese friend of his who had visited New York a short while ago had given him: Delmonico, Martin, Sherry. Carlo quickly oriented himself, then boarded a streetcar headed uptown, was once again struck by the goings-on on Broadway, and got off right in the middle of the raffish district of Manhattan named after the tenderest, juiciest cut of meat, the Tenderloin, to dine at Sherry's.

It was the epitome of cultured life, rarely to be found even in Central Europe. Deep Persian carpets, absorbing every sound, waiters, looking like aristocrats at a ball, exquisite porcelain, heavy silver, crystal glasses, voluptuous, blood-red roses on every table, soft, discreet music from a small, invisible string quartet. Carlo examined the menu on handmade paper, which the waiter for his table presented him, the order of courses almost too vast to take in.

Despite all his good intentions to save the last few thousand dollars he had brought, Carlo ordered an elaborate meal and then stretched out at ease in his armchair. In a country with such fine restaurants, surely one must be able to live a life of comfort! In a country that developed wealth like this with such natural grace, it had to be easy to make one's fortune!

Suddenly Carlo felt himself being looked at, even stared at, from the adjoining table. An elderly lady sat there with a young, pretty woman and a gentleman in a tuxedo. The young woman looked at him coldly and dismissively, the gentleman seemed agitated, the lady made attempts to get them to relax. Surely they were occupied with him, surely they too had sensed his black blood, maybe even seen his blue birthmark. Carlo, who had always been admired and honored for his foolhardy courage, ducked down like a coward and hid his hands under his napkin.

Instantly the waiter appeared next to him in polite deference and presented him an open envelope on an elegant plate of exquisite Sèvres porcelain. In the envelope was tucked a card on which in most delicate handwriting it said:

"Honored guest! According to the regulations of our establishment and much to our regret we are not able to serve you!"

Carlo raised no ruckus, did not clamor or shout, but had just one thought: Away from here, away from the stares, for if he were to catch even one scornful smile here, then he would lose all self-control, would turn into a raging beast and jump at the first white throat in reach!

Where to go now? He didn't dare go to another restaurant. For they would perhaps, even probably, likewise show him the door out of second and third class establishments and advise him to go to some nigger joint.

Without a plan, but with a throbbing, pounding pulse, he rushed downtown, down amidst the slowly waning crowd along Broadway. After an hour of running back and forth, he felt immensely tired, exhausted, dusty, and sweaty. Without thinking he breathed in, pressing his wet hand to his nose.

"So, now these dogs will not only see it in me, but also smell it on me that I'm colored." And then he saw Hella Bühler before him, the beautiful Hella, who whispered in sensuous repose: "You smell completely differently than our gentlemen—like cinnamon, nutmeg, and vinegar—"

Carlo now entered an area filled with strange hurly-burly. Behind every door were beer saloons, hard liquor bars and vaudeville theaters of the most abject sort. Music blaring from the locales, drunks on the street, and at least as many whites as Negroes among them. And every so often some broad in gaudy make-up. By the glow of a streetlight he was able to make out the street sign "Bowery." From his travel guides he knew that he was now situated in New York's sleaziest district, filled with the lowest sorts of sin. Before him loomed a mysterious restaurant bathed in garish, blue-white light. Gigantic banners read: Dinner with the best music in New York, just 50 cents! Come in, come in, come in! Five courses for 50 cents and the newest operetta hits too! In front of the open portal stood a guy with a megaphone, bellowing to the passersby an invitation to visit the finest and most unsurpassed restaurant in all New York. Carlo just stood still in the glaring light of the doorway and the screamer invited him in with a wave of his hand.

"Come in, colored gentleman, and enjoy our exquisite menu and drinks."

As if struck by a lash, Carlo flinched. So even for this scum he was at first glance nothing more than a colored person, a man of the Negro tribe, regardless of his upbringing and education! It dawned on him that he was confronting the inevitable, something he could not fight against.—

And yet, he needed to eat and rest his weary limbs. Slowly, hesitatingly, he entered the massive locale with more than a hundred tables set, buzzing fans, detestable brass music, and guests slurping and smacking noisily, mostly men who kept their hats on.

All the tables were occupied, but there was one with a gentleman sitting alone, and Carlo set out in that direction. But a gentleman in a greasy looking tuxedo was already seizing him by the arm and the manager, or even owner, of the place showed him to another table where two Negroes were already sitting.

"Here is a nice seat available for you, Sir!"

Carlo gave the disconcerted man a hard shove, turned on his heel, and dashed out of the hall onto the street.

Raging disgust and hatred for these people that he was being forced to associate with, made him clench his fist. And just then a fat Negro woman with an outrageous, comical, green feather hat hustled up close to him and cooed "Come with me big boy!" At that point, he spat, hurling an oath in her face, and ran on.

Off to Hotel St. Helena. He remembered having seen a sign in the hallway with the inscription: "Restaurant Entrance." Surely they wouldn't insult him there. But he didn't know his way around, didn't know which of the crisscrossing streetcars to take. He felt his strength waning, and so he eventually threw himself into a taxi, although he knew very well that he would again be paying an incredibly high sum when calculating in kronen.

Well, the restaurant in Hotel St. Helena did not exactly look appealing. Behind a big bar where beer was dripping on the floor stood a fellow dressed in shirt-sleeves mixing all sorts of drinks. In front of the bar stood five or six guests throwing dice for glasses of whisky. In the front there were several tables without tablecloths and he took a seat at one of them. A chewing waiter appeared in an apron that might have been white a few weeks ago, and asked him in a mixture of Italian and English what he'd like. No, there weren't any prepared meals available, but steak and potatoes could be ready in a couple minutes. Carlo nodded, eagerly reaching for the white bread and butter dish, washing down a glass of ice-cold beer in one gulp, and finally coming more or less to his senses again.

At the next table sat an elderly, corpulent gentleman. Small blue eyes shone from his rather rosy face making him look all the more comical because his thin eyebrows were as white or platinum as the hair on his head. Carlo caught his friendly gaze, smiled involuntarily and felt somehow put off. Then he delved into the giant steak and thought how he had not savored a more delicious meal in years. When he was done and looked around sated, the genial platinum blond gentleman man got up and sat down with him without asking him for permission.

"Stranger here, young man?" and when Carlo nodded and looked inquiringly:

"I can tell by the European cut of your suit. Americans wear padded shoulders, but your jacket fits like a glove. Well, anybody who has traveled the world as I have, knows his way around. By the way, you aren't fully European, are you? It seems to me that some foreign race has been mixed in with good German blood."

Carlo could not resent these words, which were accompanied by a broad, agreeable smile, and so he affirmed.

"My father was a German, my mother a mulatto!"

"Hmm," ruminated the fat man, "around here that does not always lead to the most pleasant situations." Examining him, his gaze ranged over Carlo, pausing at his flawless shoes, his heavy silk tie and his golden wristwatch. Then he said:

"Don't take my curiosity in a bad way, Sir. But I would be interested in knowing how you ended up in a dive like this. Gentlemen like you don't usually stay at the St. Helena. There's a lot of riffraff here avoiding the light of day, who've barely escaped the authorities in Marseille harbor and hide out here until someone catches them or until they find out that no wanted poster was issued. Then they lose themselves in the big city New York, go American, or hop the first ship back again."

Rage, pain, and defiance fused in Carlo. He felt virtually compelled to get things off his chest, so he told the well-intentioned gentleman, who meanwhile had ordered two cocktails and introduced himself as a Dane named Andersen, in rushing and excited words what he had experienced unsuspectingly after eight days of sea sickness. And eventually he burst forth nearly sobbing:

"What am I to do now? Do you think that even educated, refined persons will treat me like a leper here? How can I make my life here, how can I regain my sense of humanity again?"

The Dane puffed reflectively on his cigar, ordered another round of cocktails and, troubled, then offered the opinion:

"That's a hard nut to crack you've given me! If you were a nigger or a mulatto or some other person of the Negro tribe, of which there are hundreds of thousands running around here, you wouldn't lack for anything. You speak English like a Yale professor, French, as you mentioned, just as well as English, and German. You could get a good job tomorrow in a hotel as a supervisor over the black waiters or a clerk for a nigger lawyer or something like that. But now you don't want to have anything to do with Negroes, and the whites don't want anything to do with you, so the situation is devilishly difficult. The Yankees will keep on rejecting you, even more so than if you were black! They will still excuse the blacks their skin color, the mulattoes, the 'half-caste' somewhat less, and those who are even further removed from their race they hate because they instinctively suspect them of being interlopers wanting to break through their boundaries. Educated, distinguished Americans? Hm, they definitely won't insult you, but they won't want to have anything to do with you, either! You see, I'm an adjuster for a life insurance company, and so I stay in places just like this. Now, I could take you to our superintendent tomorrow and tell him: 'Here's just the man we need, a man who can process Yankees as well as foreigners.' But what would our boss say? He would take one look at you, pull me aside and whisper to me: Impossible, can't risk someone showing him the door and going complaining to the board of directors. If he wants to process the colored, then I can hire him, otherwise it won't work."

Beaten down and scarcely capable of a single clear thought, Carlo mumbled to himself in anguish:

"Oh, if I had never set foot in this country, if I had only stayed among my friends!"

The Dane leaned forward and stroked the hand with the blue stains.

"Well, you still have that opportunity! Or don't you have enough money for a return ticket?"

"O yes, enough for a return ticket and some to spare! I have a few thousand dollars, and if tomorrow brings more disappointments, then I really will board the next ship home. To be honest, it is not a pleasant thought; even in Vienna or Berlin or wherever I go, I will have to do quite a bit of scuffling with life. But I am not afraid, the main thing is: I will be a human being again, a full, complete person that no one dares look askance at!"

The day's excitement, the beer, the five or six strong drinks began to suffuse Carlo with a leaden weariness. He could barely keep his eyes open so he paid, shook the Dane's hand and explained that he needed to retire to his room. The friendly gentleman also stood up:

"If you permit, I would like to accompany you and, while you are preparing to go to bed, tell you a few more things that might come in handy for you. It's still early in the day and I have passed up meeting my party uptown for the sake of our animated conversation."

Carlo would have preferred to remain alone now, but he could not reject the friendly offer. He retired to his room with Mr. Andersen and undressed slowly while his visitor, restlessly pacing back and forth, told him about his life on the go; the hundred professions he had practiced, before he had gotten on well enough to spend his days quietly in a safe post, sufficient for his needs. The Dane spoke now so softly and monotonously that his words sounded like a murmur, lulling Carlo to sleep. He barely heard him, closed his eyes, experienced the Dane's stories as a kind of distant surf, while he poised on the threshold of deep sleep, as his guest turned out the light and left the room, closing the door behind him.

The endless noise from the street, the warm, humid air, and vermin had awakened Carlo again and again from leaden sleep. Bewildering dreams made him groan as he lay dripping with sweat. Once he saw a noose around his neck as he ran down the street, pursued by an angry crowd that bellowed behind him: "String up that Negro, he's trying to assault a white girl!" Then again he saw a thousand gigantic, black beetles crawling over him, dancing a wild dance all around him, and the black porter in the Lido Palace Hotel stroked him, his friends in Vienna ridiculed him, and Hella Bühler shouted: "Ugh, I can't stand the stench of a Negro!"

As if pummeled and battered, Carlo awakened early in the morning from knocking at the door. Startled, he said, "Come in," and a young boy opened the door and handed him a letter with the remark:

"A gentleman handed in a letter last night and said he would like this to be delivered to you today!"

Carlo jumped out of his bed, tore open the envelope and read:

"Dear young man! You must be more cautious in this country! I'm deeply sorry because I like you, but I couldn't help myself. I simply could not pass up the opportunity to make a fortune, which will keep me out of misery forever. You are young and strong and will get through this; I'm an old geezer for whom your money means the jackpot! With best wishes, yours truly, allegedly Andersen!"

With a suppressed outcry Carlo dashed to the table, where, as he was undressing, he had laid his watch and wallet in the Dane's presence. The watch was there, next to it a little pile of change, but his wallet was gone. The friendly, sympathetic Dane had taken it with him, leaving Carlo alone in a foreign, spiteful world with thirty-three cents!

Carlo railed against his fate for a minute with clenched fists, then his eyes fell on his gold watch and all his frivolousness burst forth, he gave a quick laugh and said to himself:

"May those 3,000 dollars somehow break that rogue's neck! Now's the time to do it, by hook or by crook! Lisl's uncle will bail me out somehow. And once I am earning my living, I will come out on top again." The Dane's pessimistic remarks revealed themselves to him to be the deceiving line of a swindler trying to win his trust.

At the hotel office and the restaurant he inquired after the Dane to no avail. No one knew him, no one claimed to have seen him, and Carlo, recognizing the hopelessness and absurdity of his situation, passed up making a police report, which never would succeed anyway.

He used the thirty-three cents for a cup of tea. He could pay the next day's room rent later, and so Carlo strolled uptown, meticulously searching until he came to a pawn shop whose owner, Moe Löwenstein, advertised that he paid the best price in all of North America. But in the end the appraiser only offered him 15 dollars for the watch, but then did offer to buy it for twenty. Carlo didn't ponder long, he handed over the watch and took the twenty dollars.

The residence of Mr. Ortner, Lisbeth's uncle, stood on West 75th street. Carlo got his bearings from his pocket map and immediately rushed uptown on the subway. Before his duel with Thomas Bühler and the gondola ride in Venice from the Piazzetta to the Lido, Carlo had gotten to know his every heartbeat that could evoke fear, feverish expectation, and stormy excitement. But that was nothing compared to the feelings that had his heart pounding like a hammer as he now stood before the beautiful, distinguished brownstone that harbored his love, his fate, perhaps even his life! He wiped the sweat off his brow a couple of times and took in a few deep breaths before he finally decided to press the ivory bell button with his right index finger. As he did this, the blue half-moon shone on his fingernail, even bluer and more vivid than usual, as if in warning.

At that moment a nice girl in a dainty white cap was opening the door and asked his wishes.

"Is Miss Elsbeth Ortner at home?"

It buzzed in his ears, and as if in a dream, he heard the answer:

"Yes sir, who may I say is calling?"

He stood now in the dark hallway endowed with the dignified noblesse of a single family mansion and reached toward his breast pocket wallet: Of course, the wallet had become the Dane's booty, together with his calling cards. He tore a page from his notebook and wrote with trembling fingers: "Carletto Zeller."

Carletto—How long had it been since Lisbeth, his good friends and delicate women had called him that?

The girl had him enter the parlor on the right side of the hall and offered him a seat.

Carlo stepped into the great drawing room, where a Steinway grand piano stood in the background, walked up and down; heavy, dark mission style oak furniture, good paintings on the walls, and photographs on consoles and étagères.

On one of the faces Carlo saw a strong resemblance to Elsbeth, so it was probably a photograph of Mr. Ortner. And this young, slender girl probably was her cousin. She also looked something like Elsbeth, but on her lips was that dismissive, arrogant trait which Carlo had already seen yesterday on a number of women. In a silver bowl lay images of Lisbeth herself. A large number were pictures taken in Vienna, among them snapshots he had already seen.

Carlo found the most recent photograph taken at the American resort of Newport Beach. Excited, he pressed the picture to his lips; yes, that was his dear, good Lisl with big, bright eyes! But the smile on her full mouth seemed less childlike to him, there was something more austere and her eyes gazed more coolly at the world.

Why had Lisl not come rushing down? Ten whole minutes had already passed and even if Lisl were not fully dressed she would at least have been able to extend her hand through the doorway.

A frightening feeling seized his throat. Curiously, he listened intently toward the door. There was a flurry of voices upstairs, women's voices, excited but unintelligible words, and now it seemed to him as if he were hearing sobbing. He pressed his nails into his palms and bit his lips, as his blood shot through his veins at a blinding rate.

Minute after minute passed. Things grew quiet upstairs, one could hear nothing but the ticking of the big clock over the fireplace. It felt as if his knees were made of lead; now he sat down for real and began counting. He counted to a hundred and then to one-hundred again.

Noiselessly, the door opened up and Carlo jumped up and stretched his arms out. But only the parlor maid, who looked at him amazed and with curiosity, stood in the door. She gave him a letter and said:

"The young lady offers her regrets; she has a migraine and cannot receive the gentleman."

Carlo had no idea how he got out of the house, but thinking back on it later, it came to him vaguely, that, as he exited the house, the girl twice picked up his hat, which had fallen from his hand, then, that he had stumbled down the four steps of the front entrance to the street, and was caught up by the postman laughing. Then he ran down the street pressed tightly against the wall like a thief so that people could not see him from the window, until he reached broad Columbus Avenue. Then he stopped and read:

"Carlo, you must forget me! We must not associate with one another here. Everything is different over here from the way it was over there in Vienna. Please, sir, don't be angry with me, and don't think badly of me. Carlo, it simply cannot be. Be mindful that I was a foolish little girl over there, but here I've become an American. You will eventually understand everything yourself. Farewell greetings to you, sir, Elise Ortner."

Carlo began howling like an animal. Primitive instincts overcame him. He beat his chest with his fists. With bloodshot eyes he stared at people, who stopped in startlement, so fiercely that they quickly withdrew. When a woman ran off saying: "That nigger has gone mad," Carlo laughed shrilly, white foam dribbling over his lips. Right after that he was standing in a bar, gulping down a full glass of whisky, and then one more, and then another, until everything starting spinning around him and he staggered into a corner and fell into a chair. Then the reaction set in: he felt an aching pain making him shudder and he just had the one thought: I must not cry or wail around like a child in front of these white animals. And in a flash, for the first time, a feeling overwhelmed him, that between the white people and himself there was an abyss, and that he stood on this side of the abyss with the blacks.

After days full of apathy and dissolute whisky drinking, the young immigrant's lithe and leathery resolve had banished Lisl from his brain. He put his best suits over his arm, sold them, moved from Hotel St. Helena to a small backroom on the top story, for which he paid only a dollar, and set about seeking a new life. Eventually—in a city with six million people—he had to find an opportunity for making his living, without being shoved in with the Negroes.

He got up early at five o'clock in the morning, went down to Park Row, where newspaper buildings stand one after another and, hot off the press, bought the *World* where the most help wanted ads were to be found.

He stood waiting in the increasingly cool morning hours with a hundred others in front of offices, factories, skyscrapers, and private apartments until it was his turn and he could reel off his spiel. And what disappointments! Insults, blows came crashing down rendering him completely insensate.

A large school was looking for a teacher of French and German. Barely twenty applicants were even able to apply, and Carlo, slender and still elegant in appearance, should have had the best chances.

"Impossible—my students are young ladies from the best houses—You understand———"

An advertising office was looking for bright workers with a good sense of style. The manager, who immediately recognized Carlo's superior intelligence and education, hesitated, then said: "What the heck, I'll take you!"

Full of ardor, Carlo plunged into his work, outlined marketing ideas, and delighted the manager, who had finally found in him the employee he had been seeking in vain after months of searching among young, poorly educated, unimaginative drudges. On the second day, Carlo was already badgered by hostile looks, heard whisperings and mutterings about himself in the great room, and observed how the thirty men and girls pressed into the manager's office at lunch break instead of using the short half-hour for eating. In the afternoon the manager shook his hand, expressing deep regret, and asked him to go.

"My people don't want to work with a colored person, they're threatening to get the clerk's union breathing down my neck, I have to give in whether I want to or not——"

At the largest book and magazine mail-order business in the United States there was an open position for an educated gentleman who spoke English, French, German, and also Italian, if possible. Carlo handed in a written resume in every language and was conducted to the chief executive. The executive, a German who himself had only been living in the country for a few years, did not see his blue birthmark in the poor lighting of the small office, and also did not recognize the mixed race in Carlo's face. He was delighted to be able to speak about Vienna and was convinced he had found a most valuable employee and hired Carlo at a salary of twenty dollars a week. Finally, it was Carlo himself who made the German aware of his ancestry and alerted him to the possibility of conflicts that might arise because of it.

The chief executive smiled dismissively.

"You will meet no resistance here! Half of the thousand employees I have are greenhorns who are overjoyed to be earning a living. And the others, the Americans, will be wary of raising a stink, because I will just kick them out. As a precaution, however, I will have you working in the German section in a small room together with three or four young girls."

Carlo was jubilant, and for the first time in a long time feelings of happiness rippled through his body. He walked as upright on the street, inclining at the waist, as he had done in Vienna when he strolled along the Graben, well rested after a luxurious breakfast.

As he was climbing the steps to the elevated, he collided into a young girl, who, like him, was trying to push past the official taking the tickets just so she could catch the train. He politely yielded the right of way to the lady and then they both took a seat across from each other. The girl gave a friendly smile and straightened her jet-black hair in disarray. Carlo got a jolt. A girl smiling at him, golly, that had not happened since Hamburg! Of course immediately following this inner jolt came the sobering realization. The girl with the olive complexion, great long eyelashes, shaded eyes, dazzling white teeth, and voluptuous lips was a mulatto! She was not a quadroon like him, but the child of a Negro woman and a white man.

Strange and conflicted feelings raged through him. Somehow he felt an attraction for the girl, who was barely mature, and made quite a good, proper impression. Her smile was so friendly that he surely would not experience a curt dismissal if he spoke to her. Carlo thought it over:

If all these calamities had not befallen me, if the whites weren't always shoving me into the colored camp, then I wouldn't be hesitant to speak to this pretty, charming, little girl, and maybe this very day quenching my desires on her slim, brown body. But this must not be, for this mulatto would not see in me the honored, adored white man for whom, as they say, all the black women long but would see in me a comrade in race, a man from her people, and she would pull me down to those black depths which horrify me.

The face of the man grew so distorted, so cold and dismissive, that the girl stopped smiling and looked at him with large, frightened eyes.

Zeller got out at Twenty-Third Street and dispelled his repulsive thoughts. He counted his cash. He still had three dollars left from selling his clothes and he wanted to spend two of them in comfort today. For tomorrow he would have an office and dignity. Tomorrow was Wednesday, Saturday was payday, and he would get by until then somehow. He laughed to himself with pleasure, amused by his own recklessness, he smiled at his reflection, which appeared slimmer and paler, but no less handsome, and strolled through the Tenderloin with its beautiful women, elegant men, and magnificent coaches. He was enthralled by the expensive store windows, by the crisp toiletry, by the elegant perfume which this woman or that trailed behind her, by the sparkling of gold and diamonds. He felt a lust for conquest and stretched his limbs.

And so, this and only this is my world! I will force these benighted fools to acknowledge me, I will have gotten on in life in a year and a day and prove to them that the driving strength in me originates from sublime, Germanic blood, and I have nothing in common with those people they want to force me in with, just because of this blue mark, this insidious gift from a mother I have never known!

He expanded on this train of thought. I will take revenge for every suffering they've put me through. I will seduce their women and daughters, they shall lose all racial arrogance in my arms, they shall moan with pleasure when I embrace them and they will bring my children into the world, who then shall convey the indelible blue stain into their social circles.———

A lust for life, for women, and for luxury made his muscles swell, led him into a fantasy dreamland, and endowed his dark eyes with such boldness and dreaminess that here and there a glance from a white woman's countenance swept over him, not without favor, for just a few seconds before retreating behind the dignity of a woman offended by the sight of a *colored* man.

Evening came, and Carlo went down as far as Fourteenth Street, turning off toward Second Avenue. The Viennese and Hungarian coffeehouses and restaurants stood there in a row, giving this part of Second Avenue the popular name Goulash Avenue.

Carlo knew that in these establishments, frequented by the naïve and never to be Americanized children of Vienna and Budapest, people had no interest in the Negro question and that he would be as welcome as any a guest who was able to give the waiter a five cent tip rather than sticking him with the bill.

At the Vindobona Café Carlo surrounded himself with a mountain of Viennese and Berlin newspapers, ate his fill of noodle soup, beef goulash, and apple strudel, all together for forty cents, ordered a mocha, lit an imported Austrian cigarette and felt almost as if he were at home in Vienna. All you heard spoken around here was German, genuine Viennese German, German with Czech coloration, German with Budapest accentuation, and mostly German with a strong, unmistakably Jewish accent. Billiards and tarot were played, America was bad-mouthed, and the latest news from the *Neue Freie Presse* was discussed. In short, these folks got on with life, like it or not, taking the good with the bad, perhaps more bad than good, and had created for themselves in the middle of America a Central European island, living out their lives without ever learning English and/or being Americanized in the good and bad sense of the word.

Carlo smiled ironically to himself. Actually, these brown-skinned, dark-haired Jews were also being shoved aside by the white Aryans in Vienna. The Negro question has one hell of a similarity with the Jewish question. Well, the Jews in Europe haven't let themselves be ground down and I, who am no Jew and no Negro, damned well won't let that happen to me either.

✶   ✶   ✶

"My name is Carlo Zeller from Vienna, I only arrived a few weeks ago in this country and would be thankful if you would assist me here at work!"

Three young girls were flattered and bowed, giving him their hand. Grete Möller, Erna Struve, Lilli Wegner. Grete Möller was a straw blond, robust, but already somewhat faded beauty of a woman from Hannover who had been in America for three years. Erna Struve, small and unimposing, had come a year ago with her parents from Lübeck; Lilli Wegner had been here for only a few months. Her brothers had been living in New York for years and had just recently brought over their widowed mother and eighteen-year-old sister. Carlo liked Lilli quite a lot, she was medium-sized, had soft, supple movements and kind, blue eyes. For the time being, he was to work mostly with her; he dictated to her the German letters to be typed, which he drafted, based on brief shorthand notes from the chief executive. He himself typed, albeit somewhat awkwardly, the letters in French and

Italian to book traders since he was the only one in this department who knew these languages.

The International Book Company, where Carlo was now employed, had a monopoly on the import and export of books and magazines in and out of Europe, it was a huge company with more than a thousand employees, of whom more than three quarters were involved in the mechanical work of packaging, addressing, and categorizing. These employees were tiny cogs in the giant mechanism, whereas Carlo had already become more of a mover and shaker.

Time passed quickly, and Carlo felt so blessed at being one person among others, of being able to produce profitable work for which he got paid, that he did not feel tired when the clock struck six and everybody was getting ready to leave.

Lilli lived with her mother and two brothers in a rental house on First Avenue. And it seemed in the natural course of things that Carlo join her and escort her home. They walked the relatively short distance; he sketched out for her in a few words his rich but agitated youth in Vienna, the girl complained that she felt uncomfortable in the big city whose language she had not yet mastered. All the more so, since her brothers were strangers to her and she always had to spend the evenings in her dull, wretched apartment.

"Even so," Carlo said softly, "you have your mother and brothers around. I am completely alone, don't know anyone, and I have no one with whom I could talk and exchange thoughts."

They had arrived at the door of the ugly, four-story house, and Lilli looked at him compassionately with big eyes.

"If you feel lonely, Mr. Zeller, then come visit us some evening after dinner. My brothers are rarely at home and even when they are, mother and I usually just sit around in our little room, so it will delight us very much if you would like to chat with us."

Carlo gladly accepted. When he went to the Hotel St. Helena alone, he had a slight smile.

Just a few months ago, I would not have turned to look at this small girl in her cotton blouse. Evening upon evening I spent in high society, gambling with congenial friends or spending time in the salons of beautiful women who liked me quite a lot, women whose slender, white hands trembled when I kissed them or boldly pressed my lips to their pulsing veins. Today I'm a poor clerk, one among millions, and I am happy if I can spend one evening with two simple women who have nothing to say to me and do not excite me in any way. Who would have predicted all this, who could predict today in what other directions my path will take me!?———

The next few days passed in the harmonious flow of work; the chief
executive twice took it upon himself to express his extraordinary satisfaction with Carlo, who began feeling more self-confident and secure in his
future. He paid no attention to the mistrustful and ironic glances from
other employees in the stairways or corridors and let it slide. He didn't
come into closer contact with anyone except for the three German girls,
since the room he worked in could be entered directly from the third story
staircase. He always escorted Lilli home in the evenings, but he hadn't visited her yet since she had not mentioned the invitation again and he did
not want to come without explicitly being asked once again.

On Saturday, for the first time in his life, Carlo received money in
his hands that he had earned himself, in fact, even though he had only
started on Wednesday, he got the whole week's salary of twenty dollars.
He laughed gaily as he strode with Lilli down the street and reined in his
feelings of proud satisfaction by remembering how just a short while ago
he had squandered other, quite substantial sums on passing fancies and
empty, conceited amusements.

The October days were warm and sunny. They presented Indian
summer in all its glory, the feeling was in the air that a new spring was
approaching and Carlo suggested to Lilli that they visit the famous Coney
Island, which he hadn't yet seen, on the following afternoon.

The girl happily agreed. She had been there once with her family, but it
had been terribly hot and crowded, and her mother had gotten a headache
from all the noise and hullabaloo, so she had not actually been able to have
any fun on the carousel or any of the other amusement rides.

Zeller awaited the petite girl on Sunday afternoon at the house gate,
and they rode in the vastly overcrowded elevated across the seemingly
endless Brooklyn Bridge over to Coney Island, the immense amusement
complex on the coast, which constituted almost the sole recreation for New
York's three million lower class people. Deafening noise welcomed them,
the suffocating fumes from people, of the strange corn on the cob, which
was sold out in the open, from thousands of sausage stands, from the howling of several hundred music bands, and the shrieking of people who were
tossed high up in the sky on the daring roller coasters. Vienna's amusement
park, the Wurstelprater, had been contorted into something gigantic and
grotesque, but a thousand times larger.

Next to the young gal, who still had her Mannheim ways about her,
Carlo felt just like a boy today, surrounded by a surging, frolicsome crowd.
Whooping, he wheeled with Lilli through the air in the gondola of the Ferris
wheel, climbed on wooden horses, which threw you every time, savored

the amusement of the devil's wheel, that flung you out while bystanders laughed, and got irretrievably lost with his companion in a gigantic maze, in which occasionally the eye of the Gnome lit up electrically. When he felt Lilli nestled fearfully up to him, his young, famished senses blazed up. He wrapped his arms around the girl's soft body and singed her lips with his kisses after she had first resisted. Then suddenly an electric arrow lit up before them dispelling the darkness and showing them and the other couples the way out.

Lilli cautioned him to be frugal, but to no avail. They dined at the finest restaurant on Coney Island that evening. A minor incident started there, which abruptly spoiled the pleasant mood. Two gentleman walked by to their table, remained standing for a moment, and then one of them said loudly to the other: "Ugh, a white girl is sitting with a colored man!" and walked on.

The blood drained from Carlo's face, turning him so ashen that Lilli, who had not understood the English remark, laid her hand on his arm and asked whether he felt sick. With difficulty he regained his faculties, shook his head, then paid quickly and asked Lilli, who might have preferred to stay, to leave with him. The return trip passed in apprehensive silence, while Lilli was unable to account for Zeller's disgruntlement.

*   *   *

The next morning dark, heavy clouds hung in the sky, and one glance at his dollar watch, which he had bought a few days ago, told him that he was quite late. Carlo didn't shave, dressed quickly, and was drinking a hot coffee while standing on Duane Street, where the International Book Company was located, just before eight. Since the elevator was just about to depart, Carlo wanted to take it contrary to his normal habit of taking the stairs. The elevator was almost packed, but there was still room for one more person. As he was about to squeeze inside, a huge, bull-necked fellow shoved him back, and instead squeezed himself in and jeered:

"I say, any damn nigger better yield to a white gentleman."

No Negro in America lets himself be called a "nigger" with impunity. He regards this word as an insult and prefers to be called a "colored man," or better yet, a "colored gentleman." The strange thing about what happened was that even Carlo didn't mind the word "damned," but felt "nigger," to be an outrageous insult and burning disgrace. His heart stopped for a beat, and he got that ashen coloration in his face from earlier, which in Negroes, mulattos and quadroons substitutes for blushing or turning pale.

The whites of his eyes reddened, he crouched and pounced like a predator on the man who was already standing in the elevator door opening, and tore him out; two or three workmanlike punches resounded through the halls and the guy who had insulted him, wallowed senselessly on the floor, blood streaming from his nostrils and mouth.

Americans show a commendable discipline in such fights. They don't meddle or take sides, but regard it as a private matter that does not concern a third party. This also applied here. The hundred men and women gathering around formed a ring around the two during the one minute fight, and when one of the men was unable to get up and had to be carried off, the crowd quietly dispersed: not without an admiring glance at Carlo, who took the stairs breathing heavily. Then, an older gentleman muttered to the bystanders: "That young man got it right, we don't live in the South, where anybody can just call a colored man a nigger."

Carlo arrived a full ten minutes late in his work room, but no one took note. He greeted the three employees as if nothing had happened. He shook Lilli's hand and saw now that her eyes were puffy from crying. Dismayed, he looked at her and whispered: "What's happened?" He didn't get an answer and couldn't keep asking because he felt he was being watched by two other girls, and the daily correspondence had just arrived in the office. Later, when there was a short break, Lilli quickly and furtively slipped him a note, written on the typewriter.

> "Carlo! It was horrible! My brothers saw me with you and reviled me calling me a common slut because I've been hanging around with someone descended from the black race. I had to swear that I would no longer associate with you except at the office, otherwise they will toss me out on the street! I don't understand all this; but my brothers think that a white girl is regarded worse than a streetwalker in this country if one sees her in the company of a colored man. Tell me what to do, Carlo, but only in writing, for I can't dare speak with you on the street any longer."

Carlo swallowed down tears and saliva bitter as gall and laughed to himself.

Lisl and Lilli, the rich girl and the poor one! Nothing ever changes! I know that as long as I must stay in this atrocious country, I will be utterly alone, and cut off from all the people, that I have to be satisfied if they just allow me to earn a crust of bread!

On the reverse side of the letter he wrote: "What you should do? Very simple! Don't speak with me anymore and be a good American girl!"

He shoved the note over to Lilli, sat down at the desk, wrote letters in French and Italian and worked at such a fervid pace that the hours went by like minutes for him. At five o'clock, an office boy came and requested that he come see the chief executive. The director sat in a swivel chair, visibly irritated, running his hands furiously through his thin hair. After a short while he said:

"Unfortunately, dear Zeller, you have judged conditions more correctly than I did! A few miserable swine, who I cannot catch because I don't know who they are, have agitated against you and now I'm getting this note from the Book and Music Trade Union."

He handed Zeller a letter that said:

"The Secretary of Union Local 23 has been informed that the International Book Company has been employing a man named Carlo Zeller for a short time in your workplace who is to be classified in the category Colored People. This conflicts with Paragraph 19 of our closed shop collective agreement with management, and we must request that you without delay enforce the implementation of this paragraph. We put you on notice, that a refusal on your part to fulfill these terms would by our Trade Union Bylaws force declaration of lack of good faith and boycott of the International Book Company."

Carlo had read the letter quietly and without a word. Controlling himself, he handed the letter back to the director and said in a soundless, tired voice:

"Then I guess I have to go, Mr. Director!"

The director looked at him in desperation through his glasses, commenced condemning all Americans to hell in his blunt German-American speech, but eventually conceded, shrugging his shoulders:

"There's nothing I can do, my friend! If I defy this, it would not only cost me my position, but could endanger the whole company, which would not help you either. I can only tell you that you are more valuable to me than that whole gang of rabble, and that I was about to make you my next private secretary. Now, however, our ways must part. The only thing that I could do for you is direct the payment of your salary for the whole week. But just so you don't have to endure the sneering looks of those dogs I ordered your salary, which is unfortunately so low, to be removed directly from our cash box."

Carlo took the twenty dollars, signed a receipt for it, shook the hand of the obviously relieved director, who took his hand cordially, and walked quietly and apathetically down the steps. Downstairs, in front of the elevator, dark-brown spots showed on the wooden floor: the blood of the enemy he had knocked out. A soft, thin smile scurried over Carlo's compressed lips.

"I got this one satisfaction from them, but in the end, they are stronger than I am, and I cannot knock out all of America."

Slowly, a bit unsure and shakily, Zeller went on his way, until he came to a saloon, another bar in the plushest style. He hesitated for a moment and then entered, sat down in a corner and began drinking whisky, one shot after another. Only when he felt that one more drop would render him senselessly drunk, did he exit out into the wet, cool, unfriendly night, down towards the harbor, where his burning eyes trailed a ship headed eastwards for Europe.

November had come, a fine drizzle fell, and Carlo was sitting on a bench in Battery Park. Here he was, his physical appearance neglected, unshaven, his jacket collar turned up, because he was not wearing a shirt collar. Since his tragic departure from the International Book Company he had not found work, nor had he even looked very hard, knowing that no place with whites would keep him very long. When his few dollars were used up, he sold off his clothes piece by piece except for what he wore on his body, his *toilette necessaire*, two pairs of shoes, a couple German and French books he had brought from Vienna because he loved them so, and in the end, even his razor. The only thing he kept was his little Styria repeating pistol: under no conditions did he want to part with that, because it seemed to him to be the last way out. He had spent his last five cents on a cup of coffee that morning. He now stood hungry and shivering, looking for any way to get something on his stomach.

He had long since learned the tricks of the unemployed; he knew what the vagrants had to do to make it through without starving. He slunk by several bars, peeking in until he found one that was full enough for him to proceed with his plan. He entered the big room filled only with men. At the bar people drank their sudsy beer or whisky and soda, then they went to the buffet across from the bar where there were baskets of sandwiches with sliced sausage, cheese, and bits of pickled herring. They ate as much as they wanted and then either turned back to drink another beer at the bar or walked away. Free lunch in America, the breweries for the bars supplied it so that guests got thirsty from the cheap, spicy stuff. Still, it was a blessing for someone who only had five cents and wanted to get his fill of free lunch along with a glass of beer.

Carlo mixed in with the crowd at the bar, then turned around and went over to the buffet where nice as you please he devoured maybe ten sandwiches with sausage and cheese.

He was full now, though not for long. He could quench his burning thirst at a fountain in Battery Park and then wander uptown on his torn boot soles until he came to Cooper Union Institute, where he buried himself behind books and magazines in the great library hall until six o'clock came around.

He sought out another saloon, searching around for the last cheese leftovers and then set out on the long path down to Hotel St. Helena.

When Carlo, dead-tired, tried to tiptoe past the hotel office to get up to his room he was stopped. The swaggering clerk blocked his path.

"Mr. Zeller, sorry, but you don't have a room here anymore. You haven't paid in eight days, you don't have any possessions left, and I'm holding onto your empty suitcase as collateral for the eight dollars you owe us!"

Carlo wanted to ask for a deferral, to protest, and point out that he had paid regularly for two months, but he couldn't get a word out, it felt like he had a lump in his throat, so he shrugged, turned off and went out into the gray evening.

While tired and walking aimlessly through the deserted streets of the lower city, he patted, from time to time, his back pocket where he kept his pistol hidden. He passed by a brightly lit junk store and stopped.

I could get two dollars for this pistol. I could pay for a bed in a shelter, eat my fill tomorrow and then I would be standing around tomorrow evening no better off than today! No, in this wicked, hostile world, the pistol is my last best friend. I'll part with this gun when it has done its duty and fallen out of my cold hand.

He walked westward toward the commercial docks on the Hudson. A cargo ship was just being loaded. Screaming and cursing, men rolled crates and bales toward the crane that strapped ten or twelve of them together in mighty bundles, swinging them with a screech into the air and then turning to lower them into the ship's hold.

At the mighty gate of the freight shed hung a sign: "Early departure tomorrow of the S.S. Missouri to Rotterdam. Stokers still being accepted. Free ride and twenty dollars."

Breathless, Carlo stared at the words.

He, with his young, hardened muscles, could maybe survive the hellacious work at the boilers. And twenty dollars—he could buy a suit in Rotterdam and travel to Vienna in comfort.

But what would come after that? What would his friends say when he stood before them, downtrodden, disheveled, decayed, and worn down with work-scarred hands and gaunt limbs, asking them for help?

A chill ran down his back. No, better to kick the bucket here like a dog than to have to live in sumptuous, gluttonous Vienna surviving on the mercy of others.

Carlo took the stone steps leading down to the water and gazed into the murky, dirty gray torrents hurtling to the sea.

If I bend over and blow a bullet in my temple, then it's all over. One less nigger in the world, that's all!

Was it his overactive fantasy, was it reality? The waves were carrying off a corpse, the carcass of a man with outspread arms. Filled with revulsion, Carlo kept bending forward and saw a greenish, bloated face with eyes wide open, and saw the muddy, white hair and open mouth.

"No, I can't do that," Carlo mumbled, I still have some time, tomorrow, the day after that, if I can't go on anymore!"

A dark night, the rain started up again mixing with snowflakes. A dull chill made Carlo walk faster, almost running. He ran uptown, regaining composure near Houston Street, instinctively directing his steps, impelled by strange curiosity, towards the streets that he knew almost exclusively housed Negroes.

My people, he thought grinning cunningly, the people I belong to, and with whom I could, if I wanted, probably eke out a pretty decent living.

A thought raced through his head. Where does a person belong? Wherever others put him. Here they stick me in with colored people. By rights, that's where I belong. Is it just childish pride when I put up resistance and try to join the ones I don't fit in with? What would happen if I went to a colored newspaper tomorrow and offered my services? There won't be many Negroes who are as educated as I am. I would probably be welcomed in with open arms!

But these thoughts had arisen frivolously, and Carlo smiled, laughed them off. A painful smile, for he felt ravenous, was unspeakably tired, began to stumble while walking and felt his eyelids grow heavier and heavier.

*   *   *

A Negro stood in the front door of a restaurant, open and at-ease with a garish green tie, a gigantic rhinestone on his right index finger and golden teeth yawning out into the night.

Carlo felt so miserable that he stopped right in the middle of the cone of light streaming out the open door and leaned against the wall.

"Sick, Mister?" the fat Negro asked sympathetically. His jet-black child eyes stared at the stranger with curiosity. Carlo felt so pitiful, so needy, that he stammered forth, almost unconsciously:

"I am tired, hungry, and have no place to stay!"

The black proprietor reached in his pocket, thought for a second, and then took Zeller by the arm and said quietly:

"You need to eat your fill! Come inside!"

He led Carlo to a table, clapped his hands and whispered a few words to an even fatter black woman with huge coral earrings. The Negro woman, the owner's wife, soon waddled over with a plate of soup, bread, butter and a bowl of meat and said, while she grinned from ear to ear:

"Well, just eat your fill young man! And don't be sad! More than one has been down and out and in the end came out as rich as Vanderbilt!"

She discreetly withdrew, as did her spouse, and it seemed to Carlo that the other black guests observing the incident ostentatiously looked away so as not to bother him during his meal.

Only when he had finished did the proprietor sit down next to him, a few other Negroes did likewise, his wife brought beer, and suddenly Carlo was sitting among the people who according to Americans were his kind. His humor brightened, he found the whole situation grotesque and burlesque, but also not at all discomforting. He found himself among people now who would certainly give him no offense, and would probably even understand his woes. Prompted by the Negroes' questions he briefly sketched out his life and the sad experiences that he had had in America.

The Negroes put their heads together, then looked at him almost reverentially. He heard one of them murmur: "He is a university educated man, a scholar, and over there was living only among whites."

But they couldn't really understand his distress. The proprietor slowly shook his woolly head.

"It won't be at all hard to find a good job for you. Educated people like you, who speak other languages, are not easy to find among us. For the time being, I could use you as a waiter to help in the kitchen, because otherwise my old lady will work herself to death. What do you think, mama? But I will also speak with the director of the school next door, surely he would have something for you. Like I said before, we aren't in too good of shape when it comes to education."

Carlo shook his head, distraught and discouraged. What could he do without offending them? Finally, he said hesitantly:

"Gentlemen, you must understand me! It's not as though I believe I'm any better than those who only have black blood because my father was a white man. No, but it is just that I have grown up among whites, have never felt different from any other European and don't want to be brutally thrown into a situation where, in my view, I don't fit in."

Stunned, the men looked at each other.

"Yes, but if the whites don't want to have you living among them and you can live just fine among colored people?"

A curiously respected full-blooded Negro with snow-white hair and glasses had entered and, standing close by, had heard most of the conversation. He was addressed now as Reverend Jonas, treated very respectfully, and invited to take a seat. The Methodist pastor declined, then took a long look at Carlo and said:

"Young man, just go back to Europe and enjoy the rights they grant you there, because they don't know anything there of this aspect of the race problem. However, if you want to stay here, then you have to come on over to our camp and become a Negro! Never will you be able to court a white woman here and your children would in any case be thrown back in with the coloreds. I know very well that in your heart you despise the dumb, clumsy Negro. Overcome these sentiments and help educate him instead of despising him and you will see many a grain of gold under that black skin and see that the Negro can be thankful as no other person can."

Reverend Jonas left again. The others nodded without having completely grasped all his words. Carlo grew pensive and the thoughts in his brain began to swirl in rapid succession.

The conversation turned away from Carlo and to the interests of the others. Business matters were discussed; little changes occurring in the neighborhood were recounted. The barber Sam Lincoln had unexpectedly married the daughter of shoe merchant Washington Robbin. The cabinet-maker's wife so-and-so had delivered twins, and even though her spouse is said to be a full-blood like her, the twins look more like mulattos. They laughed grinning and then started telling all kinds of risqué stories.

Carlo thought: Try as I might, I can't say that these people are any different from whites of the same social milieu and level of education. Their conversation would sound exactly the same if I were sitting in Podunk or even in Berlin or Vienna in a suburban tavern at a table together with old tailors and saddlers and the like. True, they smell different, my nose can tell that, they look different, my eyes see that, and they speak funny English, as if they hadn't quite yet overcome their savage, African dialect. But otherwise I find them just like Mueller and Schulz, like Smith and

Jones, like Boulanger and Dupont! Maybe a bit more naïve, and, as the bard said, not enfeebled by the pale hue of deep thought, but they are surely more good-natured and welcoming than the Duponts and Müllers usually are!

Carlo suddenly listened up. One Negro said that his younger brother, who at the moment was jobless, had indentured himself to go logging in Alabama. A big company had bought up huge forest tracts in the state of Alabama along the Alabama River. A virgin forest, which now had to be logged out on the one hand in order to plant cotton, and on the other hand so they could transport the lumber downstream to New Orleans where it was to be shipped to England. Everything was supposed to be completed by early next year. The company was hiring ten thousand hands under favorable terms. Free food and lodging plus three dollars a day, and for the man who stays to the end and does his work a bonus of fifty dollars. The day after tomorrow a giant company train was set to depart from New York with a few thousand people.

Carlo, who had listened intently, threw out a question:

"Are they only hiring colored?"

"No way," laughed the Negro, "white and black and yellow! Wherever there's hard work, the differences stop in this country. But they only take strong people, where they're not risking anything on somebody who might fall down sick after a couple of days."

Taking a close look, he measured Carlo with his eyes.

"That wouldn't be anything for you, I think, you look more suited for brain work."

Carlo stretched out smiling.

"Oh, I'm as strong as anybody else and I'll take anyone on in boxing, wrestling, and weightlifting, even if they outweigh me by twice as much."

He asked for the address of the recruiting office. His plan was set. Just get out of here, and not get dragged in with the Negroes. Months of hard work and work like a dog, but then next spring with a couple hundred bucks in his pockets go back to Europe, to Vienna, as a white man among whites!

It was midnight, the guests were leaving. Mama prepared a bed for Carlo on a couple chairs and the proprietor put a hard silver dollar in his hand:

"If you come back from Alabama with some money, then you can give it back to me!"

Moved, Carlo shook his black hand. Was this not the first warm hospitality that he had encountered in this country?

Carlo slept deeply and soundly on the improvised bed. The evil, dark thoughts that had pursued him relentlessly for the last while now had vanished. Adventurousness and the wish once and for all to take on and grapple with this strange life dominated him. He again had a goal and path, the Cathedral of St. Stephen shone to him from afar, the Ringstraße, the beautiful Viennese women and his circle of kindred spirits he was eager to rejoin, once he had by his own might liberated himself from America's spell.

Down on the East River, on the portal of a building stood written in chalk:

Wanted: Strong Hands for Logging in Alabama!

A few dozen men hung around in front of the door. There were those who had just signed up and didn't quite know what to do till tomorrow and others they turned away for being too weak. Inside the great hall, which normally was a warehouse and now had been rented provisionally as a recruitment office, a buzz of all kinds of the strangest voices was heard. As a confusion of tongues, English and German, Polish and Hungarian, Italian and Yiddish words came to his ear, Zeller realized with a laugh that this was just as it must have been around the tower of Babel. The recruits of the group had already organized themselves by language and nationality, and with great discomfort Carlo saw that there was a whole cluster of Negroes and mulattos standing together. So, here too he would be stuck with the colored people and thus be excluded from the white community! Be that as it may—in the wilderness of Alabama it would not matter to him at all! He would save his money and then be off to Europe—that was his plan, one he could not allow to fail because of his sensibilities.

Carlo now stood at a table behind which an American was filling out lists. The man looked up and grumbled: "I think you are too weak." He pointed with his index finger to a giant 100 pound iron ball lying beside him on the floor. "Show me what you can do with that!"

Carlo stepped sideways, lifted the ball by the handle, and lifted it ten times with an unbent arm until the man at the table was satisfied and said with a smile:

"Enough! We could use more people like you!"

The contract was quickly drawn up. Early next day at four the company train was departing for Alabama. From then on, three square meals and three dollars every day. However, the first pay would only be given out after thirty days. Whoever quit working for whatever reason before that would get nothing but the money for a return ticket. Whoever worked for four full months, would receive a fifty dollar bonus and another fifty for the return trip. Furthermore, the workers were grouped into teams of fifty men with one overseer for each team. Every team that exceeded a certain work quota would receive a premium to be evenly distributed.

Carlo signed on and was instructed to arrive back at the train station for departure at 3:00 a.m. at the latest. But he either could stay right here or come back in the evening and lie down somewhere on the floor of the hall.

Carlo went away cheerful and elated and began to calculate intensively. Three dollars every day made about 360 dollars in four months. Plus, the fifty dollar bonus and the return travel allowance. He would have about 460 dollars by mid-March if he used extra earnings for outperforming the quota to buy drinks and tobacco. The ride to the closest harbor, the purchase of decent clothing, and a trip to Europe in second-class steerage would eat up around two hundred sixty dollars, so if everything ran smoothly he could end up in Vienna with two hundred. Not a lot, but enough to rent a room and live modestly for a few weeks. And then it was just a matter of working, not with his hands, but with his brain!

Discontent crept over him again. Clemens von Ströbl and the other friends would probably treat him coolly, more or less. And the women? Hmm, they had spoiled the elegant, idly rich Carletto. How would they react to a poor Carlo, toiling at the office? Ah what the heck, I'm young and not the dumbest and will have more experience behind me than almost anybody else.

Carlo reflected on the past few years. Had he not gone through life like a little lad? From pleasure to pleasure, from toy to toy! How stupidly and pathetically he had squandered his father's inheritance and how he had allowed year after year to pass by unused! Like a Negro, that's how unaware and careless I had been, thought Carlo, smiling in self-mockery. Well, maybe this is just my mother's inheritance, this joy in whatever glitters and sparkles, in externalities and intoxicating tempo!

Zeller felt that his mood had become milder and softer today than in the last few chaotic weeks. Above all, the hate and distaste for blacks no longer raged through him. This excessive disgust and rage at being taken for a Negro had ceased. He had experienced their feelings of community starting yesterday, and—no—deep down he could not deny it—a certain comfort from last night dwelled on in him, a sort of goodwill, just like an adult senses when he sees foreign children at play.

Almost cheerfully, Carlo flipped the silver dollar in the air and caught it.

Today I am rich and free, and can go to a Viennese café on Goulash Avenue and bid culture good-bye. And then—well, I am a "strong hand," nothing more. I'll cut down trees and collect dollars, eat corned beef and beans, and lounge in the hot sun of Alabama on Sunday until the time comes when I can draw a line through the American episode.

The long train with the lumberjacks rolled for two days and two nights through Pennsylvania, over the mighty, endless Allegheny Mountain chain southwards. They had departed in rainy weather, were accompanied for a whole day by snow and cold weather, then it felt as warm as springtime, and when the thousand men from New York stepped out in Anniston, the hot, humid air of Alabama started to parboil them. Big wagons were waiting for them in Anniston as the men stowed their bundles and luggage and for a short stretch could take a seat if someone got footsore. They ate heartily. Provisions were distributed, and then they moved out, first on good country roads, later on worn cross-country paths directly across cotton plantations, over blue-green meadows, on which tens of thousands of horses were grazing, and finally through the swamps into the mighty oak forest which was to be cleared.

In the distance you could already hear the death of the forest, the groan of giant trees resisting violent death, the cracking of branches, the screeching of saws and the dull thud of the axes. They passed barracks, in which just then crews of lumberjacks were bedding down. You could hear raucous shouting, and the men were greeted by jeering and mocking until finally the leader at the head of the group signaled them to stop. They had arrived at their camp from which they were to depart for work early every morning. The whole convoy was quickly divided into groups of fifty men; every group was assigned an existing barracks consisting of a sleeping hall and a lavatory. A kettle with soup and meat stood ready; everyone could eat as much as they wanted and then go to sleep.

Carlo had associated almost exclusively with German men on the train. He believed that among them, he could be certain not to be treated as a Negro and they were also more pleasant to him than the Slavs, with whom he could not communicate, and the Irish, who were always looking for a fight and proved to be ruffians and drunkards. There were only a few native-born Americans among the lumberjacks, for over the course of a century, it so happened that Yankees would avoid hard work and make sure that fresh immigrants would do it for them.

The group Carlo belonged to was housed in Barracks number 43. The fifty men called themselves the 43s for short. Their leader, the "Boss," as he was called, was a stolid German-American who hadn't learned English and forgotten his German long ago, so he spoke a queer mishmash. Several groups of twenty were under the control of the so-called "Superintendent" who was simply called the "Super." The supervision over all the people was located in Anniston, from where the superintendents and managers and general managers drove up by car every morning.

Work began at six in the morning. From two sides, two men at the same height swung their long-handled American axes with mighty strokes into the tree trunk, until there was barely an inch-thick layer of wood separating the two axes working toward each other. Then at a great height a hawser was quickly thrown over the tree to bring it down. Immediately the lumberjacks moved on to do the next tree, while another man was assigned to chop off the branches on the felled tree. When a whole area consisted of such fallen trees, they were loaded onto a low-slung set of wheels, which the horses then pulled down to the Coosa River, a tributary of the Alabama. On mighty rafts everything went downstream for days until the Alabama reached the Bay of New Orleans, where the rafts then disappeared into the holds of mighty sailing ships bound for England.

On the first and second evenings almost all the new arrivals were so exhausted from the unaccustomed hard work that they could barely eat their meal. They dropped half-dead on their cots and slept twelve hours. After two days of felling trees they got to chop branches and load the trunks for a day, both of which tasks were significantly easier. And so it came that on the third evening the 43s did not immediately go to sleep after dinner but first sat outside in front of the barracks during the mild evening, until the mosquitoes got to them and they went inside the barracks chatting good-naturedly and exchanging stories by the glow of the kerosene lamps on the ceiling. Almost everyone had bulging blisters on their hands, had aching bones and muscles, and grumbled long and hard about the backbreaking work, but they were at the same time content with their fate. For—and this was the main thing for everyone—the food was good and more than enough, no one constantly bitched at them, and the three dollars a day made up for the ten-hour workday. They just resented the fact that the canteen workers—every twenty barracks had a canteen— throughout the week sold fruit, sweets, seltzer, soft drinks, and tobacco products, but no alcohol. Only from Saturday afternoon until Sunday noon was it permissible to sell bottles of beer, whisky, caraway schnapps, and other hard drinks, then the sales were off again.

Carlo immediately saw through the cleverness, but also the treachery of this system. The canteens had to procure all of their products from the Director-General in Anniston. During the week, the hard-earned money of the "hands" was siphoned off with useless goodies, and on Saturday evening and Sunday morning with beer and schnapps, when the alcohol no longer had an adverse effect on productivity. Carlo calculated that the company on average ran a fifty percent profit from everything that the canteens carried. Since every second man weekly consumed his whole salary in the canteen, the company took an immense cut, one that any New York department store owner would have envied.

Carlo found all kinds of Germans in Group 43: easygoing Swabians, Berliners, Hanoverians, Pomeranians, and Mecklenburgers, Bavarians with a knife in their bootleg; even two Transylvanian Saxons were there. In general, these were people who were used to hard work: peasants, wood workers, metal workers. However, there were a few people where it was easy to tell that they had seen better days. One was a former school teacher, another, a totally wasted and drink-besotted student, who had supposedly been in the Borussia fraternity; an accountant, who told straight out and openly that he fled from Frankfurt by night in the fog because he had cheated his boss, and a bookstore apprentice clerk from Dresden. All of these people who came from these so-called educated professions wanted, just like Carlo, to return to Europe and had every intention to save every dollar in order to have enough money after four months to travel. But the student and the accountant drank away their wages and the bookstore clerk regularly gambled his away. Only the schoolteacher really did save like Carlo, who for the time being did not permit himself a single penny for sundries. He often had to be amazed at himself. He, who never had any understanding of the value of money, who had been the most frivolous free-spending prodigal among all of his friends, had turned into a miser now who did not even allow himself a single cigarette. He simply experienced this whole new life as an adventure, a sporting achievement, as a kind of wager with himself over whether he would really last four months.

In vain Carlo tried to enter into closer companionship with his associates. Most were primitive, uneducated people with nothing that could connect him with them; some spoke their home dialect, which he barely understood. The school teacher was depressed, shy, spiteful, and secretive, and the others, who might otherwise have come into consideration, continually lied, bragged, swaggered and showed off, always recounting love affairs, in which of course only ladies from the highest society, if not baronesses and countesses, played leading roles.

Such talk really repelled Carlo, who was too much of a lover and romantic adorer of women to speak crudely of them, and so he just restricted himself to exchanging the customary phrases and platitudes. He would have liked to sit out late in the evening outside on the edge of the woods on a tree-stump, but this turned out to be nearly impossible because the mosquitoes appeared in massive swarms when the sun set, and soon one's whole body was stung and sore. So Carlo just had to sit on his cot like the others or at the long, rectangular, rough-hewn table in the dorm. A couple of books that the former school teacher had, among them a Russian grammar book, served as his sole distraction since after a week he had given up listening to the brainless conversations of his comrades once and for all.

And so, the others began all the more to focus their curiosity on him. Both the educated and the uneducated quickly worked out how to get at his more refined and cultured ways.—With the exception of the schoolteacher, who grew more apathetic every day, they ganged up on him. Not that they were hostile towards him, but, having tired of their own tall tales and boring conversations, they increasingly viewed him as a target for their mockery. It all started when they called him a prince in disguise and addressed him as Mr. Aristocrat until they somehow learned that he had dark blood in his veins. From then on he got the moniker, "Zulu King." In the beginning Carlo let this teasing wash over him until one day the thing went too far. A student asked him whether his mother had been a cannibal. Carlo smacked him so hard that he walked around for two days with a swollen face. From then on he had relative peace.

One evening, when it had turned especially hot, Carlo could no longer stand the barracks air filled with smoke from the kerosene lamps and tobacco. He went out in the open and got a green oak branch smoldering in order to drive away the mosquitoes. From a distant barracks, he heard the sound of a mandolin and a soft, melancholy song. He walked closer and came by a barracks that was inhabited by Negroes. They were sprawled out in front of their barracks and kept a mighty campfire going with dry twigs and soggy moss, which dispelled the mosquitoes. They huddled around the pyre and sang in chorus with the banjo player, a very handsome, slender, almost pitch-black guy.

Unending melancholy lay in these Negro melodies, whose origins no one knew, and no one even knew who first wrote them down as sheet music. It seemed as if in these monotonous melancholy melodies one could hear the unconscious longing of the Negro for his African homeland, hear the suffering of sojourning in a foreign land, hear the slave chains rattling, hear savageness mix with profound dreams.

Strangely moved, Carlo also sat down on the ground. Memories of his boyhood swirled up in him because his father had occasionally played these songs on the piano on calm, peaceful Sunday afternoons and sung them softly in his deep bass. Once his father had abruptly slammed the piano cover shut and wiped tears from his eyes. Carlo went to him then and asked, fearful and confused, why his father was crying. Professor Zeller took him on his knee, tenderly stroked him and said:

"These songs always remind me of your mother, who died giving birth to you. I loved her very much."

"Tell me about my mother," the boy asked. And Professor Zeller said with a low, soundless voice:

"Your mother was young and beautiful. She had brown cheeks and big, black eyes, in which her whole child-like spirit lay. She had not fully blossomed, when death snapped her off the stem at a time when other women are just beginning to live. One day, my boy, I will tell you the whole story of your dear, little mama, a story that sounds as touching as a fairy tale. But today you are too small for it and wouldn't understand it."

Years had passed, Professor Zeller never returned again to the story of Carlo's little mama; Carlo forgot to ask, and today, moved by the sounds of these songs, he could have howled in pain over the fact that he knew almost nothing about his mother, nothing, only that she left behind a legacy with him, which excluded him from the community of white people in this country.———

And yet an irrepressible urge to approach these dark-skinned people plagued him in this moment. He wanted to learn how they thought and felt, what they wanted from life and what they hoped for.

Their blood courses through my veins, he thought, so some of their nature must also be present in me. Blood is thicker than water, and the blood of these Negroes weighs more than the blood of the whites.

The song had ceased; the banjo player squatted next to Carlo, examined him and then shortly after asked abruptly:

"Quadroon or octoroon?"

Carlo replied to this question, which just a few weeks ago would have set his blood pounding in his temples, with complete calm and a smile:

"Quadroon, my mother was a mulatto, my father, with whom I grew up, was German."

Others joined in the conversation, and one exclaimed, grinning:

"What, you were raised by your white father? Damn, I've never heard of that! How did that happen?"

Carlo explained that his father had lived with his mother in New York, but she had died in childbirth, so his father moved to Europe, to Vienna, taking him.

"Vienna? Europe?" The questions rained down upon him.

"How big is Europe? Where is it exactly? Is it as hot as Africa there? Are there only whites in Europe? Where is Vienna?"

Carlo started explaining and, when he saw that he would not achieve much with words, he pulled a piece of paper from his bag and traced an outline of America and Europe, showing that Western Europe was roughly as far away from the Atlantic coast of North America as New York was from San Francisco. He split Europe up into its different countries and marked Vienna and Berlin. In short, he gave a rather long lecture like an elementary school teacher would have given to little children.

An older mulatto of revolting ugliness shook his head in amazement.

"You are a wise man, educated, a professor! How come you're down here chopping wood instead of teaching at a university in Virginia or Atlanta or wherever there's a university for colored people?"

For only one moment Carlo hesitated with his answer. Then he knew that he could be completely open and sincere with these big children, he had to be, if he wanted to gain their trust.

The Negroes from the entire barracks had gathered around him, as he told them of his youth, his glamorous grand life in Vienna, his trip to New York and the terrible, horrible disappointments that he experienced there. He ended with the words:

"You all must believe me that I do not scorn the colored people that the whites keep shoving me together with. But I did, after all, grow up among whites, they were my companions throughout my youth. I grew up with their manners and customs and I don't want to be forcibly excluded from the place where I belong."

A young, handsome lad leaned in over to him and spoke excitedly:

"Professor, did you consort with white women in Vienna? Did you even have some?"

Carlo, who from now on was only addressed by the coloreds as nothing other than Professor, laughed briefly:

"My friends, believe me, even if completely unadulterated Negroes came to Vienna or Berlin, the white women would have nothing against them, on the contrary, some even say that the women occasionally pursue them. No one thought of me as having Negro ancestry, they only saw in me a dark gentleman who looked more interesting than the blond men."

Now he was bombarded with their questions, in which he perceived again and again the Negro's desire to mix with white blood and their voracity for the white women they were not even allowed to look at in America. Carlo found this flight from one's own race almost painful. Then he realized something. Did not all children have the desire to be grown up? Did they not desire finally to wear adult clothing, to be allowed to drink and smoke, just like them? And weren't these blacks simply children with a deep awe for whites, who were for them the higher ones, the adults?

"Why do you all want to mix with white women," he said finally, "aren't there enough beautiful black women who want to love you? And what would be the point of this mixing, if your children and your children's children from then on are born with the blue stain that brands them as colored?"

A very young, woolly fellow about seventeen years old laughed impishly.

"Professor, every guy always wants what he can't get. And since we are not allowed to mix with white women, the desire for them is even greater. A colored man who lives in Vienna might even long for our black girls when it gets down to it."

The others in the circle nodded, grinning and laughing.

But Carlo said to himself: "This guy has made as wise and reasonable a pronouncement as any young Yankee or German might have made. And most importantly—if I think of these people on the whole as children, then they are quite obviously children capable of development who can turn into adults if one raises them up right instead of beating them down."

He moved the conversation, which he found embarrassing anyway, in another direction and began to question the men about their fate. Most hailed from Northern states since Southern Negroes usually stayed on the cotton plantations and grew up in poverty and misery. The younger ones could read and write for the most part, but the older ones, the ones over thirty, were almost all illiterate. The mulatto sighed deeply at the mention of this topic.

"I'm from Philadelphia, my mother was born into slavery back then, but even she doesn't know how she got up North after that. My father? She never knew which drunken sailor it was she slept with for a couple pennies or a colored kerchief, or whether it was because she felt it an honor to be embraced by a white man. Well, I grew up on the streets, slept out in the open or in doorways. I have never seen a school from the inside, and, if I hadn't been able to earn my own bread as a five year old, would never have been able to go to school anyway because the parents of white children would not have tolerated that. There were no Negro schools at the time. I'm ashamed of myself today because I can barely write my name. I wish I could have learned something, so that I could make something better of my life!"

Carlo's heart cringed. What a horrible crime human beings have committed who think of themselves as superior and highly sophisticated. A whole people torn by brute force out of their primitive state, bartered away like cattle, exploited and tormented in slavery, then by force of the sweet, sentimental slogan "emancipated," that is, given the freedom to starve, to stay animals or become animals, and on top of that, to be treated with contempt. He told the mulatto, whose name was Sidney Houston:

"Dear friend, reading and writing is less of an art than you believe. If it is all right with you, I would like to teach you how in the hours after work and on Sunday. I am sure that you can learn how to do it perfectly in three or four weeks."

Flushed with joy, the mulatto had no sooner agreed, when others from all sides also rushed up.

"Professor, please, please, I would like to learn as well, I beg you, I will pay you for it."

Carlo refused with a laugh.

"There will be no talk of paying me. We are brothers here, and if one man can help another, then he must do it. Very well then, starting tomorrow evening you will learn. Everyone must supply his own paper and pencil. The canteen sells all these things."

It was almost midnight when Carlo came back to his barracks. A warm feeling ran through him. Now, besides the goal of earning money, he also had a mission: to lead ignorant, uninformed people out of the deepest darkness, to share with others some of the rich gifts that fate had bestowed upon him, the child of a mulatto woman. With a mixture of pride and self-irony, Carlo felt himself to be a useful member of human society for the first time in his life.

From then on, every evening and every Sunday morning, out in front of Negro Barracks 55 and inside as well, Carlo regularly gave lectures that drew an ever greater throng of people. New students came from other barracks where colored men lived, among them were men who were over fifty as well as quite young people who had learned only very little in inferior schools and, of that little bit, had forgotten almost everything. Carlo marveled at the tough will, studiousness, and keen perception of his students. In a few hours they learned what children take weeks to learn. With clumsy fingers stiffened and almost incapable of feeling from hard work, they spent hours tracing the letters that Carlo sketched out. After three weeks there was scarcely a single person who could not read and write all the letters of the alphabet individually, and by Christmas, his class had gotten far enough along that they could write words he dictated, even if the spelling wasn't perfect.

But Carlo could not limit himself to this rudimentary class. Time and again the Tommys, Johnnys, Washingtons and Lincolns asked him after the end of the class to tell them something of the outside world. So that in the end he was giving almost every evening a short, accessible lecture about the social institutions, habits, and customs of the peoples of Europe. He got unspeakable satisfaction and joy from seeing how the people hung on the words from his lips, admired and looked up to him.

Were these really the lazy, barbaric, thievish half-animals the Americans considered them to be? At work and in class they were extremely diligent, and there was at least as much stealing among comrades in the white barracks. And no brutal excesses ever occurred, at least in Carlo's presence. They smelled different, they spoke different, they were undoubtedly more naïve and gullible, and more goofy than the whites, but time and again it became evident that there were just as many and just as few intellectual cripples, definitely fewer degenerates, just as many and just as few malicious and good-natured people, just as many imperious and just as few humble people, and arrogant ones and modest ones, as among the other people of all races.

From New Year's on, Carlo lived among the coloreds in Barracks number 55. His relationship with his white comrades in number 43 had become progressively worse. When they had learned that he spent his evenings as a teacher among the coloreds, they developed such an animosity towards him that finally he himself asked the "Boss" to let him transfer to the 55th Barracks. The boss put the matter before the "Super," who grumbled something about colored dogs who belong together anyway, and Carlo was permitted to tie up his pack and be welcomed with jubilation by his half-brothers.

Life with his new comrades was tough enough to get used to. It was a bitter recognition when he found it all too true that they had scarcely developed any sense of hygiene. In the morning they barely dipped their hands into the washbasin and dampened their face. The use of soap appeared as irrelevant to them as that of toothbrushes and nail clippers. The nightly perspiration in the sleeping quarters was so strong that Carlo could barely stand it. But he combated his disgust and dislike by extending the comparison with children again.

Aren't children by nature unclean? Don't most of them cry when you come at them with soap and water? Isn't it simply the example of adult behavior that slowly but surely has an effect on them? And wouldn't children of the most distinguished ancestry also grow up in filth if they were left to their own resources?

Without further ado, Carlo held a talk over cleanliness and personal hygiene next evening.

"Whites always accuse us of our lack of cleanliness," he said, "and unfortunately this accusation is completely justified for most of us, my friends. You all desire to ascend to the level of white people, to become their equals in the best sense. To do that, you've got to start at the bottom with the most basic things, and above all start with the care of your own body. You've offered me money for the little bit of teaching I'm doing, and I turned it down. But now you can amply pay me back by competing in who can be the cleanest. The cantina keeper has soap, nail brushes and tooth brushes. Buy these cheap things from him and let's just have before bedtime tonight and every morning a bathing contest."

A gray-haired Negro growled and protested with a peculiar justification:

"The only one who has to wash himself is someone who is dirty, and we are not dirty!"

But old Benjamin was drowned out, and everyone shouted over each other that Carlo's advice had to be followed. An hour later there was a funny splashing in the dorm, which soon stood almost completely under water. Snorting and puffing, the guys poured buckets of water over each other's naked backs. Houston got soap and brushes for the whole barracks. There was such a gurgling and snorting going on that curious people from neighboring barracks came running just to see what was going on. From then on, the coloreds pursued their washing as a kind of sport with the marvelous humor and great exuberance that is so typical of them.

Carlo felt very gratified that from that point on the obtrusive perspiration of the Negroes started fading away and transformed into a characteristic odor of nutmeg, cinnamon and vinegar, which in the past—oh, how long had it been—the strawberry blond Hella Bühler had drawn into her nostrils.

Weeks of rain came, but it wasn't any cool, refreshing rain. Instead it seemed as if warm, dirty water were saturating the air and the earth.

Toxic mists rose from the steaming soil: work was agonizing, the cases of typhus and malaria infections multiplied, hundreds of lumberjacks had to be transported out and Carlo had to muster up all his will power to stay.

In most of the barracks nearly a whole week's pay was blown every Saturday on schnapps because people believed the artificial warmth from inside could work against the skulking noxious wetness from outside. With his full power of eloquence Carlo convinced his closer comrades of the nonsensical, suicidal nature of such actions. It weakened the body, squandered hard-earned cash and would only increase the company's fortune. He even managed it that the colored lumberjacks, to the utter astonishment of the sales personnel at the cafeteria, spent much less money on alcohol than the whites, and the inhabitants of Barracks 55 spent almost nothing at all. They bought tea, sugar and lemons, prepared hot drinks over their wood fires, saved their money, and were spared more illness than the others.

By the end of February the rain stopped and sweltering heat almost immediately took its place. More and more forest tract dwindled away, while new workers set about blasting out the stumps of felled trees and turning over the soil so that it would willingly and patiently accept the cottonseeds.

By the predicted deadline, the virgin forest along the Coosa River had been transformed into a broad, open area. Carlo bade an affectionate farewell to his black and brown work comrades, who had become true friends. He strapped his small pack of clothes and linens on his back, and kept nearly five hundred dollars well secured in his breast pocket. His hand on the walking stick he had whittled himself, he took off, upbeat and light-hearted, on his march to Birmingham, Alabama, thirty miles away, where he planned to turn into a European again. There he would buy new clothing, linens and a suitcase, and then take the train to the coast so he could steam back to Europe as quickly and cheaply as possible. Three, four, five weeks still, then he would be in Vienna again and think back on the last nine months as a chaotic dream, at first horrible, in time endurable, but always highly instructive.

Carlo set out vigorously. During the day, when the heat of the sun was at its worst, he slept in shady groves. In the evenings till midnight and then from three o'clock in the morning until eight o'clock in the morning the walking was easy, and the progress both pleasant and toughening. On the third day early in the morning, he arrived in Birmingham, with its

hundred thousand residents, thousand churches, pathetic theater building and a thimble full of borrowed culture. Here he was: One colored man
among ten thousand other ones, dirty, dusty with torn clothing and boots,
covered in sweat and dust. Wisely, he never raised his eyes in the direction of a pretty girl, for he had no desire to experience the brutality of the
Southerners on his own body.

Nevertheless—there was also a large department store in Birmingham.
In an hour's time, Carlo bought everything he needed to make of himself a
new person, actually the old person. The clothing he bought he stored in a
small brown leather cabin suitcase, and Carlo carried it down the monotonous and uninteresting streets of Birmingham until he happened on a bar-
bershop that had a sign announcing available bathing rooms. And, since a
Negro was standing at the door, he could just go on in. The Negro made an
anxious face when he mentioned his desire for a bath, but eventually said:

"I only have white clientele so you may not bathe here. But it is still so
early in the day that nobody will be coming, so no harm will be done."

Carlo sat down in a tub filled with hot water, savoring the delight of
a bath with full pleasure for the first time in many, many months. He had
his hair cut and was shaved while in the tub, blissfully inhaled the scent of
Bay Rum which was poured over his head and face, then put on his new
clothes, shoes, and linens, leaving behind his old rags, and inspected with
pleasure the slim, handsome, more than usually tanned Mr. Carletto Zeller
from Vienna in the mirror.

The dark blue suit, the elegant shoes, the soft, subtly patterned shirt,
the pearl gray silk tie, as well as the bright gray, smooth fedora and his new
suitcase—looking like this I could pull up in a car in front of the Hotel
Bristol or Imperial in Vienna without further ado!

Now he felt very hungry. Knowing that a colored man could only enter
a normal restaurant here in the South if he were engaged as a waiter, he
decided—despite a subtle feeling of resistance that crept in—to look for a
place for Negroes. He found such a place in Lincoln Square, which looked
nice and bore the inscription: "Eldorado for Colored People." And in fact,
he dined very well there, it was astoundingly cheap, and was no less clean
than any other second-class restaurant.

The next day took him to a travel agency to inquire about the possibilities of traveling to Europe. He was directed to a black clerk, who readily
gave him information. Today, Thursday, at one o'clock, so in just under
an hour, a passenger train was departing for Atlanta, the largest city in
Georgia. The clerk rolled his eyes up reverently so that one could only see
the whites.

"Atlanta is a magnificent and grand city, Sir! Many coloreds live there, among them fine, well-educated gentlemen, there is a theater for us, several colleges and a university on a par with Yale and Columbia. You will be able to enjoy yourself marvelously among your peers. You will arrive in Atlanta around six o'clock, and it would be best for you to go to the Montgomery Hotel, which belongs to the honorable Moses Broocker and is reserved for us coloreds. In the morning you can make a telephone call to the office of the shipping company Lefevre Brothers in Charleston on the coast. One of the company's cargo ships is leaving from Charleston on Saturday to go to Le Havre, which I very much recommend. It's a big, beautiful, French ship, which only has a few cabins without class divisions. Even though the trip with the *La Gloire* lasts twenty days, then the best thing is that it is unlikely there will be any Yankees on board, but almost exclusively French and colored, so that no one will insult you and you will easily make contact with fellow travelers. Besides, the passenger fares are barely half the price of those on the regular passenger steamers out of New Orleans."

Carlo, who had listened to these detailed explanations with mixed feelings, half amused and also hurt somehow, thanked the clerk, bought his ticket to Atlanta and had someone show him the way to the train station.

At the door of the travel agency, he collided into a young Negro woman and then heard her request, like him, a ticket to Atlanta.

Interested and fascinated, Carlo remained standing outside until the girl came out again and walked ahead of him to the train station.

There were just as many beautiful and ugly people among the Negroes as among Aryans, and this girl was an ideal embodiment of black beauty. Taller than average, slim, her young body flexible and poised; her feet were dainty and narrow, the fullness of her blue-black hair knotted into a bun, the nose not broad and blunt, as is normally the case with Ethiopians, but thin and delicate, her cherry-red lips not protruding but voluptuous, and her big, dark eyes not unaware and dull, but smart, deep, and a little mischievous, as Carlo sensed when he noticed her flash him a fleeting glance at the next turn in the road.

As children by nature love colored things, glistening, garish colors, so too does the Negro, and especially Negro women, who generally achieve the utmost in grotesque imitation of popular style and cannot do without glaring, screaming colors. The young girl Carlo was following was most definitely an exception to this. A navy blue skirt, a plain, white blouse, a hat decorated with a few flowers, white silk gloves and patent leather shoes—a perfect lady, in clothes as well as otherwise.

Carlo pondered. What a comical, illogical world we have created for ourselves! If this young woman were to appear in Berlin or Vienna today she would be the day's celebrated beauty in an instant. The aristocrats and tycoons would kill for the favor of this black Venus. And with a little cleverness and reserve, she could easily succeed in becoming a wife to one of the greatest men in the country! But here? Here she is an outcast who may not eat at the same table with whites or sit in the same row of a theater. She is just barely good enough to quench the lust of some guy, and if she finds herself with child from a white man, then the child also becomes an outcast, a miserable mulatto who must return to his race!

He arrived at the train station and the girl disappeared in the crowd. Carlo had his ticket stamped at the ticket counter and was about to board the nearest train car when he felt a hand on his shoulder. He turned and saw a black conductor grinning from ear to ear and shouting to him:

"Hey Jimmy, that's a mistake, you belong back there in a car for our people!"

A fit of rage welled inside Carlo again. He felt the rush of blood to his ears again, but at the last moment he lowered his clenched fist.

Who am I getting mad at? At this poor guy who's only doing his detestable duty? At the ingrained prejudice of the lords and masters of this country?

Breathing deeply, he followed the order and boarded one of the two last cars bearing the inscription: "Colored People Only!" This new phrase had seized and assailed his self-esteem so much that, as he was settling down in his seat, he involuntarily spat out between his teeth:

"Lowdown dirty rabble! Damn them!"

A quiet, bright laugh made him look up. Sitting across from him at the open window was the young girl he had followed from the travel agency. She smiled right at him, bent forward, met his gaze, which was still angry and questioning, and said to him softly in the most irreproachable tone, as is never the case with Negroes up North:

"Forgive my laughing, but I saw the scene on the platform and your outraged words—you must be foreign to the South, otherwise you would not have gotten angry over such self-evident things!"

Carlo found it very pleasant to get to know this young, beautiful woman in this way, but his anger was still too great and he answered in a tone that was almost brusk:

"I'm actually a foreigner both to the South and to the North and am preparing to leave this horrible, brutal country, which I would have been better off never entering!"

The girl looked at him now with big, sympathetic eyes.

"Why so? How is it that you, a person of mixed race, do not call the United States your home? May I ask, without being indiscreet, where you come from?"

Carlo reflected for a moment. "Why should I not also tell her about my life, when I have had to explain it to so many other people who were clearly less distinguished and intelligent than this woman?"

He bowed gently and gave his name.

"Jane Morris," was the reply and then: "Carlo Zeller? A mix of Germanic and Romance. Might I now ask you?"

He was bewildered! Romance and Germanic! What strange words coming from the mouth of a female Negro! Well, he would at least be able to talk with her without having to search for the most basic vocabulary. And then, omitting overly personal matters and especially his cruel affair of the heart, he told her about his origins, his life in Europe, and the events in America.

"Now I have had enough and will be overjoyed to be able to leave a country that is governed by the basest prejudices and the most wicked race instincts!"

Jane had rested her soft, round chin into her small, brown, immaculate hand and listened to him attentively. Then, as a shadow fell over her eyes, she said:

"Have you ever considered how unjust it is of you to go away from here? Do you have any idea how desperately we need men like you?"

The man suddenly flinched. Where else had he heard these very same words? That's right, months ago, on a wet November night the black Methodist preacher at the Negro restaurant had said the same thing, when he, half-starving, had been restored.

As if she could read his thoughts, Jane said:

"Yes, Mr. Zeller, we need you badly! Very badly! We cannot do without you in these troubled and fateful times we Negroes are going through here."

Carlo reared up as if to escape fetters wrapped around him.

"You need me? What for, if I may ask? Aren't there enough black, brown and yellow Negroes to serve the white man, shave him, shine his boots, be his slaves! Or should I pick cotton here in the South or better yet become a preacher and sermonize about gloom, humility, and reverence?"

He had spoken so loud that the other passengers had taken notice. Jane whispered to him:

"Since you speak French, it would be much better if we were to continue this conversation in that language."

Carlo was baffled again. So the girl spoke French! And the thought raced through his brain that he had still not experienced various things well worth knowing. Even this unspoken thought Jane picked up on.

"You are far and away more educated than most Americans," she said fluently in French, though not with a faultless accent, "but you seem to know very little about the Negro issue and have experienced only the crude externalities. If I don't bore you, I would like to tell you a few things you don't know. Listen and see how the United States has seen developments in a ridiculously short amount of time, barely within half a century, that world history has never before experienced with the same rapidity and intensity. Put yourself in this situation: Wretched slave-traders packed Negroes up in Africa and peddled them off in America. These people in Africa lived virtually in a primitive state, naked, wild, nourished by the fruits of the untended earth, relying solely on their dull instincts. However, these were human beings who had the spark of godliness buried somewhere deep within them. As involuntary slaves and beasts of burden they lost much of their inborn nature but gained nothing by way of intellectual growth or cultural refinement. At best, they were trained so as not to offend too grossly the aesthetic tastes of their white masters. Then the war between the North and the South came, with its so-called 'Emancipation' of black slaves. Since that time little more than fifty years have passed. And do you know what those of us, that is, only a few selected among us and a handful of wise, energetic Americans have achieved here in the South, where the great mass of Negroes has remained? Did you know that there were scarcely any Negroes around in 1850 who could read and write? In 1890, still 90 percent were illiterate, and today it is barely twenty percent. These are mainly older people who did not go to school, whereas there are scarcely any black children in the South today who don't go to school. Today we have 40,000 teachers, and apart from the elementary students, there are 100,000 students at schools somewhat comparable to the German *Gymnasium*. We have doctors, men and women, in the thousands. We have homes for infants and children. We have big, strong Negro banks with excellent, well-educated officials and managers. We have become entrepreneurs and proprietors and no less than 900,000 Negroes own real estate that they manage themselves as landlords. Today, just fifty years after our liberation, Negroes own, according to precise statistics, one billion dollars. Last year, at the Medical Congress in Atlanta more than five hundred black doctors and dentists attended. We have about one hundred newspapers that are written, managed, and edited by colored people. We have big libraries and 36 insurance companies which only employ Negroes. All of these figures are increasing year by year despite white Americans clamoring and raging in opposition to it and us. In light of these unprecedented advances, even more hate us than ever before."

Jane Morris had spoken with excitement. Now she leaned back, fanning herself and quietly smiling. Carlo was in a daze.

"That is indeed colossal! How was this even possible?"

Jane straightened herself up and in her bell-like voice rang enthusiasm:

"How was this possible? All of this is the work of the National Association for the Advancement of Colored People, a wonderful creation by our leaders Corvoy and DuBoy [sic]. Shortly after this miserable Booker Washington had been unmasked as a creature bought by the whites, young, wise, educated Negroes founded this association and since then we have struggled with all the weapons of our intellect for our advancement, our unity, and our true liberation. Do you now still not believe that we need men like you?"

Conflicting feelings strangled Carlo. Too many new things assailed him at once. It took a few minutes before he could think clearly again.

"Where is all this leading? Evidently simply in the end toward a terrible struggle between blacks and whites! Because Americans will never voluntarily recognize Negro equality. The more equal they become, the less likely the Americans will recognize them as such!"

"These words have been repeated a thousand times in history, and they have always been disproven by the facts. The lords used these phrases against farmers and workers, the French against the Germans, and two hundred years ago virtually all Christians were agreed that the Jews should never be granted equal rights. I, or more precisely, the men who are my teachers and educators, believe that the problem is easier than it seems. We actually want the same thing that Americans want. They shrink in horror at the thought of mixing their race with ours. They have a point; because each type should develop its own specific potential, not change it. We aim to create racial pride in the Negro and preserve his kind. There should be no more mulattoes and quadroons, but only Negroes, the blacker the better! We preach it to our girls every day in school that they should never give in to a white man because by this they stain and degenerate their race. Unfortunately it is true that the mulatto usually receives the evil instincts of both parents and only becomes a splendid person if both the mother and father were blameless. Once the whites realize that we never want to over-step the bounds of our race—not out of fear, but out of pride—then they will more easily accept our existence and learn to respect us. We shall educate ourselves unremittingly, compete with them in entrepreneurial spirit, and raise the standards of the masses year by year, as my brief retrospective adequately demonstrates."

"Fine, Miss Morris, but you still haven't answered my question. The Negro breeds faster than the average American, who is burdened by the millennium of culture of his forefathers. This is why there might be thirty million Negroes in America in another fifty years, and in a hundred years there will be a hundred million descended from the millions of today. Do you then consider it even possible that two equally strong peoples could live next to each other without natural borders and without mixing? Must things not end up in a terrible test of strength, in a life and death struggle?"

The train proceeded along the railroad embankment and through endless fields of cotton. Negroes with giant straw hats waved happily, whole hordes of black children stood and played in front of small mud shacks and miserable wooden houses.

Shading her eyes with her hand, Jane had glanced out over the countryside roasting under the sun and said:

"Within our great NAACP there are two groups: the smaller group has set its sights on returning to Africa; the other one, which constitutes three-quarters of our members, contemplates a peaceful and automatic conquest of America's Southern states. I belong to this group. Step by step, we will become the masters of this country because we are young, unspent, tougher and more strong-willed than the lazy, white Southerners who still call themselves "Colonel" and dream outmoded dreams of being the masters. The horrific crimes of their forefathers will take revenge on them. They will lose to us all their property, their land, and their wealth until we one day will constitute such an overwhelming majority, qualitatively and quantitatively, that we will be able to claim the South as our own. But all of this lies far off and is actually immaterial for those of us living now. For us there is only one thing: indefatigable work by us and for us! And do you still not want to believe that we need men like you? Do you still not believe that you are called to something great here and could lead a life rich in success and esteem?"

Carlo experienced these words like a ponderous burden which made his head droop. He closed his eyes; struggled with himself, saw his past in Europe, full of glitz and glamour, his future gloomy and grim, clouds over him, the abyss at his side. He sighed deeply and tried hard to fight back against this young, blossoming, black woman.

"But what if you're wrong, and it is really true that Negroes are half-animals and that a gap persists between them and the Caucasians that can never be bridged?"

"The best evidence against that is myself, my friends and the leaders of our movement. I know plenty of white men and women and know very well that they aren't smarter or better than the more advanced among us. I know the literature of the European peoples and know very well that they have achieved an enormously high level of civilization. But I also know books by our young scholars and poets and can see that they are building on this foundation and not starting afresh. I am a teacher in a home for abandoned colored girls and have students who are dumb and malicious and others who are smart and sweet, lazy and studious, some who comprehend the most difficult material quickly and others who can't understand anything. I'm having exactly the same experiences that every teacher in a white school has."

Carlo took a new approach.

"And how about the morals of the Negro, especially the sexual morals? Are they not in a dismal state?"

Jane smiled.

"Dismal? We are more passionate, our blood is hotter, we are less speculative regarding eroticism and our people are young, thoughtless, and uneducated! That's all! But the genuine moral instruction we are providing in our schools is falling on fertile ground. Already, our girls are becoming vigilant about too easily falling prey to a man. And I do fear that in a few decades eroticism will become intertwined with the dowry of the woman and the career of the man, just as is the case with white people."

Carlo, delighted by the priceless irony of these words, burst out laughing and then played his last trump card.

"Aren't all of your theories destroyed by the example of Haiti? Long ago, the Negroes there fought for full freedom and self-rule, and what became of it? A world scandal, a caricature, a despicable monkey farce!"

"Brilliant, one can tell that you eagerly read American newspapers! Oh, how shallow it is always to fling Haiti at us! I always emphasize, however, that we are a people without tradition, history, and past. A people still in its infancy! Now take this example: If it were to occur to someone to pack up twenty thousand or more children who cannot read or write off to some fertile island and tell them: 'All right, now you can live in total freedom just as you see fit!' Wouldn't these twenty thousand European or American children develop into semi-animals despite the culture of their parents? Wouldn't this infant republic also become a joke and fall prey to the most wicked and savage among those children? Let the Haitian Negroes develop under the guidance of well-intentioned whites or our educated Negroes and in fifty years Haiti will be able to boast at least as much culture as there is in Australia today!"

The train stopped at one of larger stations. Peddlers carried fruit, newspapers, and baked goods through the train cars. A pause in the conversation ensued. Later, Carlo entreated the girl:

"I have told you much, nearly everything, about me. May I ask you now about your upbringing and education? Don't you want to explain how it was possible to develop from a Negro child to a lady, and who in education is undoubtedly the equal of all but a very few European women and whose spirit is greater than most."

With these words Carlo took Jane's hand and brought it to his lips, following an inspiration and forgetting the customs of the country. Jane hastily withdrew her hand, a gentle red blush colored the soft smooth brown of her cheeks, and then she said laughingly:

"From the kiss of the hand alone I should have recognized that you are Viennese. Namely, I have read a few charming novels by Arthur Schnitzler, unfortunately in bad English translations. But now I will certainly learn German! So, would you like to know my life story? I have not experienced all that much on the surface. More than seventy years ago, my grandparents were both hauled on the same ship like wild animals to America. Both came as slaves to the same plantation owner in Virginia. There they lived together, and, as my parents believe, were even lawfully married in church by a pastor. Incidentally, the masters of my grandparents were halfway decent people who treated their slaves well. When my mother was born, the Civil War was already about to start, but my grandparents also stayed on even after the war with their little daughter on the farm in Virginia, where my grandparents died.

"Relatively late, only at age twenty, my mother married a young man, my father, who had reason to believe he was the grandson of a Negro king. In any case, he was more confident, intelligent, and adventurous than most of his kind were at that time. And when I was born twenty years ago, he moved with my mother to Atlanta in Georgia, where he opened a small fruit and newspaper stand, while my mother was a wet nurse for the wife of a professor at the new university in Atlanta. She was allowed to keep me with her, however.

"I grew up with the professor's children, half companion and half servant. Indeed, I had to attend the relatively primitive Negro school but learned at home with the other white children with an ardent zeal. I probably even learned more than they did. For example, I astonished the French private tutor with my good intellectual grasp. At age ten I could speak perfect French, while the professor's children, my foster sister and a fourteen-year-old boy, could only sputter a few sentences with the greatest of difficulty.

"When I turned fourteen, a terrible event occurred which was decisive for my future life. As I said, my father had a stand where he sold fruit, candy, and newspapers. One day a white man stopped by his stand and had his fruit wrapped up, took several newspapers and then was about to leave without paying. A big altercation arose and when my father threatened to call the police, the thug punched him. Now, quick to anger as anyone might be, my father lunged at his throat and clobbered him. The man ran away, but came back fifteen minutes later with a horde of men, and after desperate resistance, my poor father lay dead, pierced by three bullets. A victim of lynch justice, like thousands of others before him. A murder victim that no judge or law cares one whit about.

"At that time, six years ago, the Negro movement had already developed into a very considerable force, and kind, educated, colored people took an interest in my mother, helping her with the modest capital my father had left behind to buy a small house with a yard, so she could rent out rooms, to our racial kin only, of course, and continue to live with me. A young professor at the first university for coloreds in Atlanta, and his wife, who was a doctor, were our first renters, and other educated men and women followed. I now had an opportunity to educate myself, to read good books, and to devote myself heart and soul to our national movement. Three years ago I took my teacher exams. Today I am the first teacher at the home for abandoned colored girls, and I am also a regular correspondent for the largest daily newspaper of our movement, *The Crisis*. So, my income is good enough that my mother and I can live by ourselves in our small home. As always, all the leaders of the intellectual Negro community in Atlanta frequent our home."

Both remained silent, each of them in their own thoughts, when Carlo suddenly looked at the girl with big, fearful eyes and expressed his inner strife in words.

"What am I to do now? What you have told me moves me deeply, makes me vacillate, causes new possibilities to rise up before me, and displaces me completely and utterly from the path that I had at least imagined for myself. Should I stay here and devote my life to something that was unknown to me only yesterday, but already has begun stirring a number of things in me today? Or should I board the *La Gloire* on Saturday and leave all these chaotic, frightening problems behind me and return to where I don't have to fight because no one attacks me?"

A sharp, dismissive expression came over the black girl's beautiful face.

"Oh, I well know that people there don't do any wrongs to the Negro and the Negro race there. Because they hold him in high regard? Not one bit! Because he is a rare curiosity! Take ten thousand Negroes to Vienna or Berlin, then hate will suddenly flare up against them and the Negro issue will explode there from the same mire and mucky perspective as here. So, you'd actually be taking the coward's way out!"

Carlo shuddered and again took the girl's hand in his.

"Miss Jane, please don't be so harsh in your opinion of me. Consider that all this is so new for me and please don't forget that I bear hate in my heart for this country where I have experienced almost nothing but bitterness. Even my heart has been most grievously wounded and mistreated here!"

Softly, Carlo told the story of Lisl, whom he had loved, who was attached to him with the passion of a young woman, and whom he would have been able to take if he had wanted. And who, in his hour of bitter need, spurned him like a beggar on the threshold.

Jane nodded mutely, caressed his hand and said: "Poor boy!" and then abruptly turned towards the window, through which one could see the suburbs of Atlanta. Shortly before the arrival at the station, they took leave of one another. Jane tolerated his repeatedly squeezing her hand and said as she fixed her gaze on him:

"Mr. Zeller, think about it, argue it out with yourself! And if you are not already on the train to Charleston tomorrow to board the *La Gloire*, then I'll be expecting you for dinner at six o'clock at our place. I would be delighted to see you again and to discuss much, much more with you. We live on Sunflower Street, Number 72."

Carlo took lodgings in the Montgomery Hotel as he had been advised, obtained a small, clean room quite inexpensively, and soon went to bed.

Next mid-morning Carlo got in touch with the office of the shipping company in Charleston and found out that the *La Gloire* would not be departing the day after tomorrow on account of a minor mechanical problem, but would weigh anchor on Thursday of next week. By all means a cabin would be reserved for him until Wednesday.

Carlo breathed a sigh of relief. So now he had time to think and most importantly—he could visit Jane today. His heart beat wilder when he thought of her. He longed for her, and the hours of the afternoon stretched endlessly. When he stood at six o'clock sharp before the one-story house with a trim front yard on Sunflower Street, he was almost as agitated as he had been many months ago when he stood before the palatial brownstone of the affluent Mister Ortner.

Jane extended both hands to him. He was delighted to see how pleased the girl was at his visit. The feeling of familiar, bourgeois comfort surrounded him. Jane's mother's black skin and white hair would have made a grotesque impression on him just months ago, but today, having gotten accustomed to other skin colors, he saw in her nothing but a lovely, old woman cordially welcoming him.

The rooms of the small one-story home were nicely furnished, a small piano stood in the parlor, bookshelves lined one wall, and the library could just as well have belonged to any distinguished, educated European lady.

Jane placed a third setting on the meticulously clean dining table. Carlo was delighted at the graceful, charming movements with which she served them at the table. It was a typical Southern dinner: ice-chilled raw tomatoes topped with grated cheese; baked oysters, a gigantic turkey with cranberry sauce and apple pie with whipped cream.

Jane did not let any weighty table conversation arise. She asked Carlo about his impressions of Atlanta, agreeing with him that probably any little German town of ten thousand inhabitants had more genuine culture to show than this metropolis of nearly a quarter million, but she subtly drew his attention to various lovely places about the city, especially Atlanta's central park, Piedmont Park, whose rich tropical flora made it a sight to behold.

Both had no clue that more than a quarter century earlier in this park, on a hot summer night a German professor and a poor, unprotected mulatto girl lay in intimate embrace, and that the fruit was Carlo———

When black coffee was served on the screen porch, three more guests arrived. All three were full-blood Negroes. Isidor Pope, Professor of Law at the Negro university of Atlanta, Dr. Samuel Thompson, Doctor and Director of the Surgical Department of the Hospital for Coloreds, and Abel Crawford, Editor in Chief of the daily, *The Crisis*.

Jane briefly told the gentlemen Zeller's story and after a conversation about European relations and Carlo's comical description of his voluntary teaching activities in the barracks of the woods, the three Negroes almost simultaneously shouted:

"You will stay with us, won't you? We could use men like you!"

A lively, often agitated conversation with wild temperamental out-bursts ensued. Carlo felt at home in this circle of educated people. It ful-filled an exquisite need in him to lay out his intellect and his knowledge. On the other hand, he struggled with his last ounce of strength and utmost force of will against Jane and the three men who welcomed him with open arms so as to draw him over to them.

All the aspects of the Negro problem were discussed, illuminating all the dangers and prospects for the future, the biological and the historical aspects, and the economic and social side of the Negro issue. Every one of Carlo's objections, every qualm that he expressed, shattered on the statistics they put forward and on the successes they pointed to. Until, sighing heavily, Carlo gave in:

"You have convinced me! Even I can no longer doubt the inner pos-sibility of the equality of our race, and I now also believe that the American Negro by dint of systematic education will quickly traverse all the phases of development until he has reached the level the German, Anglo-Saxon, Romance, and Slavic peoples have attained."

"At least in regard to civilization," Jane objected, "for I don't believe the black race will provide geniuses to the world until centuries have passed."

Now they all put positive proposals to Carlo. Professor Isidor Pope volunteered to provide Zeller a chair of German and French language and literature at the university; Abel Crawford asked him to join the editorial staff of his paper.

Carlo was still vacillating, and it was Jane herself who asked him to reflect in peace and quiet and to do nothing that he would later regret. Eventually, Carlo made an agreement with the editor to write a series of articles describing his impressions of America and recounting his experi-ences among black lumberjacks from the perspective of a colored person raised in Europe. The honorarium that Abel Crawford offered to him was so great that Carlo could simply go ahead and stay on in Atlanta for two more weeks.

It was midnight when Carlo departed along with the three other guests. In the dark of the front yard he bade goodbye to Jane. He once again kissed her hand, his lips trembling when they pressed against Jane's slender, warm hand. He also felt the shiver running through her body.

Carlo was too agitated and excited to even think about sleeping. He fetched paper from the reading room and began to write the articles he had promised. Fluently, without the least linguistic difficulty he filled page after page until the rays of the morning sun outshone the electric light and he went to bed dead-tired and exhausted, only to awake in the afternoon following dreamless sleep.

It was oppressively muggy. A damp, east wind swirled in from the sea when Carlo washed and dressed. A peculiar feeling of anxiousness seized his chest; dull feelings of impending disaster generated an oppressive feeling in him. Suddenly he heard clearly the rattling of gunfire, interspersed with the crack of pistol bullets and dull muttering, as one typically hears from masses of people.

Baffled, he rushed to the window and leaned out over the street. It was overrun with gesticulating, fleeing people massed together. In the air two, three airplanes flew, converging on a point, and then flying apart again. A small pointy object separated from the airplane, followed by a whistling as if the crack of a mighty whip had come down.

Confused and frightened, Carlo completed his dressing. And while he was storming down the three flights of stairs his thoughts were of revolution, war, and gigantic strikes.

In the hotel hall about a hundred people stood screaming and gesticulating. The portal was barricaded. He pushed through the Negroes in order to open the portal.

Excited hands pulled him back.

"Stop! Do you want to get shot outside?"

"What's happened? I don't know anything, I just woke up!"

Now he was surrounded by people and from all sides they shouted at him until he finally extricated himself and got clarification from a colored man who seemed to have maintained his calm.

At the city's finest hotel, the Lincoln House, the horrible events had started. At noon, the wife of one of the richest men in the area, Mrs. Arabella Stockton, left her lodgings and took the elevator to the ground floor. On the way down, the black elevator operator allegedly stepped violently on her foot and instead of offering due apology, had gotten impudent. When the woman smacked him in the face with her parasol, he snatched the umbrella and broke it, as she alleged. Mr. Stockton immediately made a fuss, and summoned a policeman to haul the elevator boy off to prison. But Mrs. Stockton was not content with that. She went to her husband's office. He alarmed members of the notorious anti-Negro group, and an armed band of Ku Klux Klan people, mixed with other white riffraff, marched on the city prison to force the handing over of the Negro so that he could of course be lynched. The prison warden refused to turn him over, whereupon the mob began storming the prison, shooting down some Negroes who by chance were coming that way.

At this, all the young Negroes in the city began to gather and for their part to march on the prison. At this time, a grisly battle between whites and blacks was in full swing, some pilots got in their planes and began to bomb the prison, Negro churches and schools. There were already reports of several dead, panic prevailed in the Negro districts, the whole city was in a huge riot.

Horrified and unsettled, Carlo had listened to this. Was he awake or was he dreaming? Was he in the highly-civilized America or in Patagonia, where savages overran each other with war? An elevator attendant had stepped on a lady's foot, and because of that bloodshed, murder, and man-slaughter! This was too much for a European's brain. Carlo clasped his hands at his temples. He could not understand the inconceivable.

A mob rushed past the Hotel Montgomery, throwing stones against the glass windows that shattered.

Suddenly a new terrifying message started circulating, delivered by a Negro with blood pouring out of a bullet wound, who had succeeded in escaping in through the hotel's back door.

As he told it, dozens of dead bodies were lying in the square in front of the courthouse; the blacks had had to yield to superior forces. The prison had been stormed and the elevator attendant lay brutally murdered next to a dozen other black prisoners. Now, following a new call to action, the white mob was moving on towards the home for abandoned colored girls, not far from the park, to seize the youthful occupants.

Carlo saw through a black and red fog arising in him, his saliva turned to bile, beads of sweat popped out on his forehead, his mouth foamed. While he swung out through one of the broken windows onto the street, one single, massive, overwhelming thought arose in him:

I am one of them now! I'm a Negro now, nothing but a Negro!

Instinctively he pulled the brim of his hat over his face so as not to be recognized immediately as having Negro blood. Then he ran down amidst the surging mob to where the white men were running with their revolvers.

"Jane!" he shouted to himself, "Jane! These beasts are getting ready to storm the home where you lead these young souls from darkness into the light. They're preparing to ravage poor, defenseless children just in order to set degenerate half-breeds into the world who will be afflicted with the animal instincts of their fathers!"

Suddenly it occurred to him that Jane would be dwelling among the children, that the fate of these adolescent girls would also become the fate of that beautiful young girl.

Raging fear spurred his steps, as he held his pistol in his hand, ready to fire.

Then he came to the central park fence, one block off to the side, and there stood a modest red brick building with the inscription:

"Home for Orphan Colored Girls."

A vast crowd surrounded the building, shots were fired, gun smoke blew by, the shrill cries of raving mad people resounded, the painful cries of casualties could be heard.

Carlo quickly climbed up on a lamppost in order to survey the situation before he could be recognized as being a colored man.

A cohort of three or four hundred black men pushed against the immense masses of whites attempting to push them away from the closed portal. The Negroes shot, the whites did the same, here and there Carlo saw a man with his hands in the air falling.

Suddenly, a shout arose among the whites:

"Out of the way! Our boys are attacking!"

Carlo watched as about twenty white men carried a lamppost and began ramming it against the door. With immense power the iron post crashed against the portal. Only three or four more impacts and the portal would be smashed open for those men on whose dehumanized faces brutish lust and bloodthirstiness was inscribed.

Carlo slid off the lamppost where he was observing.

He crouched down on the ground, crawling between the legs of the men cursing and thrusting at him, but not recognizing him, until by superhuman effort he got behind those holding the lamppost, wedged in by the mass of the lynch mob.

He thought it over in a flash. If he attacked the lynchers here, then he would be a corpse in an instant without having prevented anything. He pushed his hat deep over his face again and pushed forward until he passed the horizontal post that was being thrust a second time as a ram and stood next to the building's portal. There was no time to think any more, it would be too late.

Carlo raised one hand and shouted to several Negro guys who were held off by only a thin layer of whites: "Hey boys, follow me!" He threw himself against those whites carrying the lamppost, socked one of them down, and with his pistol shot down a second, third, and fourth one.

Horrified and not knowing what had actually happened, the white mob pulled back, dropping the lamppost. In these brief moments of confusion, the Negroes advanced with their last ounce of strength. Dozens of whites fell from gunfire. Chaos ensued and Carlo vaguely saw how the coloreds in compact masses occupied the portal while the mounted militia came rushing in with shrill whistles. Then he felt a terrible blow to his skull, a sharp pain in his chest and his eyes went dark.

Carlo awakened in a white bed, saw flowers standing on the windowsill and heard a canary chirping in a brass cage.

Where was he, what had happened to him? He wanted to sit up, but sank back groaning, and felt his head and upper body covered in bandages.

His memory slowly returned, the uncertain awareness of battle with gunshots and bloodshed dawned. But where was he now?

The door opened and a Negro who seemed familiar to him bent over him:

"You don't recognize me, do you? Doctor Thompson, I saw you the day before yesterday at Miss Jane Morris' house! Darn, wouldn't have expected that we'd see each other again this way! Well, for you things turned out lucky. You took a hit from a revolver butt on your skull and got a small concussion, and also took a shot underneath your right shoulder, just missing the lung. The bullet is already out, the wound cleaned and no threat. In three, four days you can leave your bed."

"Where am I?" Carlo asked while his eyes heavy with fever fell shut.

"You're in good hands, with good friends," the doctor smiled. "Now drink this and sleep!"

When Carlo awoke for the second time, the morning sun shone in his room and next to him sat—Jane.

Refreshed, free of fever, with lust for life and a feeling of euphoria coursing through his veins, he snatched her hand, pulling it to his lips.

"Jane, you're here! How happy I am that nothing happened to you! Now tell me, where am I, what happened when I fell?"

Jane bent over him. Her whole body trembled; a tear fell from her eye onto his forehead.

"Carlo, oh, you dear, good man! You did not want to join us poor blacks and now you nearly sacrificed your life for us!"

Then she recounted, amidst sobs and laughs, how his deed had actually saved the home and probably her life and the girl's lives. When he set the battering ram column in retreat with fearsome losses on their part, the Negroes then regained courage, used the confusion to throw back the lynch mob and held the portal until the mounted militia, who had come at the urging of editor Crawford, was able to clear the whole square. All together, seventy Negroes and fifty whites had died from the battles in front of the courthouse and orphan girls' home. Today all is calm because a regiment of Federal solders was keeping order.

"And how did I get away from there?" Carlo asked shuddering.

"I was watching the whole scene through a crack in the closed shutter. When the square was cleared, I immediately rushed down with the school porter, and before the soldiers had noticed, we pulled you in. At first I thought you were dead. But when I saw that you were alive I was probably as happy as I will ever be in my entire life!"

Jane sobbed and a few minutes passed in silence before she could speak again.

"After that I provisionally bandaged your wounds, then Doctor Thompson and I brought you here to our house by car inconspicuously under the cover of night. We did not want to take you to the hospital because otherwise it might have come out in the investigation that you participated in the fighting. So now you are my and my mother's guest, and we will nurse you to health. Doctor Thompson said it won't take long. Then you maybe can even set sail on the *La Gloire* and leave this country forever."

Questioningly, in amazement, and uncomprehendingly Carlo looked at her.

"Now Carlo, I truly can't expect it of you any longer to stay here with us! Not in the least bit will I take it amiss if you turn your back on this country and return to your peaceful, calm, beautiful Vienna!"

Carlo sat up in bed.

"No Jane, now more than ever it is not right for me to leave. I am yours, for better or worse. I know now that I belong to the race of my mother, to true black blood! I will stay here and devote my life to these poor people! And I will take a lovely, black woman to wife and have children who will become darker than me, and these children will grow up as civilized humans and have children, who will barely know that white blood courses through their veins. Jane, do you want to be this black girl, do you want to become my faithful, good, brave wife?"

With a bright smile, Jane threw her arms around him and kissed his eyes and lips.

AFTERWORD

Kenneth R. Janken

A melodramatic novel that moves at a breathless pace, Austrian journalist Hugo Bettauer's *The Blue Stain* has much in common with the
modernist literature of the Harlem Renaissance era, as it plumbs the alienation of its mixed-race protagonist Carlo Zeller. Carletto, as he comes to
be called, is the child of a German botany professor and a barely literate
mulatto daughter of Georgia tenant farmers. The title is a reference to the
myth that no matter how light-complexioned an African American might
be, she or he can always be identified by the allegedly blueish tinge to the
lunula of the fingernail. (More about this detection method anon, along
with another foolproof method employed by whites for detecting African
Americans who tried to pass: using their noses to sniff the suspect for blacks'
telltale unpleasant odor.) As an avowedly anti-racist Bildungsroman, it
shares a conceit with other writings of the time that Europe and Europeans
were more hospitable to African Americans than the United States generally and the American South in particular. And like that other writing, it
caricatures southern whites as possessing the outward trappings of civilization but being essentially morally depraved and prone to outbursts of violence for the purposes of punishing and terrorizing African Americans and
as a source of entertainment and diversion in small-town life. And yet, for
all its efforts to embrace a forward-looking point of view, including notably
its closing embrace of the civil rights program of the National Association
for the Advancement of Colored People, *The Blue Stain* trades in the casual
racism that infects the works of many of the moderns and promotes retrograde stereotypes of the unchecked sexual urges of black women and men

and the race's uncivilized nature generally. This mixed and unstable legacy of an ostensibly anti-racist novel is the central concern of this afterword.

The Blue Stain is replete with restless characters trying either to escape their pasts or to come to terms with new worlds they find unwelcoming and alien. Michael North in his suggestive *Reading 1922* (1999) and Clare Corbould in her excellent *Becoming African American* (2009) identify peripatetic behavior as a hallmark of the modern. In the first of this three-part novel, Dr. Rudolf Zeller, a distinguished botany professor at a prominent German university, travels across Georgia and the Deep South to catalog and collect exotic flora, including hybrids not found elsewhere. (Adding to the restlessness that defines the modern sensibility is Zeller's background: Swiss-born but German-educated, he has enjoyed university appointments in Göttingen, Prague, and Vienna, and developed a German self-identity.) Not coincidentally or subtly, he comes under the spell of the exotic and hybrid (mulatto) adolescent girl, Karola, with whom he has a furtive dalliance. Enjoying the hospitality of large landowners, including Col. Henry Whilcox of Irvington, Georgia, he is nevertheless alarmed by their treatment of their black tenants and the material and moral squalor that the blacks are forced to endure. Zeller's timorous objections to this treatment are met with intense hostility by the white upper crust, whose lascivious and boorish behavior is cataloged in the novel and marks southern whites as degenerates themselves. At a gathering of the local gentry in Zeller's honor, Zeller's query about southern whites' aversion to blacks is met with incredulity. Blacks are "thieving, lying, greedy, and, if one does not keep them on a short leash—impudent." The local physician suggests that all newborn black boys be castrated, a suggestion at which the women present pretend to be scandalized but still laugh heartily. Another guest excuses Zeller's observations because he is a foreigner but assures him that his comments are unwelcome and that if he were a Yankee and had uttered them in the presence of ladies they would be considered fighting words. Mrs. Whilcox declaims on blacks' licentiousness while shamelessly flirting with Zeller.

Zeller is initially aroused by Mrs. Whilcox's advances—which says something about him as well, though Bettauer chooses not to explore it. But he is more taken by Karola, and over the course of a sultry southern summer, their passions for one another grow—his because he finds her strangely attractive, hers because, she says, she wants nothing to do with the "stupid and ugly" black adolescents on the plantation and because she wants to be a "white lady" and presumes that Zeller is the key to her escape. When Zeller hears rumors of an imminent lynching directed at Karola and her family, he spirits her out of Georgia to New York, where she bears his son but pays for her indiscretions by dying in childbirth. Heartbroken, Dr. Zeller, having received an appointment at the University of Vienna, returns to Europe with his mulatto son named after his mother so that he can raise him in an atmosphere of refined culture with no trace of overt racial prejudice.

The reader is introduced to the young-adult Carletto in the novel's second and third parts. Rudolph died young, and Carletto is now orphaned and studying indifferently for the bar in Vienna. Having inherited his father's intellectual nimbleness, including his facility for foreign languages, but also a distracted and self-indulgent impulsiveness that the author attributes to the intrinsic nature of uncivilized Negroes like Karola, Carletto is at loose ends. Lacking the discipline or motivation to complete his studies and without substantial contacts to land an executive job in the banking industry, Carletto falls in with a dissolute crowd of well-to-do young adult men—children of coupon clippers, a term Lenin used to describe those wealthy persons who derived their income mainly from collecting interest payments on bonds rather than engaging in any productive enterprise—and their female hangers-on, including stage and concert performers and socialites. Carletto's inheritance is much more modest, and he overextends himself, eventually falling into debt to a loan shark. When he can no longer keep up his carefree pretenses, his social circle noticeably cools toward him.

And yet his alienation is only partly due to his straitened circumstances. Carletto becomes aware that the women in his circle are attracted to him because of racial difference: he is mysterious, exotic, other, even slightly dangerous. This disorients Carletto, because he so thoroughly identifies as a cultured German and rejects any association with Negroes, whom he considers uncivilized. Unease turns to despair after another failed romance, this time with Lisl Ortner, a young woman from a downwardly mobile Austrian military family who at first displayed no racial prejudice. The family's precarious finances force Lisl to move to the United States to find work and live with relatives. She and Carletto carry on a short and intense transatlantic correspondence, which ends abruptly when Lisl ceases to answer Carletto's missives that profess his desire for her. He is nonplussed. Carletto, partially for love but also to avoid the loan shark, books passage to New York, and looks her up, hoping to rekindle the relationship he thought they had. But she is in the process of Americanizing, part of which includes embracing American racism, and tells him to leave her alone. He has an encounter with similar results with another

German immigrant, Lilli Wegner, whom he met when he worked briefly for a German book printer. (The printer was willing to employ him but was forced by his white American unionized workers to fire him.) Stuck in New York and without the means to return to Europe, Carletto learns the harshest lessons of racial discrimination. Employers will not hire him, whites-only restaurants will not serve him, and whites-only hotels will not accommodate him. European immigrants who might have tolerated him back home are openly hostile—it is the way to show they are becoming American. Only black folks—porters, janitors, cooks, domestic servants, and others with the "blue stain"—show him any compassion. But Carletto rejects them summarily, feeling not even attenuated kinship, and resenting the forced association foisted on him by white Americans. He is adrift.

Ground down to the point of destitution, Carletto stumbles upon the only work opportunity available to him: signing on to fell timber in an Alabama lumber camp. When Carletto is initially assigned to a gang of German laborers, his secret of having a mulatto mother—and thus now being classified as a Negro under American racist nomenclature—is discovered, and he gets into fights with the others. Fairly quickly he is ostracized and shifts his allegiances to a black labor crew, whose sexual mores and hygiene practices are flimsy at best but who are more humane and warm. Still holding himself apart from his race brothers, Carletto nonetheless begins to engage in a bit of racial uplift by teaching his fellow workers to read and write and bathe. While his attitude softens, he still plots to return to Austria where, against his plain experiences, he feels he still belongs. But on his Jim Crow train ride from Alabama to the port of Savannah to catch a steamer to Europe, he encounters Jane Morris, an educated African American who speaks to him in fluent French and eventually convinces him not to run back to Europe but rather cast his lot with the struggle for racial equality under the leadership of the NAACP. After much wrestling with his conscience and an episode in which he confronts a lynch mob to save Jane's life, Carletto agrees to stay in Georgia and proposes marriage. With the love of a woman, Carletto's racial rootlessness is resolved, and he obtains a purpose in life.

Bettauer's *The Blue Stain* shares many similarities with the race literature of the Harlem Renaissance produced by African American authors. Among the most important is the protagonist's journey from racial isolation and denial through an epiphany and on to solidarity and community. The journey is an exercise in self-exploration, but it often has a geographic dimension as well, with the protagonists searching for fulfillment and belonging in the American South, the North, and Europe. Like Carletto Zeller, Helga Crane, the Afro-Danish protagonist of Nella Larsen's *Quicksand* (1928), bristled at her forced inclusion among African Americans, and especially among those stodgy, status-conscious middle-class blacks who incessantly discussed the race problem in America while simultaneously struggling to adhere to a standard of bourgeois respectability and extirpating any hint of popular cultural difference, whether in spoken language or comportment or fashion. Like Carletto, Helga desires to be considered as an individual and not a type, and flees the United States for Copenhagen. Denmark is initially exhilarating and welcoming, and Helga has wide latitude for self-expression. But over the months she spends abroad she comes to realize that the Danes regard her as different and exotic—as a specimen. Their curiosity is not the splenetic variety practiced in the United States, but it is nevertheless oppressive, especially when her potential suitor Axel Olsen, a highly regarded modern artist and Copenhagen celebrity, reveals himself as a boor who makes insulting assumptions about Helga's sexuality based on her racial ancestry. Restless once more, Helga flees back to the United States, where she throws her lot in with her people, whom she now identifies as African Americans.

Kenneth Harper, the northern- and European-trained doctor who is at the center of Walter White's fast-paced *The Fire in the Flint* (1924), the second published novel of the Harlem Renaissance, returns to his native Georgia after the First World War to open a hospital and begin a medical practice among African Americans. He is a convinced disciple of Booker T. Washington who believes that racial prejudice can be reduced by blacks working hard to make themselves useful and not raising a ruckus. He disparages agitation and is the opposite of his brother, whose run-ins with the local white supremacists have convinced him of agitation's essential importance. Like Carletto, Kenneth Harper clings as long as he can to notions of civility and bourgeois respectability and disdains the masses, but the unremitting discrimination and racial violence he encounters—and his desire to impress a woman who is more race conscious than he—leads to enlightenment and to him using force to redeem himself and forge bonds of solidarity with the black race.

Even for African Americans who never doubted their racial identity or loyalties, there was a conceit that Europe was safely removed from the poison of American race relations. In his autobiography *Along This Way* (1933) the outstanding poet, diplomat, and NAACP leader James Weldon Johnson wrote of his time in Europe that he could breathe freer. The great dancer Josephine Baker felt as if she had to leave the United States to pursue her career, because remaining in America meant resigning herself to clowning roles on stage. Robert Abbott, the publisher of the influential *Chicago Defender* weekly, wrote extensively and favorably of his continental travels. Not only were Europeans friendly, they also afforded great opportunities for material, educational, and social advancement to African-descended people. Middle-class African Americans eagerly sought passage to Europe to participate in both secular and religious world meetings because they knew they would be treated as sisters and brothers by Europeans—who would also work diligently to contain or neutralize visiting white Americans' propensity to spread Jim Crow wherever they went. Countee Cullen wrote admiringly of Europe in his poetry, and Langston Hughes, though he had a tough time making a living in Europe, nevertheless wrote fondly of the continent in his two memoirs, *The Big Sea* (1940) and *I Wonder as I Wander* (1956). Cultural arbiters like Alain Locke and Mercer Cook gravitated to the circle of francophone West Indians and Africans that produced *La Revue du Monde Noir*, which for a time regularly published material written by African Americans as well as articles by leading European social scientists advocating racial equality. That such a journal existed and promoted the distinct cultural attributes of Africans and African-descended people was proof that Europe offered a more tolerant climate in which to live and thrive than the United States.

The exaltation of Europe is understandable. In the Harlem Renaissance era of the 1920s and 1930s especially, Europe *was* more tolerant and welcoming to African Americans than the United States. At a time when black Americans faced an epidemic of lynching, other forms of racial violence, legal discrimination, and disfranchisement, Europe lauded African American culture and was largely hospitable to black Americans, especially expatriate and touring musicians and performers. Elevating Europe had value as a psychic ploy and as propaganda. The continent could be both a salve for the frayed nerves of African Americans and offer an alternative way to organize society along non-racialist lines. In this regard, Bettauer's *The Blue Stain* shares many traits of the prose and poetry of the Harlem Renaissance.

The Harlem Renaissance writers' lack of discernment had a cost, too. While they enjoyed the hospitality willingly accorded them, they largely overlooked the horrid treatment of African immigrants. The efforts of dockworkers in Marseilles to earn a decent living were forcibly suppressed after World War I. While Africans who embraced, for example, France's *mission civilisatrice* were incorporated in varying degrees in civil society, those who opposed colonialism were labeled subversive by the state and subjected to harassment and disruption of their activities. African Americans who travelled to Europe generally found it convenient not to take notice when *La Revue* was forced to shut down because of its agitation against France's colonial policies. Nor did they take much notice of the protests against Josephine Baker's appearances in Vienna, where Austrians decried the decay of civilization that accompanied her. With the notable exception of Nella Larsen, none questioned the insidious prejudice that was embedded in many Europeans' attraction to African American culture: a belief in the vitality of the primitive, which would save enervated and over-civilized Europe. Advertisements, performance reviews, and entertainment and cultural news were saturated with these forms of racism.

African American writers of the Harlem Renaissance era might be forgiven for overlooking these less aggressive forms of cultural superiority expressed by Europeans. In the United States they were, after all, faced daily with the virulent racism of the Ku Klux Klan. At the same time, they did confront and critique many of the dominant cultural tropes that prevented the formation of bonds of racial solidarity. Rudolph Fisher's novel *The Walls of Jericho* (1928) shares with *The Fire in the Flint* and *The Blue Stain* the plot convention of a good woman turning the life of the respective novel's protagonist around. They also lampoon whites' parochialism and self-congratulatory puffery. But that is where the similarity between the African American authors and Bettauer ends. Both Fisher and White critically examine the modes of thought that keep the black race from closing ranks, with particular emphasis on the craven nature of middle-class respectability. And though they might gently mock black working-class expressiveness and nomenclature, they always do so with familiarity and with good humor.

Shine Jones, the massive piano-mover protagonist of *The Walls of Jericho*, is a hard-working and knowledgeable employee of a black-owned furniture-moving business. He is also a hard drinker who has great difficulty understanding, let alone revealing the full range of his considerable and strong feelings. His wounds are deep and come from multiple sources. Whites—and more particularly wealthy whites—have managed to exploit him and his fellow black workers. But in an American society stratified by race and dominated by whites, this was not a surprise to Shine, and he dealt with this fact simply by steering clear of whites wherever and whenever possible. He could not avoid them altogether, though, because through their alleged philanthropy they supported the efforts of black middle-class uplifters who in turn tried to regulate the behavior of African American workers, particularly by directing their leisure activities away from convivial entertainment and toward more respectable pursuits. Moreover, by employing the services of upwardly-mobile black attorneys or bootleggers—highfalutin African Americans that Shine calls "dickties"—wealthy whites created another layer of social control over the black masses. Shine displays more contempt for the dickties than he reserves for the whites. He is enraged by them, and they cause him to think and act irrationally, as he blames them for his oppressed lot in life. Over the course of *The Walls of Jericho*, Shine learns that in order to realize his dream of economic independence in the form of business ownership he has to come to terms with his blind hatred for the black middle class. He has to learn to differentiate among the different types of strivers, for there are some who do indeed share his racial affinity, while there are a great many others who are indeed parasites who blindly link their fortunes to the dominant race. Rudolph Fisher makes clear another, more important point: An intra-racial cross-class alliance was the only productive way forward and could be accomplished only if the dickties abandoned their snootiness and supported an alliance that proceeded under the guidance of black workers.

Similarly, Walter White's *The Fire in the Flint* inspects the black middle class's rectitude and emphasis on respectability and finds it painfully lacking as a strategy for overcoming white supremacy and Jim Crow in the South. White knew firsthand of the ineffectuality of this strategy. He shared his parents' and siblings' light complexion and blonde hair. He grew up in a family of working-class strivers and as a young teen lived through the terror of the Atlanta Race Riot of 1906, in which mob violence was especially directed at African Americans who were perceived as trying to live their lives above their place. A graduate of the historically black Atlanta University, as a young adult, White gave up a potentially lucrative career in the insurance business to become the assistant secretary of the National Association for the Advancement of Colored People and risk his life as an undercover investigator of lynchings. And though White also pokes fun at black workers and sharecroppers for their irregular grammar and their fondness for establishing social organizations with long and over-grandiose names, his account of them is largely sympathetic. They understand that hard work is no guarantee of reward and respect. Just the opposite was the case, in fact: Hard work and attempts to achieve prosperity and material independence threatened the superior position of the ruling whites and would be met with cheating, chicanery, and violence to prevent blacks from flourishing. In other words, the masses might not say it properly, but they had a native understanding of how the system was rigged against them. People like the protagonist Kenneth Harper, who advocated hard work and submission to the larger order while trying to find less abrasive and marginally more paternalist white patrons, were bound to fail. As in *The Walls of Jericho*, their only hope was to join their destinies with the black masses and fight directly for their dignity and improved circumstances.

The Harlem Renaissance was not an unadulterated proletarian affair. There were more advocates among African American artists and patrons for refined culture who preferred operatic and symphonic music to the blues singers and jazz orchestras. They praised the Georgia-born and classically-trained tenor Roland Hayes (whose own tastes in music were remarkably catholic) and winced at the rough-edged Bessie Smith, whom they hoped few would note. At the same time, there was sincere and vigorous debate coursing through the Harlem Renaissance over issues of class, racial representation, gender, and the proper relationships between art and politics. One need only peruse the anthology edited by Alain Locke, *The New Negro* (1925), Langston Hughes's "The Negro Artist and the Racial Mountain" (1926), W. E. B. Du Bois's "Criteria of Negro Art" (1926), Richard Wright's "Blueprint for Negro Writing" (1937), George Schuyler's "The Negro-Art Hokum" (1926), or any of several other interventions to conclude that those who produced these works of art were vitally concerned with the portrayal of the race and the race's constituent parts.

Such critical reflection is absent from *The Blue Stain*, which reflexively retails in the basest racial stereotypes. Bettauer seems to want to soften the brickbats with pseudo-explanations of how blacks' incontinent emotional state and uncivilized, childlike nature was due to their having been only recently released from bondage. And he does scold southern whites for their debauchery and in particular southern white women for their sexual laxness and willingness when caught in flagrante delicto to create a diversion that focused violence on blacks. But it is difficult to escape the conclusion that Bettauer's novel, however much it appeals for less brutal treatment of African Americans, accepts the notions of the mass of African Americans as imbecilic, unaware, self-hating, and fundamentally different from other human beings.

Bettauer reveals this limitation at the very beginning, with the title, which, like Carl Van Vechten's controversial *Nigger Heaven* (1926) was an insult to all the Harlemites who welcomed him to their neighborhood and world. Their objection was not simply to the use of an epithet by someone who was white and an outsider despite his pretense that he was a consummate insider and honorary Harlemite. Rather, it was that presumption combined with Van Vechten's portrayals of various unflattering racial types as authentic representations of African American life that angered the critics. Similarly, Bettauer seems to accept as truth—unfortunate, yes, but truth nevertheless—markers of physical difference between the races that have no basis in fact but were used to justify the branding of blacks as inferior. Whites invented the concept of the blue stain—the putative dark pigment visible at the base of the fingernail of light-complexioned African Americans—as a way to police racial boundaries. It gave whites who were concerned with racial purity—or more exactly, white males who were concerned with preserving the racial purity of white females—some false comfort that they could identify and stop African American men who tried to pass for white and infiltrate the white race. The assumption, of course, was that this was black men's ultimate desire.

African American writers like Walter White, George Schuyler, and Rudolph Fisher had in their different ways discussed the blue stain or variations of it, almost always to mock it and the whites who swore by it. Schuyler's satirical novel *Black No More* is merciless in its lampooning of this literal, racial essentialist notion. In *The Walls of Jericho*, the lawyer Merrit, a blond-haired, blue-eyed African American whose race loyalty and hatred of whites is unimpeachable, mischievously engages in a long conversation with the wealthy white dilettante philanthropist, who not only asserts white superiority but also stupidly insists that she can discern blacks from whites—though she is clearly incapable of doing so with the person sitting beside her. Walter White, who was also able to pass for white and did so to infiltrate lynch mobs and report on their barbarity for the NAACP, punctures the notion of the blue stain in his fiction and in many trenchant anti-lynching essays. In his autobiography *A Man Called White* (1948), White recounts a train trip in which he was engaged in an animated conversation with a cultured white southerner who was incessantly preoccupied with the race question. The man offered White, who was traveling incognito as a white man, his surefire way to detect a Negro trying to pass for white: he grabbed Whites hand and said all you had to do was check the fingernails for the telltale crescent mark. The man's observational acumen, of course, failed him and earned him and all such proponents nothing but public ridicule.

Bettauer's Carletto, however, considers the blue stain a tangible and permanent mark of inferiority, not a figment of the white mind. At different points in the novel, he curses it for its power to bind him to a racial group that he disdains and to prevent him, despite his obvious breeding and intellectual faculties, from assuming a prominent station in society. Likewise, the body scent of blacks is allegedly distinct and redolent, at least to the white nose, of something between slightly jarring like "cinnamon, nutmeg, and vinegar" and utterly repulsive. Carletto's father, when he sojourned through the Georgia countryside collecting plant specimens and becoming involved with Karola, was told by his hostess Mrs. Whilcox that she could tell he was out trolling the black quarters because she could smell the scent of a black woman on him. She said this to him not only because she was vindictive and dissolute, which we know from other incidents in *The Blue Stain*, but also because she was determined to do her part to police the borders of racial intimacy. Carletto's many lovers in Vienna commented on his scent as a way to keep him in line and prevent him from feeling entirely comfortable in his relationship with them; Carletto was thus held in their thrall, effectively at their mercy. As he travelled through the eastern and southern United States trying to find a way to return to Europe, Carletto was faced with the fact of his and his race's body smell—and he was tortured by it. The alleged sourness seemed to be baked into the body, and there was nothing he could do to remove it.

It is not a big leap from the distress felt by the black characters in *The Blue Stain* on account of their alleged marks of alleged inferiority to their wishing they were white or could have intimate associations with whites. Karola tells Rudolf Zeller matter-of-factly that she wishes she were a white lady. This is heartbreaking to the novel's narrator, who attributes such sentiment to black people's uncomplicated and childlike psychological makeup, their lack of resiliency and a concomitant tendency to self-hatred. This dynamic is demonstrated again when Carletto works in the Alabama lumber camp. When it becomes widely known that he is descended from a black woman, he is shunned by native white and European immigrant workers alike, and finds a refuge in a gang of black laborers. His new companions resist his efforts to clean them up and wash away their smell. They, however, are intensely interested in Carletto's sexual encounters with European women. They explain to him that they dream of getting such a chance because men want what they are denied. Carletto concludes from this that black men have a "voracious" desire for white women—thus confirming the insidious stereotype that African Americans lack self-control and are not fit to take their place in public life. Such lack of self-mastery is further confirmed by Carletto's growing frustration and anger at being rejected by white business owners, including hoteliers who refused to shelter him, restauranteurs who denied him service, and employers who fired him when white employees objected to his presence, as well as a European woman who expressed desire for him at home but revulsion for him when she immigrated to America. Bettauer accurately and potently captures the indignity and outrage that Carletto and African Americans felt at this rejection. Claude McKay's poem "The White House" (1922) eloquently explored the same feelings and expressed a determination to struggle to overthrow the system that promoted such oppression. But Carletto's solution was instead to vindictively redouble his efforts at the sexual conquest of white women and leave them soon afterward. Bettauer accepts and spreads rather than critiques and condemns some of the most dangerous racial calumnies in circulation at that time.

There is much to commend *The Blue Stain*. To the extent it identifies slavery and the continual racial oppression after its overthrow as *the* root cause of the submission of African Americans, this novel is an anti-racist document worthy of an audience. Written during a politically and socially unstable time in German and Austrian history, it must surely have had a salubrious effect on the citizens of those two countries who read it. Given its significant overlap with racial and modernist themes explored by Harlem Renaissance-era writers, *The Blue Stain* helped extend the reach and influence of that important and vital cultural movement. At the same time, it is a deeply flawed novel that demonstrates the staying power of racist ideas and notions in popular culture, even among the modernists whose conceit was that they were bringing forth something new and revolutionary. Racial epithets appear liberally and casually—sometimes even gratuitously—in the prose of Faulkner, Dos Passos, Fitzgerald, Van Vechten, and other American authors, as well as in that of the Austrian Hugo Bettauer. It is, however, not only the appearance of the words themselves that contain the power to shock, though they are indeed jarring even to the contemporary eye. Rather, the epithets' presence in the text speaks to the power of the thoughts behind the words. Even authors who espouse in their works points of view that are anti-racist (or anti-sexist, or against other forms of oppression) have to be aware of and vigilant against retrograde ideologies that insinuate themselves into popular discourse so that they do not end up being reflected or represented in those works.

ABOUT THE
CONTRIBUTORS

PETER HÖYNG, Associate Professor of German Studies at Emory University, studied *Germanistik* and European history in Germany, and received his PhD in German literature at the University of Wisconsin-Madison. After years on the faculty at the University of Tennessee-Knoxville, he joined the German Studies Department at Emory University in 2005. His research focuses on German literature and culture since 1750 with a particular emphasis on cultural creations emanating from Austria. He has published forty essays and a monograph on historical representations in late eighteenth century drama, and has edited a volume on the Jewish dramatist George Tabori.

CHAUNCEY J. MELLOR, Professor Emeritus of German at The University of Tennessee-Knoxville, received his BA, MA, and PhD in German linguistics from the University of Chicago, and joined the faculty of the University of Tennessee in 1970. He has been an exchange student at the Johann Wolfgang University in Frankfurt, a recipient of Fulbright awards, and was elected to the Executive Committee of the American Association of Teachers of German (AATG) in the 1980s. He edited the AATG's journal, *Die Unterrichtspraxis-Teaching German*, from 2000 to 2004. He has published on pedagogy and on oral proficiency testing.

KENNETH R. JANKEN, Professor of African American and Diaspora Studies, and Director of the Center for the Study of the American South at the University of North Carolina-Chapel Hill, received his BA and MA in History from Hunter College of the City University of New York and his PhD in American History from Rutgers University. His research focuses

on twentieth-century African American history, and his most recent pub-
lication is *The Wilmington Ten: Violence, Injustice, and the Rise of Black
Politics in the 1970s* (2016). He is also the author of two biographies: *Walter
White: Mr. NAACP* (2003); and *Rayford W. Logan and the Dilemma of the
African-American Intellectual* (1993).

The complex question of American racism in the age of Jim Crow rarely obsessed Europeans. In 1922 the Austrian Jewish novelist Hugo Bettauer's *The Blue Stain* captured the complex struggles of American Blacks in a system that relegated them to the status of nonpersons. Höyng and Mellor's brilliantly accessible translation makes this novel, an important precursor to Toni Morrison's *The Bluest Eye* and Philip Roth's *The Human Stain*, available to readers of English for the first time. A vital book to understand racism in Europe at the moment the Nazis were beginning their ascent.

—Sander L. Gilman, Distinguished Professor of the
Liberal Arts and Sciences, Emory University

Through his novel *The Blue Stain*, Hugo Bettauer delivers an evocative representation of race relations in the United States in the early twentieth century. Thanks to Peter Höyng and Chauncey J. Mellor's masterful translation, we now have another essential text to inform our ongoing national conversation on race and citizenship.

—Mark A. Sanders, Professor of English, Emory University

This superbly contextualized and thoughtful translation of Hugo Bettauer's overlooked novel offers a welcome expansion of this vital author's writings available in English. In highlighting Bettauer's lamentable reliance on racial stereotypes he aimed to critique, this book provides fresh insight on the power and persistence of prejudice and racism in the United States and Europe.

—Lisa Silverman, Associate Professor of History,
University of Wisconsin-Milwaukee

[M]erits the attention of several audiences and is a valuable resource for those interested in the Harlem Renaissance. Recommended. Upper-division undergraduates through faculty.

—*CHOICE*